In the Reign of Terror

A Story of the French Revolution

G. A. Henty

In the Reign of Terror: A Story of the French Revolution

Copyright © 2019 Indo-European Publishing

The present edition is a reproduction of previous publication of this classic work. Minor typographical errors may have been corrected without note, however, for an authentic reading experience the spelling, punctuation, and capitalization have been retained from the original text.

ISBN: 978-1-64439-295-9

PREFACE

MY DEAR LADS,

This time only a few words are needed, for the story speaks for itself. My object has been rather to tell you a tale of interest than to impart historical knowledge, for the facts of the dreadful time when "the terror" reigned supreme in France are well known to all educated lads. I need only say that such historical allusions as are necessary for the sequence of the story will be found correct, except that the Noyades at Nantes did not take place until a somewhat later period than is here assigned to them.

Yours sincerely,
G.A. HENTY

CONTENTS

CHAPTER I

A JOURNEY TO FRANCE

"I don't know what to say, my dear."

"Why, surely, James, you are not thinking for a moment of letting him go?"

"Well, I don't know. Yes, I am certainly thinking of it, though I haven't at all made up my mind. There are advantages and disadvantages."

"Oh, but it is such a long way, and to live among those French people, who have been doing such dreadful things, attacking the Bastille, and, as I have heard you say, passing all sorts of revolutionary laws, and holding their king and queen almost as prisoners in Paris!"

"Well, they won't eat him, my dear. The French Assembly, or the National Assembly, or whatever it ought to be called, has certainly been passing laws limiting the power of the king and abolishing many of the rights and privileges of the nobility and clergy; but you must remember that the condition of the vast body of the French nation has been terrible. We have long conquered our liberties, and, indeed, never even in the height of the feudal system were the mass of the English people more enslaved as have been the peasants of France.

"We must not be surprised, therefore, if in their newly-recovered freedom they push matters to an excess at first; but all this will right itself, and no doubt a constitutional form of government, somewhat similar to our own, will be established. But all this is no reason against Harry's going out there. You don't suppose that the French people are going to fly at the throats of the nobility. Why, even in the heat of the civil war here there was no instance of any personal wrong being done to the families of those engaged in the struggle, and in only two or three cases, after repeated risings, were any even of the leaders executed.

"No; Harry will be just as safe there as he would be here. As to the distance, it's nothing like so far as if he went to India, for example. I don't see any great chance of his setting the Thames on fire at home. His school report is always the same—'Conduct fair; progress in study moderate'—which means, as I take it, that he just scrapes along. That's it, isn't it, Harry?"

"Yes, father, I think so. You see every one cannot be at the top of the form."

"That's a very true observation, my boy. It is clear that if there are twenty boys in a class, nineteen fathers have to be disappointed. Still, of course, one would like to be the father who is not disappointed."

"I stick to my work," the boy said; "but there are always fellows who seem to know just the right words without taking any trouble about it. It comes to them, I suppose."

"What do you say to this idea yourself, Harry?"

"I don't know, sir," the boy said doubtfully.

"And I don't know," his father agreed. "At anyrate we will sleep upon it. I am clear that the offer is not to be lightly rejected."

Dr. Sandwith was a doctor in Chelsea. Chelsea in the year 1790 was a very different place to Chelsea of the present day. It was a pretty suburban hamlet, and was indeed a very fashionable quarter. Here many of the nobility and personages connected with the court had their houses, and broad country fields and lanes separated it from the stir and din of London. Dr. Sandwith had a good practice, but he had also a large family. Harry was at Westminster, going backwards and forwards across the fields to school. So far he had evinced no predilection for any special career. He was a sturdy, well-built lad of some sixteen years old. He was, as his father said, not likely to set the Thames on fire in any way. He was as undistinguished in the various sports popular among boys in those days as he was in his lessons. He was as good as the average, but no better; had fought some tough fights with boys of his own age, and had shown endurance rather than brilliancy.

In the ordinary course of things he would probably in three or four years' time have chosen some profession; and, indeed, his father had already settled in his mind that as Harry was not likely to make any great figure in life in the way of intellectual capacity, the best thing would be to obtain for him a commission in his Majesty's service, as to which, with the doctor's connection among people of influence, there would not be any difficulty. He had, however, said nothing as yet to the boy on the subject.

The fact that Harry had three younger brothers and four sisters, and that Dr. Sandwith, who was obliged to keep up a good position, sometimes found it difficult to meet his various expenses, made him perhaps more inclined to view favourably the offer he had that morning received than would otherwise have been the case. Two years before he had attended professionally a young French nobleman attached to the embassy. It was from him that the letter which had been the subject of conversation had been received. It ran as follows:

"Dear Doctor Sandwith,—Since my return from Paris I have frequently spoken to my brother, the Marquis of St. Caux, respecting the difference of education between your English boys and our own. Nothing struck me more when I was in London than your great schools. With us the children of good families are almost always brought up at home. They learn to dance and to fence, but have no other exercise for their limbs, and they lack the air of manly independence which struck me in English boys. They are more gentil—I do not know the word in your language which expresses it—they carry themselves better; they are not so rough; they are more polite. There are advantages in both systems, but for myself I like yours much the best. My brother is, to some extent, a convert to my view. There are no such schools to which he could send his sons in France, for what large schools we have are under the management of the fathers, and the boys have none of that freedom which is the distinguishing point of the English system of education. Even if there were such schools, I am sure that madame my sister-in-law would never hear of her sons being sent there.

"Since this is so, the marquis has concluded that the best thing would be to have an English boy of good family as their companion. He would, of course, study with them under their masters. He would play and ride with them, and would be treated as one of themselves. They would learn something of English from him, which would be useful if they adopt the diplomatic profession. He would learn French, which might also be useful to him; but of course the great point which my brother desires is that his sons should acquire something of the manly independence of thought and action which distinguishes English boys.

"Having arranged this much, I thought of you. I know that you have several sons. If you have one of from fourteen to sixteen years, and you would like him to take such a position for two or three years, I should be glad indeed to secure such a companion for my nephews. If not, would you do me the favour of looking round among your acquaintances and find us a lad such as we need. He must be a gentleman and a fair type of the boy we are speaking of. I may say that my brother authorizes me to offer in his name, in addition to all expenses, two thousand francs a year to the young gentleman who will thus benefit his sons. I do not think that the political excitement which is agitating Paris need be taken into consideration. Now that great concessions have been made to the representatives of the nation, it is not at all probable that there will be any recurrence of such popular tumults as that which brought about the capture of the Bastille. But in any case this need not weigh in the decision, as my brother resides for the greater part of the year in his chateau near Dijon in Burgundy, far removed from the troubles in the capital."

The more Dr. Sandwith thought over the matter the more he liked it. There were comparatively few Englishmen in those days who spoke the French language. It was, indeed, considered part of the education of a young man of good family to make what was called the grand tour of Europe under the charge of a tutor, after leaving the university. But these formed a very small proportion of society, and, indeed, the frequent wars which had, since the Stuarts lost the throne of England, occurred between the two countries had greatly interfered with continental travel.

Even now the subjects of France and England were engaged in a desperate struggle in India, although there was peace between the courts of Versailles and St. James's. A knowledge of the French language then would be likely to be of great utility to Harry if he entered the army; his expenses at Westminster would be saved, and the two hundred and forty pounds which he would acquire during his three years' stay in France would be very useful to him on his first start in life. After breakfast next morning Dr. Sandwith asked Harry to take a turn in the garden with him, for the holidays had just begun.

"What do you think of this, Harry?"

"I have not thought much about it one way or the other, sir," Harry said, looking up with a smile. "It seemed to me better that you should do the thinking for both of us."

"I might perhaps be better able to judge whether it would be advantageous or otherwise for you to accept the offer, but you must be the best judge as to whether you would like to accept it or not."

"I can't quite make up my mind as to that, sir. I like school very much and I like being at home. I don't want to learn Frenchified ways, nor to eat frogs and snails and all sorts of nastiness; still, it would be fun going to a place so different to England, and hearing no English spoken, and learning all their rum ways, and getting to jabber French."

"It might be very useful to you in the army, Harry;" and then the doctor stopped suddenly.

"The army!" Harry exclaimed in a tone of astonished delight.

"Oh, sir, do you really think of my going into the army? You never said a word about that before. I should like that immensely."

"That slipped out, Harry, for I did not mean to say anything about it until you had left school; still, if you go to France I do not know why you should not keep that before you. I don't think the army is a very good profession, but you do not seem to have any marked talent for anything else. You don't like the idea of medicine or the church, and you were almost heart-broken when I wanted you to accept the offer of your uncle John of a seat in his counting-house. It seems to me that the army would suit you better than anything else, and I have no doubt that I could get you a commission. Now, whenever we fight France is sure to be on the other side, and I think that it would be of great advantage to you to have a thorough knowledge of French—a thing which very few officers in our army possess. If you accept this offer you will have the opportunity of attaining this, and at the same time of earning a nice little sum which would pay for your outfit and supply you with pocket-money for some time."

"Yes, sir, it would be first rate!" Harry exclaimed excitedly. "Oh, please, accept the offer; I should like it of all things; and even if I do get ever so skinny on frogs and thin soup, I can get fat on roast beef again when I get back."

"That is all nonsense, Harry, about frogs and starving. The French style of cookery differs from ours, but they eat just as much, and although they may not, as a rule, be as broad and heavy as Englishmen, that is simply a characteristic of race; the Latin peoples are of slighter build than the Teutonic. As to their food, you know that the Romans, who were certainly judges of good living, considered the snail a great luxury, and I dare say ate frogs too. A gentleman who had made the grand tour told me that he had tasted them in Paris and found them very delicate eating. You may not like the living quite at first, but you will soon get over that, and once accustomed to it you will like it quite as well as our solid joints. My principal objection to your going lies quite in another direction. Public opinion in France is much disturbed. In the National Assembly, which is the same as our Parliament, there is a great spirit of resistance to the royal authority, something like a revolution has already been accomplished, and the king is little more than a prisoner."

"But that would surely make no difference to me, sir!"

"No, I don't see that it should, Harry. Still, it would cause your mother a good deal of anxiety."

5

"I don't see it could make any difference," Harry repeated; "and you see, sir, when I go into the army and there is war, mother would be a great deal more anxious."

"You mean, Harry," the doctor said with a smile, "that whether her anxiety begins a little sooner or later does not make much difference."

"I don't think I quite meant that, sir," Harry said; "but yes," he added frankly, after a moment's thought, "I suppose I did; but I really don't see that supposing there were any troubles in France it could possibly make any difference to me; even if there were a civil war, such as we had in England, they would not interfere with boys."

"No, I don't see that it would make any difference, and the chance is so remote that it need not influence our decision. Of course if war broke out between the two countries the marquis would see that you were sent back safely. Well, then, Harry, I am to consider that your decision is in favour of your accepting this appointment."

"If you please, sir. I am sure it will be a capital thing for me, and I have no doubt it will be great fun. Of course at first it will be strange to hear them all jabbering in French, but I suppose I shall soon pick it up."

And so Mrs. Sandwith was informed by her husband that after talking it over with Harry he had concluded that the proposed arrangement would really be an excellent one, and that it would be a great pity to let such an opportunity slip.

The good lady was for a time tearful in her forebodings that Harry would be starved, for in those days it was a matter of national opinion that our neighbours across the Channel fed on the most meagre of diet; but she was not in the habit of disputing her husband's will, and when the letter of acceptance had been sent off, she busied herself in preparing Harry's clothes for his long absence.

"He ought to be measured for several suits, my dear," she said to her husband, "made bigger and bigger to allow for his growing."

"Nonsense, my dear! You do not suppose that clothes cannot be purchased in France! Give him plenty of under-linen, but the fewer jackets and trousers he takes over the better; it will be much better for him to get clothes out there of the same fashion as other people; the boy will not want to be stared at wherever he goes. The best rule is always to dress like people around you. I shall give him money, and directly he gets there he can get a suit or two made by the tailor who makes for the lads he is going to be with. The English

6

are no more loved in France than the French are here, and though Harry has no reason to be ashamed of his nationality there is no occasion for him to draw the attention of everyone he meets to it by going about in a dress which would seem to them peculiar."

In due time a letter was received from Count Auguste de St. Caux, stating that the marquis had requested him to write and say that he was much gratified to hear that one of the doctor's own sons was coming over to be a companion and friend to his boys, and that he was sending off in the course of two days a gentleman of his household to Calais to meet him and conduct him to Paris. On young Mr. Sandwith's arrival at Calais he was to go at once to the Hotel Lion door and ask for M. du Tillet.

During the intervening time Harry had been very busy, he had to say good-bye to all his friends, who looked, some with envy, some with pity, upon him, for the idea of a three years' residence in France was a novel one to all. He was petted and made much of at home, especially by his sisters, who regarded him in the light of a hero about to undertake a strange and hazardous adventure.

Three days after the arrival of the letter of the marquis, Dr. Sandwith and Harry started by stage for Dover, and the doctor put his son on board the packet sailing for Calais. The evening before, he gave him much good advice as to his behaviour.

"You will see much that is new, and perhaps a good deal that you don't like, Harry, but it is better for you never to criticize or give a hostile opinion about things; you would not like it if a French boy came over here and made unpleasant remarks about English ways and manners. Take things as they come and do as others do; avoid all comparisons between French and English customs; fall in with the ways of those around you; and adopt as far as you can the polite and courteous manner which is general among the French, and in which, I must say, they are far ahead of us. If questioned, you will, of course, give your opinion frankly and modestly; it is the independence of thought among English boys which has attracted the attention and approval of Auguste de St. Caux.

"Be natural and simple, giving yourself no airs, and permitting none on the part of the lads you are with; their father says you are to be treated as their equal. But, upon the other hand, do not be ever on the lookout for small slights, and bear with perfect good temper any little ridicule your, to them foreign, ways and manners may excite. I need not tell you to be always straightforward, honest, and true, for of those qualities I think you possess a fair share. Above all things restrain any tendency to use your fists; fighting comes naturally to English boys, but in France it is considered as brutal and degrading—a blow is a deadly insult, and would never be forgiven.

"So, whatever the provocation, abstain from striking anyone. Should you find that in any way your position is made intolerable, you will of course appeal to the marquis, and unless you obtain redress you will come home—you will find no difficulty in travelling when you once understand the language—but avoid anything like petty complaints. I trust there will be no reason for complaints at all, and that you will find your position an exceedingly pleasant one as soon as you become accustomed to it; but should occasion arise bear my words in mind."

Harry promised to follow his father's advice implicitly, but in his own mind he wondered what fellows did when they quarrelled if they were not allowed to fight; however, he supposed that he should, under the circumstances, do the same as French boys, whatever that might be.

As soon as the packet was once fairly beyond the harbour Harry's thoughts were effectually diverted from all other matters by the motion of the sailing boat, and he was soon in a state of prostration, in which he remained until, seven hours later, the packet entered Calais harbour.

Dr. Sandwith had requested the captain to allow one of his men to show Harry the way to the Lion door. Harry had pulled himself together a little as the vessel entered the still water in the harbour, and was staring at the men in their blue blouses and wooden shoes, at the women in their quaint and picturesque attire, when a sailor touched him on the shoulder:

"Now, young sir, the captain tells me I am to show you the way to your hotel. Which is your box?"

Harry pointed out his trunk; the sailor threw it on his shoulder, and Harry, with a feeling of bewilderment, followed him along the gangway to the shore. Here he was accosted by an officer.

"What does he say?" he asked the sailor.

"He asks for your passport."

Harry fumbled in his breast pocket for the document which his father had obtained for him from the foreign office, duly viseed by the French ambassador, notifying that Henry Sandwith, age sixteen, height five feet eight, hair brown, eyes gray, nose short, mouth large, was about to reside in France in the family of the Marquis de St. Caux. The officer glanced it over, and then returned it to Harry with a polite bow, which Harry in some confusion endeavoured to imitate.

8

"What does the fellow want to bow and scrape like that for?" he muttered to himself as he followed his guide. "An Englishman would just have nodded and said 'All right!' What can a fellow want more, I should like to know? Well I suppose I shall get accustomed to it, and shall take to bowing and scraping as a matter of course."

The Lion door was close at hand. In reply to the sailor's question the landlord said that M. du Tillet was within. The sailor put down the trunk, pocketed the coin Harry gave him, and with a "Good luck, young master!" went out, taking with him, as Harry felt, the last link to England. He turned and followed the landlord. The latter mounted a flight of stairs, knocked at a door, and opened it.

"A young gentleman desires to see M. du Tillet," he said, and Harry entered.

A tall, big man, whose proportions at once disappointed Harry's preconceived notions as to the smallness and leanness of Frenchmen, rose from the table at which he was writing.

"Monsieur—Sandwith?" he said interrogatively. "I am glad to see you."

Harry did not understand the latter portion of the remark, but he caught the sound of his name.

"That's all right," he said nodding. "How do you do, M. du Tillet?"

The French gentleman bowed; Harry bowed; and then they looked at each other. There was nothing more to say. A smile stole over Harry's face, and broke into a frank laugh. The Frenchman smiled, put his hand on Harry's shoulder, and said:

"Brave garcon!" and Harry felt they were friends.

M. du Tillet's face bore an expression of easy good temper. He wore a wig with long curls; he had a soldier's bearing, and a scar on his left cheek; his complexion was dark and red, his eyebrows black and bushy. After a pause he said:

"Are you hungry?" and then put imaginary food to his mouth.

"You mean will I eat anything?" Harry translated. "Yes, that I will if there's anything fit to eat. I begin to feel as hungry as a hunter, and no wonder, for I am as hollow as a drum!"

His nod was a sufficient answer. M. du Tillet took his hat, opened the door, and bowed for Harry to precede him.

Harry hesitated, but believing it would be the polite way to do as he was told, returned the bow and went out. The Frenchman put his hand on his shoulder, and they went down stairs together and took their seats in the salon, where his companion gave an order, and in two or three minutes a bowl of broth was placed before each of them.

9

It fully answered Harry's ideas as to the thinness of French soup, for it looked like dirty water with a few pieces of bread and some scraps of vegetables floating in it. He was astonished at the piece of bread, nearly a yard long, placed on the table. M. du Tillet cut a piece off and handed it to him. He broke a portion of it into his broth, and found, when he tasted it, that it was much nicer than it looked.

"It's not so bad after all," he thought to himself. "Anyhow bread seems plentiful, so there's no fear of my starving." He followed his companion's example and made his way steadily through a number of dishes all new and strange to him; neither his sight nor his taste gave him the slightest indication as to what meat he was eating.

"I suppose it's all right," he concluded; "but what people can want to make such messes of their food for I can't make out. A slice of good roast beef is worth the lot of it; but really it isn't nasty; some of the dishes are not bad at all if one only knew what they were made of." M. du Tillet offered him some wine, which he tasted but shook his head, for it seemed rough and sour; but he poured himself out some water. Presently a happy idea seized him; he touched the bread and said interrogatively, "Bread?" M. du Tillet at once replied "Pain," which Harry repeated after him.

The ice thus broken, conversation began, and Harry soon learned the French for knife, fork, spoon, plate, and various other articles, and felt that he was fairly on the way towards talking French. After the meal was over M. du Tillet rose and put on his hat, and signed to Harry to accompany him. They strolled through the town, went down to the quays and looked at the fishing-boats; Harry was feeling more at home now, and asked the French name for everything he saw, repeating the word over and over again to himself until he felt sure that he should remember it, and then asking the name of some fresh object.

The next morning they started in the post-waggon for Paris, and arrived there after thirty-six hours' travel. Harry was struck with the roads, which were far better tended and kept than those in England. The extreme flatness of the country surprised him, and, except in the quaintness of the villages and the variety of the church towers, he saw little to admire during the journey.

"If it is all like this," he thought to himself, "I don't see that they have any reason for calling it La belle France."

Of Paris he saw little. A blue-bloused porter carried his trunk what seemed to Harry a long distance from the place where the

10

conveyance stopped. The streets here were quiet and almost deserted after the busy thoroughfares of the central city. The houses stood, for the most part, back from the street, with high walls and heavy gates.

"Here we are at last," his guide said, as he halted before a large and massive gateway, surmounted by a coat of arms with supporters carved in stone work. He rang at the bell, which was opened by a porter in livery, who bowed profoundly upon seeing M. du Tillet. Passing through the doorway, Harry found himself in a spacious hall, decorated with armour and arms. As he crossed the threshold M. du Tillet took his hand and shook it heartily, saying, "Welcome!" Harry understood the action, though not the words, and nodded, saying:

"I think I shall get on capitally if they are all as jolly as you are."

Then they both laughed, and Harry looked round wondering what was coming next.

"The marquis and his family are all away at their chateau near Dijon," his companion said, waving his hand. "We shall stay a day or two to rest ourselves after our journey, and then start to join them."

He led Harry into a great salon magnificently furnished, pointed to the chairs and looking-glasses and other articles of furniture, all swathed up in coverings; and the lad understood at once that the family were away. This was a relief to him; he was getting on capitally with M. du Tillet, but shrank from the prospect of meeting so many strange faces.

A meal was speedily served in a small and comfortably-furnished apartment; and Harry concluded that although he might not be able to decide on the nature of his food, it was really nice, and that there was no fear whatever of his falling away in flesh. M. du Tillet pressed him to try the wine again, and this he found to be a vast improvement upon the vintage he had tasted at Calais.

After breakfast next morning they started for a walk, and Harry was delighted with the Louvre, the Tuileries, the Palais Royal, and other public buildings, which he could not but acknowledge were vastly superior to anything he had seen in London. Then he was taken to a tailor's, the marquis having commissioned his guide to carry out Dr. Sandwith's request in this matter. M. du Tillet looked interrogatively at Harry as he entered the shop, as if to ask if he understood why he was taken there.

Harry nodded, for indeed he was glad to see that no time was to be lost, for he was already conscious that his dress differed

11

considerably from that of French boys. Several street gamins had pointed at him and made jeering remarks, which, without understanding the words, Harry felt to be insulting, and would, had he heard them in the purlieus of Westminster, have considered as a challenge to battle. He had not, however, suffered altogether unavenged, for upon one occasion M. du Tillet turned sharply round and caught one offender so smartly with his cane that he ran howling away.

"They are awful guys!" Harry thought as he looked at the French boys he met. "But it's better to be a guy than to be chaffed by every boy one meets, especially if one is not to be allowed to fight." It was, therefore, with a feeling of satisfaction that he turned into the tailor's shop. The proprietor came up bowing, as Harry thought, in a most cringing sort of way to his companion. M. du Tillet gave some orders, and the tailor unrolled a variety of pieces of cloth and other materials for Harry's inspection.

The lad shook his head and turned to his guide, and, pointing to the goods, asked him to choose the things which were most suitable for him; M. du Tillet understood the appeal and ordered four suits. Two of these were for ordinary wear; another was, Harry concluded, for the evening; and the fourth for ceremonial occasions.

The coats were cut long, but very open in front, and were far too scanty to button; the waistcoats were long and embroidered; a white and ample handkerchief went round the throat and was tied loosely, with long ends edged with lace falling in front; knee-breeches, with white stockings, and shoes with buckles, completed the costume.

Harry looked on with a smile of amusement, and burst into a hearty laugh when the garments were fixed upon, for the idea of himself dressed out in these seemed to him ludicrous in the extreme.

"How they would laugh at home," he thought to himself, "if they could see me in these things! The girls would give me no peace. And wouldn't there be an uproar if I were to turn up in them in Dean's Yard and march up school!"

Harry was then measured. When this was done he took out his purse, which contained fifty guineas; for his father had thought it probable that the clothes he would require would cost more than they would in London, and he wished him to have a good store of pocket-money until he received the first instalment of his pay. M. du Tillet, however, shook his head and motioned to him to put up his purse; and Harry supposed that it was not customary to pay for things in France until they were delivered. Then his companion took him into another shop, and pointing to his own ruffles intimated that Harry would require some linen of this kind to be worn when in full dress. Harry signified that his friend should order what was necessary; and half a dozen shirts, with deep ruffles at the wrist and breast, were ordered. This brought their shopping to an end.

They remained three days in Paris, at the end of which time Harry's clothes were delivered. The following morning a carriage with the arms of the marquis emblazoned upon it came up to the door, and they started. The horses were fat and lazy; and Harry, who had no idea how far they were going, thought that the journey was likely to be a long one if this was the pace at which they were to travel.

Twelve miles out they changed horses at a post-station, their own returning to Paris, and after this had relays at each station, and travelled at a pace which seemed to Harry to be extraordinarily rapid. They slept twice upon the road.

The third day the appearance of the country altogether changed, and, instead of the flat plains which Harry had begun to think extended all over France, they were now among hills higher than anything he had ever seen before. Towards the afternoon they crossed the range and began to descend, and as evening approached M. du Tillet pointed to a building standing on rising ground some miles away and said:

"That is the chateau."

CHAPTER II

A MAD DOG

It was dark before the carriage drove up to the chateau. Their approach had been seen, for two lackeys appeared with torches at the head of the broad steps. M. du Tillet put his hand encouragingly on Harry's shoulder and led him up the steps. A servant preceded them across a great hall, when a door opened and a gentleman came forward.

"Monsieur le Marquis," M. du Tillet said, bowing, "this is the young gentleman you charged me to bring to you.

"I am glad to see you," the marquis said; "and I hope you will make yourself happy and comfortable here."

Harry did not understand the words, but he felt the tone of kindness and courtesy with which they were spoken. He could, however, only bow; for although in the eight days he had spent with M. du Tillet he had picked up a great many nouns and a few phrases, his stock of words was of no use to him at present.

"And you, M. du Tillet," the marquis said. "You have made a good journey, I hope? I thank you much for the trouble you have taken. I like the boy's looks; what do you think of him?"

"I like him very much," M. du Tillet said; "he is a new type to me, and a pleasant one. I think he will make a good companion for the young count."

The marquis now turned and led the way into a great drawing-room, and taking Harry's hand led him up to a lady seated on a couch.

"This is our young English friend, Julie. Of course he is strange at present, but M. du Tillet reports well of him, and I already like his face."

The lady held out her hand, which Harry, instead of bending over and kissing, as she had expected, shook heartily. For an instant only a look of intense surprise passed across her face; then she said courteously:

"We are glad to see you. It is very good of you to come so far to us. I trust that you will be happy here."

"These are my sons Ernest and Jules, who will, I am sure, do all in their power to make you comfortable," the marquis said.

The last words were spoken sharply and significantly, and their tone was not lost upon the two boys; they had a moment before been struggling to prevent themselves bursting into a laugh at Harry's reception of their mother's greeting, but they now instantly composed their faces and advanced.

"Shake hands with him," the marquis said sharply; "it is the custom of his country."

Each in turn held out his hand to Harry, who, as he shook hands with them, took a mental stock of his future companions.

"Good looking," he said to himself, "but more like girls than boys. A year in the fifth form would do them a world of good. I could polish the two off together with one hand."

"My daughters," the marquis said, "Mesdemoiselles Marie, Jeanne, and Virginie."

Three young ladies had risen from their seats as their father entered, each made a deep curtsy as her name was mentioned, and Harry bowed deeply in return. Mademoiselle Marie was two years at least older than himself, and was already a young lady of fashion. Jeanne struck him as being about the same age as his sister Fanny, who was between fourteen and fifteen. Virginie was a child of ten. Ernest was about his own age, while Jules came between the two younger girls.

"Take M. Sandwith to the abbe," the marquis said to Ernest, "and do all in your power to set him at his ease. Remember what you would feel if you were placed, as he is, among strange people in a strange country."

The lad motioned to Harry to accompany him, and the three boys left the room together.

"You can go to your gouvernante," the marquise said to the two younger girls; and with a profound curtsy to her and another to the marquis, they left the room. Unrestrained now by their presence, the marquise turned to her husband with a merry laugh.

"But it is a bear you have brought home, Edouard, a veritable bear—my fingers ache still—and he is to teach manners to my sons! I always protested against the plan, but I did not think it would be as bad as this. These islanders are savages."

The marquis smiled.

"He is a little gauche, but that will soon rub off. I like him, Julie. Remember it was a difficult position for a boy. We did not have him here to give polish to our sons. It may be that they have even a little too much of this at present. The English are not polished, everyone knows that, but they are manly and independent. That boy bore himself well. He probably had never been in a room like this in his life, he was ignorant of our language, alone among strangers, but he was calm and self-possessed. I like

15

the honest straightforward look in his face. And look at the width of the shoulders and the strength of his arms; why, he would break Ernest across his knee, and the two boys must be about the same age."

"Oh, he has brute strength, I grant," the marquise said; "so have the sons of our peasants; however, I do not want to find fault with him, it is your hobby, or rather that of Auguste, who is, I think, mad about these English; I will say nothing to prevent its having a fair trial, only I hope it will not be necessary for me to give him my hand again."

"I do not suppose it will until he leaves, Julie, and by that time, no doubt, he will know what to do with it; but here is M. du Tillet waiting all this time for you to speak to him."

"Pardon me, my good M. du Tillet," the marquise said. "In truth that squeeze of my hand has driven all other matters from my mind. How have you fared? This long journey with this English bear must have been very tedious for you."

"Indeed, Madame la Marquise," M. du Tillet replied, "it has been no hardship, the boy has amused me greatly; nay, more, he has pleased me. We have been able to say little to each other, though, indeed, he is quick and eager to learn, and will soon speak our language; but his face has been a study. When he is pleased you can see that he is pleased, and that is a pleasure, for few people are pleased in our days. Again, when he does not like a thing you can also see it. I can see that he says to himself, I can expect nothing better, these poor people are only French. When the gamins in Paris jeered him as to his dress, he closed his hands and would have flown at them with his fists after the manner of his countrymen had he not put strong restraint on himself. From the look of his honest eyes I shall, when he can speak our language, believe implicitly what he says. That boy would not tell a lie whatever were the consequences. Altogether I like him much. I think that in a very little while he will adapt himself to what goes on around him, and that you will have no reason ere long to complain of his gaucheries."

"And you really think, M. du Tillet, that he will be a useful companion for my boys?"

"If you will pardon me for saying so, madam, I think that he will—at any rate I am sure he can be trusted to teach them no wrong."

"You are all against me," the marquise laughed. "And you, Marie?"

"I did not think of him one way or the other," the girl said coldly. "He is very awkward; but as he is not to be my companion that does not concern me. It is like one of papa's dogs, one more or less makes no difference in the house so long as they do not tread upon one's skirt."

"That is the true spirit of the French nobility, Marie," her father said sarcastically. "Outside our own circle the whole human race is nothing to us; they are animals who supply our wants, voila tour. I tell you, my dear, that the time is coming when this will not suffice. The nation is stirring; that France which we have so long ignored is lifting its head and muttering; the news from Paris is more and more grave. The Assembly has assumed the supreme authority, and the king is a puppet in its power. The air is dark as with a thunder-cloud, and there may be such a storm sweep over France as there has not been since the days of the Jacquerie."

"But the people should be contented," M. du Tillet said; "they have had all the privileges they ever possessed given back to them."

"Yes," the marquis assented, "and there lies the danger. It is one thing or the other. If as soon as the temper of the third estate had been seen the king's guards had entered and cleared the place and closed the door, as Cromwell did when the parliament was troublesome to him in England, that would have been one way. Paris would have been troublesome, we might have had again the days of the Fronde, but in the end the king's party would have won.

"However, that was not the way tried. They began by concessions, they go on with concessions, and each concession is made the ground for more. It is like sliding down a hill; when you have once begun you cannot stop yourself, and you go on until there is a crash; then it may be you pick yourself up sorely wounded and bruised, and begin to reclimb the hill slowly and painfully; it may be that you are dashed to pieces. I am not a politician. I do not care much for the life of Paris, and am well content to live quietly here on our estates; but even I can see that a storm is gathering; and as for my brother Auguste, he goes about shaking his head and wringing his hands, his anticipations are of the darkest. What can one expect when fellows like Voltaire and Rousseau were permitted by their poisonous preaching to corrupt and inflame the imagination of the people? Both those men's heads should have been cut off the instant they began to write.

"The scribblers are at the root of all the trouble with their pestilent doctrines; but it is too late now, the mischief is done. If we had a king strong and determined all might yet be well; but Louis is weak in decision, he listens one moment to Mirabeau and the next to the queen, who is more firm and courageous. And so things drift on from bad to worse, and the Assembly, backed by the turbulent scum of Paris, are masters of the situation."

For some time Harry lived a quiet life at the chateau. He found his position a very pleasant one. The orders of the marquis that he should be treated as one of the family were obeyed, and there was no distinction made between himself and Ernest. In the morning the two boys and himself worked with the abbe, a quiet and gentle old man; in the afternoon they rode and fenced, under the instructions of M. du Tillet or one or other of the gentlemen of the marquis establishment; and on holidays shot or fished as they chose on the preserves or streams of the estate. For an hour each morning the two younger girls shared in their studies, learning Latin and history with their brothers. Harry got on very well with Ernest, but there was no real cordiality between them. The hauteur and insolence with which the young count treated his inferiors were a constant source of exasperation to Harry.

"He thinks himself a little god," he would often mutter to himself. "I would give a good deal to have him for three months at Westminster. Wouldn't he get his conceit and nonsense knocked out of him!"

At the same time he was always scrupulously polite and courteous to his English companion—much too polite, indeed, to please Harry. He had good qualities too: he was generous with his money, and if during their rides a woman came up with a tale of distress he was always ready to assist her. He was clever, and Harry, to his surprise, found that his knowledge of Latin was far beyond his own, and that Ernest could construct passages with the greatest ease which altogether puzzled him. He was a splendid rider, and could keep his seat with ease and grace on the most fiery animals in his father's stables.

When they went out with their guns Harry felt his inferiority keenly. Not only was Ernest an excellent shot, but at the end of a long day's sport he would come in apparently fresh and untired, while Harry, although bodily far the most powerful, would be completely done up; and at gymnastic exercises he could do with ease feats which Harry could at first not even attempt. In this respect, however, the English lad in three months' time was able to rival him. His disgust at finding himself so easily beaten by a French boy nerved him to the greatest exertions, and his muscles, practised in all sorts of games, soon adapted themselves to the new exercises.

Harry picked up French very rapidly. The absolute necessity there was to express himself in that language caused him to make a progress which surprised himself, and at the end of three months he was able to converse with little difficulty, and having learned it entirely by ear he spoke with a fair accent and pronunciation. M. du Tillet, who was the principal instructor of the boys in their outdoor exercises, took much pains to assist him in his French, and helped him on in every way in his power.

In the evening there were dancing lessons, and although very far from exhibiting the stately grace with which Ernest could perform the minuet or other courtly dances then in fashion, Harry came in time to perform his part fairly. Two hours were spent in the evening in the salon. This part of the day Harry at first found the most tedious; but as soon as he began to speak fluently the marquis addressed most of his conversation to him, asking him questions about the life of English boys at school and about English manners and customs, and Harry soon found himself chatting at his ease.

"The distinction of classes is clearly very much less with you in England than it is here," the marquis said one day when Harry had been describing a great fight which had taken place between a party of Westminster boys and those of the neighbourhood. "It seems extraordinary to me that sons of gentlemen should engage in a personal fight with boys of the lowest class. Such a thing could not happen here. If you were insulted by such a boy, what would you do, Ernest?"

"I should run him through the body," Ernest said quietly.

"Just so," his father replied, "and I don't say you would be wrong according to our notions; but I do not say that the English plan is not the best. The English gentleman—for Monsieur Sandwith says that even among grown-up people the same habits prevail—does not disdain to show the canaille that even with their own rough weapons he is their superior, and he thus holds their respect. It is a coarse way and altogether at variance with our notions, but there is much to be said for it."

"But it altogether does away with the reverence that the lower class should feel for the upper," Ernest objected.

"That is true, Ernest. So long as that feeling generally exists, so long as there is, as it were, a wide chasm between the two classes, as there has always existed in France, it would be unwise perhaps for one of the upper to admit that in any respect there could be any equality between them; but this is not so in England, where a certain equality has always been allowed to exist. The Englishman of all ranks has a certain feeling of self-respect and independence, and the result is shown in the history of the wars which have been fought between the two nations.

"France in early days always relied upon her chivalry. The

horde of footmen she placed in the field counted for little. England, upon the other hand, relied principally upon her archers and her pikemen, and it must be admitted that they beat us handsomely. Then again in the wars in Flanders, under the English general Marlborough their infantry always proved themselves superior to ours. It is galling to admit it, but there is no blinking the facts of history. It seems to me that the feeling of independence and self-respect which this English system gives rise to, even among the lowest class, must render them man for man better soldiers than those drawn from a peasantry whose very lives are at the mercy of their lords."

"I think, du Tillet," the marquis said later on on the same evening, when the young people had retired, "I have done very well in taking my brother Auguste's advice as to having an English companion for Ernest. If things were as they were under the Grand Monarque, I do not say that it would have been wise to allow a young French nobleman to get these English ideas into his head, but it is different now.

"We are on the eve of great changes. What will come of it no one can say; but there will certainly be changes, and it is a good thing that my children should get broader ideas than those in which we were brought up. This lad is quiet and modest, but he ventures to think for himself. It scarce entered the head of a French nobleman a generation back that the mass of the people had any feelings or wishes, much less rights. They were useful in their way, just as the animals are, but needed no more consideration. They have never counted for anything.

"In England the people have rights and liberties; they won them years ago. It would be well for us in the present day had they done so in France. I fancy the next generation will have to adapt themselves to changed circumstances, and the ideas that Ernest and Jules will learn from this English lad will be a great advantage to them, and will fit them for the new state of things."

It was only during lessons, when their gouvernante was always present, at meal times, and in the salon in the evening, that Harry had any communication with the young ladies of the family. If they met in the grounds they were saluted by the boys with as much formal courtesy as if they had been the most distant acquaintances, returning the bows with deep curtsies.

These meetings were a source of great amusement to Harry, who could scarcely preserve his gravity at these formal and distant greetings. On one occasion, however, the even course of these meetings was broken. The boys had just left the tennis-court where they had been playing, and had laid aside the swords which they carried when walking or riding.

The tennis-court was at some little distance from the house, and they were walking across the garden when they heard a scream. At a short distance was the governess with her two young charges. She had thrown her arms round them, and stood the picture of terror, uttering loud screams.

Looking round in astonishment to discover the cause of her terror, Harry saw a large wolf-hound running towards them at a trot. Its tongue was hanging out, and there was a white foam on its jaws. He had heard M. du Tillet tell the marquis on the previous day that this dog, which was a great favourite, seemed strange and unquiet, and he had ordered it to be chained up. It had evidently broken its fastening, for it was dragging a piece of chain some six feet long behind it.

It flashed across him at once that the animal was mad, but without an instant's hesitation he dashed off at full speed and threw himself in front of the ladies before the dog reached them. Snatching off his coat, and then kneeling on one knee, he awaited the animal's attack. Without deviating from its course the hound sprang at him with a short snarling howl. Harry threw his coat over its head and then grasped it round the neck.

The impetus of the spring knocked him over, and they rolled together on the ground. The animal struggled furiously, but Harry retained his grasp round its neck. In vain the hound tried to free itself from its blinding encumbrance, or to bite his assailant through it, and struggled to shake off his hold with its legs and claws. Harry maintained his grasp tightly round its neck, with his head pressed closely against one of its ears. Several times they rolled over and over. At last Harry made a great effort when he was uppermost, and managed to get his knees upon the animal's belly, and then, digging his toes in the ground, pressed with all his weight upon it.

There was a sound as of cracking of bones, then the dog's struggles suddenly ceased, and his head fell over, and Harry rose to his feet by the side of the dead hound just as a number of men, with pitch-forks and other weapons, ran up to the spot from the stables, while the marquis, sword in hand, arrived from the house.

The gouvernante, too, paralysed by fear, had stood close by with her charges while the struggle was going on. Ernest had come up, and was standing in front of his sisters, ready to be the next victim if the dog had overpowered Harry. Less accustomed to running than the English boy, and for a moment rooted to the ground with horror at his sisters' danger, he had not arrived at the spot until the struggle between Harry and the dog was half over, and had then seen no way of rendering assistance; but believing that the dog was sure to be the conqueror, he had placed himself before his sisters to bear the brunt of the next assault.

Seeing at a glance that his daughters were untouched, the marquis ran on to Harry, who was standing panting and breathless, and threw his arms round him.

"My brave boy," he exclaimed, "you have saved my daughters from a dreadful death by your courage and devotion. How can I and their mother ever thank you? I saw it all from the terrace—the speed with which you sprang to their assistance—the quickness of thought with which you stripped off your coat and threw it over its head. After that I could see nothing except your rolling over and over in a confused mass. You are not hurt, I trust?"

"Not a bit, sir," Harry said.

"And you have killed it—wonderful!"

"There was nothing in that, sir. I have heard my father, who is a doctor, say that a man could kill the biggest dog if he could get it down on its back and kneel on it. So when I once managed to get my knees on it I felt it was all right."

"Ah, it is all very well for you to speak as if it were nothing!" the marquis said. "There are few men, indeed, who would throw themselves in the way of a mad dog, especially of such a formidable brute as that. You too have behaved with courage, my son, and I saw you were ready to give your life for your sisters; but you had not the quickness and readiness of your friend, and would have been too late."

"It is true, father," Ernest said in a tone of humility. "I should have been too late, and, moreover, I should have been useless, for he would have torn me down in a moment, and then fallen upon my sisters. M. Sandwith," he said frankly, "I own I have been wrong. I have thought the games of which you spoke, and your fighting, rough and barbarous; but I see their use now. You have put me to shame. When I saw that dog I felt powerless, for I had not my sword with me; but you—you rushed to the fight without a moment's hesitation, trusting in your strength and your head. Yes, your customs have made a man of you, while I am a boy still."

"You are very good to say so," Harry said; "but I am quite sure that you would be just as quick and ready as me in most circumstances, and if it had been a matter of swords, very much more useful; but I am glad you see there is some advantage in our rough English ways."

The marquis had put his hand approvingly upon Ernest's

shoulder when he addressed Harry, and then turned to his daughters. The governess had sunk fainting to the ground when she saw that the danger was over. Virginie had thrown herself down and was crying loudly; while Jeanne stood pale, but quiet, beside them.

The marquis directed one of the men to run up to the chateau and bid a female servant bring down water and smelling-salts for the governess, and then lifted Virginie up and tried to soothe her, while he stretched out his other hand to Jeanne.

"You are shaken, my Jeanne," he said tenderly, "but you have borne the trial well. I did not hear you cry out, though madame, and the little one screamed loudly enough."

"I was frightened enough, father," she said simply, "but of course I wasn't going to cry out; but it was very terrible; and oh, how noble and brave he was! And you know, papa, I feel ashamed to think how often I have been nearly laughing because he was awkward in the minuet. I feel so little now beside him."

"You see, my dear, one must not judge too much by externals," her father said soothingly as she hid her face against his coat, and he could feel that she was trembling from head to foot. "Older people than you often do so, and are sorry for it afterwards; but as I am sure that you would never allow him to see that you were amused no harm has been done."

"Shall I thank him, papa?"

"Yes, presently, my dear; he has just gone off with Ernest to see them bury the dog."

This incident caused a considerable change in Harry's position in the family. Previously he had been accepted in consequence of the orders of the marquis. Although compelled to treat him as an equal the two boys had in their hearts looked upon him as an inferior, while the girls had regarded him as a sort of tutor of their brothers, and thus as a creature altogether indifferent to them. But henceforth he appeared in a different light. Ernest acted up to the spirit of the words he had spoken at the time, and henceforth treated him as a comrade to be respected as well as liked. He tried to learn some of the English games, but as most of these required more than two players he was forced to abandon them. He even asked him to teach him to box, but Harry had the good sense to make excuses for not doing so. He felt that Ernest was by no means his match in strength, and that, with all his good-will, he would find it difficult to put up good-naturedly with being knocked about. He therefore said that it could not be done without boxing-gloves, and these it would be impossible to obtain in France; and that in the next place he should hardly advise him to learn even if he procured the gloves, for that in such contests severe bruises often were given.

"We think nothing of a black eye," he said laughing, "but I am sure madame your mother would not be pleased to see you so marked; besides, your people would not understand your motive in undertaking so rough an exercise, and you might lose somewhat of their respect. Be content, Count Ernest; you are an excellent swordsman, and although I am improving under M. du Tillet's tuition I shall never be your match. If you like; sometime when we are out and away from observation we can take off our coats, and I can give you a lesson in wrestling; it is a splendid exercise, and it has not the disadvantages of boxing."

Little Jules looked up to Harry as a hero, and henceforth, when they were together, gave him the same sort of implicit obedience he paid to his elder brother. The ceremonious habits of the age prevented anything like familiarity on the part of the younger girls; but Jeanne and Virginie now always greeted him with a smile when they met, and joined in conversation with him as with their brothers in the evening.

The marquise, who had formerly protested, if playfully, against her husband's whim in introducing an English boy into their family circle, now regarded him with real affection, only refraining from constant allusions to the debt she considered she owed him because she saw that he really shrank from the subject.

The marquis shortly after this incident went to Paris for a fortnight to ascertain from his friends there the exact position of things. He returned depressed and angry.

The violence of the Assembly had increased from day to day. The property of all the convents had been confiscated, and this measure had been followed by the seizure of the vast estates of the church. All the privileges of the nobility had been declared at an end, and in August a decree had been passed abolishing all titles of nobility. This decree had taken effect in Paris and in the great towns, and also in some parts of the country where the passions of the people were most aroused against the nobility; but in Burgundy it had remained a dead letter. The Marquis de St. Caux was popular upon his estates, and no one had ever neglected to concede to him and to the marquise their titles. He himself had regarded the decree with disdain. "They may take away my estates by force," he said, "but no law can deprive me of my title, any more than of the name which I inherited from my fathers. Such laws as these are mere outbursts of folly."

But the Assembly continued to pass laws of the most sweeping description, assuming the sovereign power, and using it as no monarch of France had ever ventured to do. Moderate men were shocked at the headlong course of events, and numbers of those who at the commencement of the movement had thrown themselves heart and soul into it now shrank back in dismay at the strange tyranny which was called liberty.

"It seems to me that a general madness has seized all Paris," the marquis said to his wife on his return, "but at present nothing can be done to arrest it. I have seen the king and queen. His majesty is resolved to do nothing; that is, to let events take their course, and what that will be Heaven only knows. The Assembly has taken all power into its hands, the king is already a mere cipher, the violence of the leaders of these men is beyond all bounds; the queen is by turns hot and cold, at one moment she agrees with her husband that the only hope lies in conceding everything; at another she would go to the army, place herself in its hands, and call on it to march upon Paris.

"At anyrate there is nothing to be done at present but to wait. Already numbers of the deputies, terrified at the aspect of affairs, have left France, and I am sorry to say many of the nobles have also gone. This is cowardice and treachery to the king. We cannot help him if he will not be helped, but it is our duty to remain here ready to rally round him when he calls us to his side. I am glad that the Assembly has passed a law confiscating the estates of all who have emigrated."

Although the marquise was much alarmed at the news brought by her husband she did not think of questioning his decision. It did not seem to her possible that there could be danger for her and hers in their quiet country chateau. There might be disturbance and bloodshed, and even revolution, in Paris; but surely a mere echo of this would reach them so far away.

"Whenever you think it is right to go up and take your place by the king I will go and take mine by the queen," she said quietly. "The children will be safe here; but of course we must do our duty."

The winter passed quietly at the chateau; there was none of the usual gaiety, for a deep gloom hung over all the noble families of the province; still at times great hunting parties were got up for the chase of the wolves among the forests, for, when the snow was on the ground, these often came down into the villages and committed great depredations.

CHAPTER III

THE DEMON WOLF

Upon the first of these occasions Harry and Ernest were in high spirits, for they were to take part in the chase. It was the first time that Ernest had done so, for during the previous winter the marquis had been in attendance on the court. At an early hour the guests invited to take part in the chase began to assemble at the chateau. Many who lived at a distance had come overnight, and the great court-yard presented a lively aspect with the horses and attendants of the guests. A collation was spread in the great hall, and the marquise and her eldest daughter moved about among the guests saying a few words of welcome to each.

"Who is that young man who is talking to mademoiselle your sister, Ernest?" Harry asked, for since the adventure with the mad dog the ceremonious title had been dropped, and the boys addressed each other by their Christian names.

"That is Monsieur Lebat; he is the son of the Mayor of Dijon. I have not see him here before, but I suppose my father thinks it is well in these times to do the civil thing to the people of Dijon. He is a good-looking fellow too, but it is easy to see he is not a man of good family."

"I don't like his looks at all," Harry said shortly. "Look what a cringing air he puts on as he speaks to madame la marquise. And yet I fancy he could be insolent when he likes. He may be good-looking, but it is not a style I admire, with his thick lips and his half-closed eyes. If I met him at home I should say the fellow was something between a butcher and a Jew pedlar."

"Well done, monsieur the aristocrat!" Ernest said laughing. "This is your English equality! Here is a poor fellow who is allowed to take a place our of his station, thanks to the circumstances of the time, and you run him down mercilessly!"

"I don't run him down because he is not a gentleman," Harry said. "I run him down because I don't like his face; and if he were the son of a duke instead of the son of a mayor I should dislike it just as much. You take my word for it, Ernest, that's a bad fellow."

"Poor Monsieur Lebat!" Ernest laughed. "I daresay he is a very decent fellow in his way.

"I am sure he is not, Ernest; he has a cruel bad look. I would not have been that fellow's fag at school for any money.

"Well, it's fortunate, Harry, that you are not likely to see much of him, else I should expect to see you flying at his neck and strangling him as you did the hound."

Harry joined in the laugh.

"I will restrain myself, Ernest; and besides, he would be an awkward customer; there's plenty of strength in those shoulders of his, and he looks active and sinewy in spite of that indolent air he puts on; but there is the horn, it is time for us to mount."

In a few minutes some thirty gentlemen were in the saddle, the marquis, who was grand louvetier of the province, blew his horn, and the whole cavalcade got into motion, raising their hunting caps, as they rode off, to the marquise and her daughters, who were standing on the step of the chateau to see them depart. The dogs had already been sent forward to the forest, which was some miles distant.

On arriving there the marquis found several woodmen, who had been for the last two days marking the places most frequented by the wolves. They had given their reports and the party were just starting when a young forester rode up.

"Monsieur le marquis," he said, "I have good news for you; the demon wolf is in the forest. I saw him making his way along a glade an hour since as I was on my way thither. I turned back to follow him, and tracked him to a ravine in the hills choked with undergrowth."

The news created great excitement.

"The demon wolf!" the marquis repeated. "Are you sure?"

"Quite sure, monsieur. How could I mistake it! I saw him once four years ago, and no one who had once done so could mistake any other wolf for him."

"We are in luck indeed, gentlemen," the marquis said. "We will see if we can't bring this fellow's career to an end at last. I have hunted him a score of times myself since my first chase of him, well-nigh fifteen years ago, but he has always given us the slip."

"And will again," an old forester, who was standing close to Harry, muttered. "I do not believe the bullet is cast which will bring that wolf to earth."

"What is this demon wolf?" Harry asked Ernest.

"It is a wolf of extraordinary size and fierceness. For many years he has been the terror of the mothers of this part of France. He has been known to go into a village and boldly carry off an infant in mid-day. Every child who has been killed by wolves for years is always supposed to have been slain by this wolf. Sometimes he is seen in one part of the province, and sometimes in another.

"For months he is not heard of. Then there is slaughter among the young lambs. A child going to school, or an old woman carrying home a faggot from the forest is found torn and partly devoured, and the news spreads that the demon wolf has returned to the neighbourhood. Great hunts have over and over again been got up specially to slay him, but he seems to lead a charmed life. He has been shot at over and over again, but he seems to be bullet-proof.

"The peasants regard him not as an ordinary wolf but as a demon, and mothers quiet their children when they cry by saying that if they are not good the demon wolf will carry them off. Ah, if we could kill him to-day it would be a grand occasion!"

"Is there anything particular about his appearance?"

"Nothing except his size. Some of those who have seen him declare that he is as big as three ordinary wolves; but my father, who has caught sight of him several times, says that this is an exaggeration, though he is by far the largest wolf he ever saw. He is lighter in colour than other wolves, but those who saw him years ago say that this was not the case then, and that his light colour must be due to his great age."

The party now started, under the guidance of the forester, to the spot where he had seen the wolf enter the underwood.

It was the head of a narrow valley. The sides which inclosed it sloped steeply, but not too much so for the wolf to climb. During the last halt the marquis had arranged the plan of action. He himself, with three of the most experienced huntsmen, took their stations across the valley, which was but seventy or eighty yards wide. Eight of the others were to dismount and take post on either side of the ravine.

"I am sorry, gentlemen, that I cannot find posts for the rest of you, but you may have your share of the work. Over and over again this wolf has slipped away when we thought we had him surrounded, and what he has done before he may do again. Therefore, let each of you take up such a position as he thinks best outside our circle, but keeping well behind trees or other shelter, so as to cover himself from any random shot that may be fired after the wolf. Do you, on your part, fire only when the wolf has passed your line, or you may hit some of us."

The two lads were naturally among those left out from the inner circle.

"What do you think, Ernest; shall we remain on our horses here in the valley or climb the hills?"

"I should say wait here, Harry; in the first place, because it is the least trouble, and in the second, because I think he is as likely to

28

come this way as any other. At any rate we may as well dismount here, and let horses crop that piece of fresh grass until we hear the horn that will tell us when the dogs have been turned into the thicket to drive him out."

It was half an hour before they heard the distant note of the horn.

"They have begun," Ernest exclaimed; "we had better mount at once. If the brute is still there he is just as likely, being such an old hand at the sport, to make a bolt at once, instead of waiting until the dogs are close to him."

"What are we to do if we see him?" Harry asked.

"We are to shoot him if we can. If we miss him, or he glides past before we can get a shot, we must follow shouting, so as to guide the rest as to the direction he is taking."

"My chance of hitting him is not great," Harry said. "I am not a very good shot even on my feet; but sitting in my saddle I do not think it likely I should get anywhere near him."

A quarter of an hour passed. The occasional note of a dog and the shouts of the men encouraging them to work their way through the dense thicket could be heard, but no sound of a shot met their ears.

"Either he is not there at all, or he is lying very close," Ernest said.

"Look, look!" Harry said suddenly, pointing through the trees to the right.

"That is the wolf, sure enough," Ernest exclaimed. "Come along."

The two lads spurred their horses and rode recklessly through the trees towards the great gray beast, who seemed to flit like a shadow past them.

"Mind the boughs, Ernest, or you will be swept from your saddle. Hurrah! The trees are more open in front."

But although the horses were going at the top of their speed they scarcely seemed to gain on the wolf, who, as it seemed to them, kept his distance ahead without any great exertion.

"We shall never catch him," Harry exclaimed after they had ridden for nearly half an hour, and the laboured panting of the horses showed that they could not long maintain the pace.

Suddenly, ten yards ahead of the wolf, a man, armed with a hatchet, stepped out from behind a tree directly in its way. He was a wood-cutter whose attention being called by the sound of the galloping feet of the horses, had left his half-hewn tree and stepped out to see who was coming. He gave an exclamation of surprise and alarm as he saw the wolf, and raised his hatchet to defend himself. Without a moment's hesitation the animal sprang upon him and carried him to the ground, fixing its fangs into his throat. There was a struggle for a few moments, and then the wolf left its lifeless foe and was about to continue its flight.

"Get ready to fire, Harry," Ernest exclaimed as the wolf sprang upon the man, "it is our last chance. If he gets away now we shall never catch him."

They reined in their horses just as the wolf rose to fly. Harry fired first, but the movement of his panting horse deranged his aim and the bullet flew wide. More accustomed to firing on horseback, Ernest's aim was truer, he struck the wolf on the shoulder, and it rolled over and over. With a shout of triumph the boys dashed forward, but when they were within a few paces the wolf leapt to its feet and endeavoured to spring towards them. Harry's horse wheeled aside so sharply that he was hurled from the saddle.

The shock was a severe one, and before he could rise to his feet the wolf was close upon him. He tried as he rose to draw his hunting-sword, but before he could do so, Ernest, who had, when he saw him fall, at once leaped from his horse, threw himself before him, and dealt the wolf a severe blow on the head with his weapon.

Furious with rage and pain the wolf sprang upon him and seized him by the shoulder. Ernest dropped his sword, and drawing his hunting-knife struck at it, while at the same moment Harry ran it through the body.

So strong and tenacious of life was the animal that the blows were repeated several times before it loosed its hold of Ernest's shoulder and fell dead.

"Are you hurt, my dear Ernest?" was Harry's first exclamation.

"Oh, never mind that, that's nothing," Ernest replied. "Only think, Harry, you and I have killed the demon wolf, and no else had a hand in it. There is a triumph for us."

"The triumph is yours, Ernest," Harry said. "He would have got away had you not stopped him with your bullet, and he would have made short work of me had you not come to my rescue, for I was half stunned with the fall, and he would have done for me as quickly as he did for that poor fellow there."

"That is true, Harry, but it was you who gave him his mortal wound. He would have mastered me otherwise. He was too strong for me, and would have borne me to the ground. No, it's a joint business, and we have both a right to be proud of it. Now let us fasten him on my horse; but before we do that, you must bind up my shoulder somehow. In spite of my thick doublet he has bit me very sharply. But first let us see to this poor fellow. I fear he is dead."

It was soon seen that nothing could be done for the woodman, who had been killed almost instantly. Harry, therefore, proceeded to cut off Ernest's coat-sleeve and bathed the wound. The flesh was badly torn, and the arm was so useless that he thought that some bones were broken. Having done his best to bandage the wound, he strapped the arm firmly across the body, so as to prevent its being shaken by the motion of the riding. It was with the greatest difficulty that they were able to lift the body of the wolf, but could not lay it across the horse, as the animal plunged and kicked and refused to allow it to be brought near. Ernest was able to assist but little, for now that the excitement was over he felt faint and sick with the pain of his wound.

"I think you had better ride off, Harry, and bring some one to our assistance. I will wait here till you come back."

"I don't like to do that," Harry said. "They must be seven or eight miles away, and I may not be able to find them. They may have moved away to some other part of the forest. Ah! I have an idea! Suppose I cut a pole, tie the wolf's legs together and put the pole through them; then we can hoist the pole up and lash its ends behind the two saddles. The horses may not mind so much if it's not put upon their backs."

"That might do," Ernest agreed; "but you mustn't make the pole more than six or seven feet long, or we shall have difficulty in riding between the trees."

The pole was soon cut and the wolf in readiness to be lifted, but the horses still refused to stand steady.

"Blindfold them, Harry," Ernest said suddenly, "and tie them up to two trees a few feet apart."

This was soon done, and the boys then patted and soothed them until they became quiet. The pole was now lifted, and this time they managed to lay it across the saddles and to lash it securely to the cantles. Then they mounted, and taking the bandages off the horses' eyes set out on their way. The horses were fidgety at first, but presently fell into a quiet walk.

For upwards of an hour they heard nothing of the huntsmen. Not a sound broke the stillness of the forest; the sun was shining through the leafless trees, and they were therefore enabled to shape their course in the direction in which they had come. Presently they heard the sound of a shot, followed by several others, and then the bay of hounds. The sound came from their left.

31

"They have been trying a fresh place," Ernest said, "and I expect they have come upon two wolves; one they have shot, the hounds are after the other."

They turned their horses' heads in the direction of the sounds, and presently Harry said:

"They are coming this way."

Louder and louder grew the sounds of the chase; then the deep tones of the hounds were exchanged for a fierce angry barking.

"The wolf is at bay!" Ernest exclaimed.

A minute later some notes were sounded on the horn.

"That is the mort, Harry. We shall arrive before they move on again."

Five minutes later they rode into a glade where a number of horsemen were assembled. There was a shout as they were seen.

"Why, Ernest," the marquis called as they approached, "we thought you had lost us. You have missed some rare sport; but what's the matter with your arm, and what have you got there?"

"We have got the demon wolf," Ernest replied; "so you haven't had all the sport to yourselves."

There was a general exclamation of surprise and almost incredulity, and then every one rode over to meet them, and when it was seen that the object slung between the two horses was really the demon wolf there was a shout of satisfaction and pleasure. Again the notes of the mort rang out through the woods, and every one crowded round the lads to congratulate them and to examine the dead monster. Ernest was lifted from his horse, for he was now reeling in the saddle, and could not have kept his seat many minutes longer. His wound was carefully examined, and the marquis pronounced the shoulder-bone to be broken. A litter was made and four of the foresters hoisted him upon their shoulders, while four others carried the wolf, still slung on its pole, behind the litter. While the preparations were being made Harry had given the history of the slaying of the wolf, saying that he owed his life to the quickness and courage of Ernest.

"And I owe mine to him," Ernest protested from the bank where he was lying. "The wolf would have killed me had he not slain it. I was lucky in stopping it with a ball, but the rest was entirely a joint affair."

The slaying of the demon wolf was so important an event that no one thought of pursuing the hunt further that day. The other two wolves were added to the procession, but they looked small and insignificant beside the body of that killed by the boys. Harry learned that no one had suspected that they had gone in pursuit of the wolf. A vigilant look-out had been kept all round the thicket, while the dogs hunted it from end to end, but no signs had been seen of it, and none were able to understand how it could have slipped between the watchers unseen.

After the ravine had been thoroughly beaten the party had moved off to another cover. On their way there the marquis had missed the two boys. No one had seen them, and it was supposed that they had loitered behind in the forest. Two or three notes of recall had been blown, and then no one had thought more of the matter until they rode into the glade when the second wolf had just been pulled down by the pack.

It was afternoon when the hunting party arrived at the chateau. Before they started homewards the marquis had sent off two horsemen; one to Dijon to bring a surgeon with all speed to the chateau, the other to tell the marquise that Ernest had been hurt, and that everything was to be got in readiness for him; but that she was not to make herself uneasy, as the injury was not a serious one. The messengers were charged strictly to say nothing about the death of the demon wolf.

The marquise and her daughters were at the entrance as the party arrived. The sight of the litter added to the anxiety which Ernest's mother was feeling; but the marquis rode on a short distance ahead to her.

"Do not be alarmed, Julie," he said; "the lad is not very seriously hurt. He has been torn a bit by a wolf, and has behaved splendidly."

"The messenger said he had been hurt by a wolf, Edouard; but how came he to put himself in such peril?"

"He will tell you all about it, my dear. Here he is to speak for himself."

"Do not look so alarmed, mother," Ernest said as she ran down to the side of the litter. "It is no great harm, and I should not have minded if it had been ten times as bad."

"Bring up the wolf," the marquis said, "and Harry, do you come here and stand by Ernest's side. Madam la marquise," he went on, "do you see that great gray wolf? That is the demon wolf which has for years been the terror of the district, and these are its slayers. Your son and M. Sandwith, they, and they alone, have reaped the glory which every sportsman in Burgundy has been so long striving to attain; they alone in the forest, miles away from the hunt, pursued and slew this scourge of the province."

He put his horn to his lips. The others who carried similar

33

instruments followed his example. A triumphant traralira was blown. All present took off their hunting-caps and cheered, and the hounds added their barking to the chorus.

"Is it possible, Edward," the marquise said, terrified at the thought of the danger her son must have run in an encounter with the dreaded beast, "is it possible that these two alone have slain this dreadful wolf?"

"It is quite possible, my dear, since it has been done, though, had you asked me yesterday, I should almost have said that it could not be; however, there it is. Ernest and his brave young friend have covered themselves with glory; they will be the heroes of the department. But we must not stay talking here. We must get Ernest into bed as soon as possible. A surgeon will be here very shortly. I sent a messenger on to Dijon for one at the same time I sent to you."

The marquis stayed outside for a few minutes while the domestics handed round great silver cups full of spiced wine, and then bidding good-bye to his guests entered the chateau just as the surgeon rode up to the entrance.

"Please tell us all about it," his daughters asked him when, having seen the surgeon set the broken bone and bandage the wound, operations which Ernest bore with stoical firmness, he went down to the salon where his daughters were anxiously expecting him. "All about it, please. We have heard nothing, for Harry went upstairs with Ernest, and has not come down again."

The marquis told the whole story, how the wolf had made his escape unseen through the cordon round his lair, and had passed within the sight of the two boys some distance away, and how they had hunted it down and slain it. The girls shuddered at the story of the death of the wood-cutter and the short but desperate conflict with the wolf.

"Then Ernest has the principal honour this time," the eldest girl said.

"It is pretty evenly divided," the marquis said. "You see Ernest brought the wolf to bay by breaking its shoulder, and struck the first blow as it was flying upon Harry, who had been thrown from his horse. Then, again, Ernest would almost certainly have been killed had not Harry in his turn come to his assistance and dealt it its mortal blows. There is not much difference, but perhaps the chief honours rest with Ernest."

"I am glad of that, papa," Mademoiselle de St. Caux said; "it is only right the chief honour should be with your son and not with this English boy. He has had more than his share already, I think."

"You would not think so if he had saved your life, sister," Jeanne broke in impetuously. "It was very brave of them both to kill the wolf; but I think it was ever, ever so much braver to attack a great mad dog without weapons. Don't you think so, papa?"

"I don't think you should speak so warmly to your elder sister, Jeanne," the marquis said; "she is a grown-up young lady, and you are in the school-room. Still, in answer to your question, I admit that the first was very much the braver deed. I myself should have liked nothing better than to stand before that great wolf with my hunting sword in my hand; but although if I had been near you when the hound attacked you, I should doubtless have thrown myself before you, I should have been horribly frightened and should certainly have been killed; for I should never have thought of or carried so promptly out the plan which Harry adopted of muzzling the animal. But there is no need to make comparisons. On the present occasion both the lads have behaved with great bravery, and I am proud that Ernest is one of the conquerors of the demon wolf. It will start him in life with a reputation already established for courage. Now, come with me and have a look at the wolf. I don't think such a beast was ever before seen in France. I am going to have him stuffed and set up as a trophy. He shall stand over the fireplace in the hall, and long after we have all mouldered to dust our descendants will point to it proudly, telling how a lad of their race, with another his own age, slew the demon wolf of Burgundy."

Ernest was confined to his bed for nearly a month, and during this time Harry often went long rides and walks by himself. In the evening the marquis frequently talked with him over the situation of the country and compared the events which had taken place with the struggle of the English parliament with the king.

"There was one point of difference between the two cases," he said one evening. "In England the people had already great power in the state. The parliament had always been a check upon the royal authority; and it was because the king tried to overrule parliament that the trouble came about. Here our kings, or at least the ministers they appointed, have always governed; often unwisely I admit, but is it likely that the mob would govern better? That is the question. At present they seem bent on showing their incapacity to govern even themselves."

The Marquis de St. Caux had, in some respects, the thoughts and opinions of the old school. He was a royalist pure and simple. As to politics, he troubled his head little about them. These were a matter for ministers. It was their business to find a remedy for the general ills. As to the National Assembly which represented only the middle class and people, he regarded it with contempt.

"Why, it was from the middle class," he said, "that the oppressors of the people were drawn. It is they who were farmers-general, collectors, and officials of all kinds. It is they who ground down the nation and enriched themselves with the spoil. It is not the nobles who dirtied their hands with money wrung from the poor. By all means let the middle class have a share in the government; but it is not a share they desire. The clergy are to have no voice; the nobility are to have no voice; the king himself is to be a cipher. All power is to be placed in the hands of these men, the chosen of the scum of the great towns, the mere mouthpieces of the ignorant mob. It is not order that these gentry are organizing, it is disorder."

Such were the opinions of the marquis, but he was tolerant of other views, and at the gatherings at the chateau Harry heard opinions of all kinds expressed.

During his rambles alone he entered as much as he could into conversation with the peasants, with woodcutters, foresters, and villagers. He found that the distress which prevailed everywhere was terrible. The people scarcely kept life together, and many had died of absolute starvation. He found a feeling of despair everywhere, and a dull hatred of all who were above them in the world. Harry had difficulty in making them talk, and at first could obtain only sullen monosyllables. His dress and appearance showed him to belong to the hated classes, and set them against him at once; but when he said that he was English, and that in England people were watching with great interest what was passing in France, they had no hesitation in speaking.

Harry's motives in endeavouring to find out what were the feelings of the people at large, were not those of mere curiosity. He was now much attached to the marquis and his family; and the reports which came from all parts of France, as well as from Paris, together with the talk among the visitors at the chateau, convinced him that the state of affairs was more serious than the marquis was inclined to admit. The capture of the Bastille and the slaughter of its defenders—the massacres of persons obnoxious to the mob, not only in the streets of Paris but in those of other great towns, proved that the lower class, if they once obtained the upper hand, were ready to go all lengths; while the number of the nobility who were flocking across the frontier showed that among this body there existed grievous apprehensions as to the future.

Harry had read in a book in the library of the chateau an account of the frightful excesses perpetrated by the Jacquerie. That dreadful insurrection had been crushed out by the armour-clad knights of France; but who was to undertake the task should such a flame again burst out? The nobles no longer wore armour, they had no armed retainers; they would be a mere handful among a multitude. The army had already shown its sympathy with the popular movement, and could not be relied upon. That the marquis himself should face out any danger which might come seemed to Harry right and natural; but he thought that he was wrong not to send his wife and daughters, and at any rate Jules, across the Rhine until the dangers were passed.

But the marquis had no fears. Some one had mentioned the Jacquerie in one of their conversations, but the marquis had put it aside as being altogether apart from the question.

"The Jacquerie took place," he said, "hundreds of years ago. The people then were serfs and little more than savages. Can we imagine it possible that at this day the people would be capable of such excesses?"

The answer of the gentleman he addressed had weighed little with the marquis, but Harry thought over it seriously.

"Civilization has increased, marquis, since the days of the Jacquerie, but the condition of the people has improved but little. Even now the feudal usages are scarce extinct. The lower class have been regarded as animals rather than men; and the increase of civilization which you speak of, and from which they have received no benefit, makes them hate even more bitterly than of old those in position above them.

"I am a reformer; I desire to see sweeping changes; I want a good, wise, and honest government; and I desire these things because I fear that, if they do not come peacefully they will come in a tempest of lawlessness and vengeance."

"Well, they are getting all they want," the marquis said peevishly. "They are passing every law, however absurd, that comes into their hands. No one is opposing them. They have got the reins in their own hands. What on earth can they want more? There might have been an excuse for rebellion and riot two years since—there can be none now. What say you, abbe?"

The abbe seldom took part in conversations on politics, but, being now appealed to, he said mildly:

"We must allow for human nature, monsieur. The slave who finds himself free, with arms in his hands, is not likely to settle down at once into a peaceful citizen. Men's heads are turned with

37

the changes the last two years have brought about. They are drunk with their own success, and who can say where they will stop? So far they find no benefit from the changes. Bread is as dear as ever, men's pockets are as empty. They thought to gain everything—they find they have got nothing; and so they will cry for more and more change, their fury will run higher and higher with each disappointment, and who can say to what lengths they will go? They have already confiscated the property of the church, next will come that of the laity."

"I had no idea you were such a prophet of evil, abbe," the marquis said with an uneasy laugh, while feelings of gloom and anxiety fell over the others who heard the abbe's words.

"God forbid that I should be a prophet!" the old man said gravely. "I hope and trust that I am mistaken, and that He has not reserved this terrible punishment for France. But you asked me for my opinion, marquis, and I have given it to you."

Despite these forebodings the winter of 1790 passed without disturbance at the chateau.

In the spring came news of disorder, pillage, and acts of ruffianism in various parts. Chateaux and convents were burned and destroyed, and people refused to pay either their taxes or rents to their landlords. In the south the popular excitement was greater than in other parts. In Burgundy there was for the most part tranquility; and the marquis, who had always been regarded as an indulgent seigneur by the people of his estate, still maintained that these troubles only occurred where the proprietors had abused their privileges and ground down the people.

CHAPTER IV

THE CLOUDS GATHER

Occasionally and at considerable intervals Harry received letters from his father. The latter said that there was great excitement in England over the events which had taken place in France, and that his mother was rendered extremely anxious by the news of the attacks upon chateaux, and the state of tumult and lawlessness which prevailed. They thought he had better resign his situation and return home.

Harry in his replies made light of the danger, and said that after having been treated so kindly it would be most ungrateful of him to break the engagement he had made for three years, and leave his friends at the present moment. Indeed, he, like all around him, was filled with the excitement of the time. In spite of the almost universal confusion and disorder, life went on quietly and calmly at the chateau. The establishment was greatly reduced, for few of the tenants paid their rents; but the absence of ceremonial brought the family closer together, and the marquis and his wife agreed that they had never spent a happier time than the spring and summer of 1791.

The news of the failure of the king's attempt at flight on the 20th of June was a great shock to the marquis. "A king should never fly," he said; "above all, he should never make an abortive attempt at flight. It is lamentable that he should be so ill-advised."

At the end of September the elections to the Legislative Assembly as it was now to be called, resulted in the return of men even more extreme and violent than those whom they succeeded.

"We must go to Paris," the marquis said one day towards the end of October. "The place for a French nobleman now is beside the king."

"And that of his wife beside the queen," the marquise said quietly.

"I cannot say no," the marquis replied. "I wish you could have stayed with the children, but they need fear no trouble here. Ernest is nearly seventeen, and may well begin, in my absence, to represent me. I think we can leave the chateau without anxiety, but even were it not so it would still be our duty to go."

"There is another thing I want to speak to you about before we start," the marquise said. "Jeanne is no longer a child, although we still regard her as one; she is fifteen, and she is graver and more earnest than most girls of her age. It seems ridiculous to think of such a thing, but it is clear that she has made this English lad her hero. Do you not think it better that he should go? It would be unfortunate in the extreme that she should get to have any serious feelings for him."

"I have noticed it too, Julie," the marquis said, "and have smiled to myself to see how the girl listens gravely to all he says, but I am not disposed to send him away. In the first place, he has done a great deal of good to the boys, more even than I had hoped for. Ernest now thinks and speaks for himself, his ideas are broader, his views wider. He was fitted before for the regime that has passed; he is rapidly becoming fit to take his part in that which is to come.

"In the next place, my dear, you must remember the times have changed. Mademoiselle Jeanne de St. Caux, daughter of a peer and noble of France, was infinitely removed from the son of an English doctor; but we seem to be approaching the end of all things; and although so far the law for the abolition of titles has been disregarded here, you must prepare yourself to find that in Paris you will be no longer addressed by your title, and I shall be Monsieur de St. Caux; or may be they will object both to the de and the St., and I shall find myself plain Monsieur Caux."

"Oh, Edouard!" the marquise exclaimed aghast.

"I am quite in earnest, my dear, I can assure you. You will say she is still the heiress of a portion of our estates, but who can say how long the estates will remain after the title is gone? Just as the gentlemen of the pave object to titles because they have none themselves, so being penniless they will object to property, and for aught I know may decree a general division of lands and goods."

"Impossible, Edouard!"

"Not at all impossible, Julie. The beggars are on horseback, and they intend to ride. Last week I called in from my bankers, all the cash at my disposal, about five thousand louis, and to-morrow du Tillet is going to start for Holland. He will hand it over to a banker there to forward to Dr. Sandwith, to whom I have written asking him to undertake the charge. If you will take my advice you will forward at the same time all your jewelry. If things go wrong it will keep us in our old age and furnish a dot for our daughters.

"The jewels of the St. Caux have always been considered as equal to those of any family in France, and are certainly worth half a million francs even to sell. Keep a few small trinkets, and send all the others away. But I have wandered from my subject. Under these circumstances I think it as well that we should not interfere in the matter you speak of. Personally one could not wish for a better husband for one of our daughters than this young Englishman would make.

"His father is a gentleman, and so is he, and in such times as are coming I should be glad to know that one of my girls had such a protector as he would make her; but this is, as you said at first, almost ridiculous. He is two years older than she is, but in some respects she is the elder; he regards her as a pretty child, and all his thoughts are given to his studies and his sports.

"He has something of the English barbarian left in him, and is absolutely indifferent to Jeanne's preference. A French lad at his age would be flattered. This English boy does not notice it, or if he notices it regards it as an exhibition of gratitude, which he could well dispense with, for having saved her life.

"You can leave them with a tranquil heart, my dear. I will answer for it that never in his inmost heart has the idea of his ever making love to Jeanne occurred to this English lad. Lastly I should be sorry for him to leave, because his good spirits and cheerfulness are invaluable at present. Ernest is apt to be gloomy and depressed, and cheerfulness is at a premium in France at present. Moreover, should there be any difficulty or danger while we are absent I trust very much to that lad's good sense and courage. That incident of the dog showed how quick he is to plan and how prompt to carry his plans into effect. It may seem absurd when there are several of our staunch and tried friends here to rely in any way on a lad, but I do so. Not, of course, as before our faithful friends, but as one whose aid is not to be despised."

Thus it happened that on the same day that the marquis started for Paris, M. du Tillet set out from the chateau taking with him some trunks and packages which appeared but of little value and were not likely to attract attention, but which contained a considerable sum of money and the famous St. Caux jewels.

Life at the chateau was dull after the departure of its heads. They had few visitors now; the most frequent among them being Victor de Gisons. The estates of the duke, his father, adjoined those of the marquis, and between him and Marie a marriage had long before been arranged by their parents. For once the inclination of the young people agreed with the wishes of the elders, and they were warmly attached to each other. No formal betrothal, however, had as yet taken place, the troubles of the times having caused its postponement, although formerly it had been understood that in the present autumn the marriage should be celebrated.

The young count had at the assembly of the States General been a prominent liberal, and had been one of those who had taken his seat with the third estate and had voted for the abolition of the special privileges of the nobility, but the violence of the Assembly had alarmed and disgusted him, and in the winter he had left Paris and returned to his father's estates.

Ernest and Harry studied with the abbe, and fenced and rode as usual with M. du Tillet after his return from Holland. The ever-darkening cloud weighed upon their spirits, and yet life at the chateau was pleasant. The absence of their parents and the general feeling of anxiety knit the rest of the family closer together. Much of the ceremonial observance which had, on his first arrival, surprised and amused Harry was now laid aside. Marie, happy in the visits of her lover and at the prospect of her approaching marriage, did her best to make the house cheerful. Harry, who had not much liked her at first, now found her most pleasant and agreeable, and the younger girls walked in the grounds with their brothers and chatted when they were gathered in the evening just as Harry's sisters had done at home. Jeanne was, if the group broke up, generally Harry's companion. Ever since the affair of the mad dog she had treated him as her special friend, adopting all his opinions and falling in with any suggestion he might make with a readiness which caused Ernest one day to say laughingly to Harry:

"One would think, Harry that you were Jeanne's elder brother, not I. She listens to you with a good deal more deference than she does to me."

The winter came and went. From time to time letters arrived from Paris, but the news was always in the same strain. Things were going worse and worse, the king was little more than a prisoner in the hands of the people of Paris. The violence of the Assembly was ever on the increase, the mob of Paris were the real masters of the situation, the greater part of the nobility had fled, and any who appeared in the streets were liable to insult.

The feeling in the provinces kept pace with that in Paris. Committees were formed in every town and village and virtually superseded the constituted authorities. Numbers of chateaux were burned, and the peasants almost universally refused any longer to pay the dues to their seigneurs. But at present none dreamt of personal danger. The nobles who emigrated did so because they found the situation intolerable, and hoped that an army would be

42

shortly raised and set in motion by foreign powers to put down the movement which constituted a danger to kings, nobles, and property all over Europe. But as yet there was nothing to foreshadow the terrible events which were to take place, or to indicate that a movement, which began in the just demand of an oppressed people for justice and fair treatment, would end in that people becoming a bloodthirsty rabble, eager to destroy all who were above them in birth, education, or intellect.

Therefore, although the Marquis de St. Caux foresaw the possibility of confiscation of the property and abolition of all the privileges of the nobility, he was under no uneasiness whatever as to the safety of his children. His instructions were precise: that if a small party of peasants attacked the chateau, and it was evident that a successful resistance could be made, M. du Tillet should send word down to the mayor of Dijon and ask for help, and should, with the servants of the chateau, defend it; if it was attacked by a large mob, no resistance was to be offered, but he was to abandon it at once and journey to Paris with the children. But the time went on without disturbance. In Dijon as elsewhere a committee had been formed and had taken into its hands the entire control of the management of the town. At its head was the son of the mayor, Monsieur Lebat.

"I do not understand that young fellow," M. du Tillet said one day on his return from Dijon. "I do not like him; he is ambitious and pushing, he is the leader of the advanced party in Dijon, and is in communication with the most violent spirits in Paris, but I am bound to say that he appears most anxious to be of service to the family. Whenever I see him he assures me of his devotion to the marquis. To-day, Mademoiselle Marie, he prayed me to assure you that you need feel no uneasiness, for that he held the mob in his hand, and would answer for it that no hostile movement should be made against the chateau, and in fact I know, for I have taken the precaution of buying the services of a man who is upon the committee, that Lebat has actually exerted himself to benefit us.

"It has several times been urged by the most violent section that the mob should be incited to attack the chateau, but he has each time successfully opposed the proposition. He has declared that while no one is more hostile than himself to the privileges of seigneury, and while he would not only abolish the nobles as a class but confiscate their possessions, he considers that in the case of the marquis nothing should be done until a decree to that effect is passed by the Assembly.

"Until that time, he argues, the people should discriminate. The chateaux of tyrants should be everywhere levelled to the ground, but it would be unworthy of the people to take measures of vengeance against those who have not notably ground down those dependent upon them, and that, as the marquis has not pushed the privilege of his class to the utmost, his chateau and property should be respected until the Assembly pass a decree upon the subject."

"I am sure we are much indebted to this Monsieur Lebat," Marie said. "He was here at the hunting party and seemed a worthy young man of his class. Of course he was out of place among us, but for a man in his position he seemed tolerable."

"Yes," Monsieur du Tillet agreed, but in a somewhat doubtful tone of voice. "So far as assurances go there is nothing to be desired, and he has, as I said, so far acted loyally up to them, and yet somehow I do not like him. It strikes me that he is playing a game, although what that game is I cannot say. At anyrate I do not trust him; he speaks smoothly but I think he has a double face, and that he is cruel and treacherous."

"That is not like you, Monsieur du Tillet," Marie laughed, "you who generally have a good word for everyone. It seems to me that you are hard upon the young man, who appears to be animated by excellent sentiments towards us."

Spring came again. M. du Tillet learned that the mob of Dijon were becoming more and more violent, and that spies and watchmen had been told off to see that none of the family attempted to fly for the frontier. He therefore wrote to the marquis urging that it would be better that the family should move to Paris, where they would be in no danger. In reply he received a letter begging him to start as soon as the roads were fit for travel.

About the same time Victor de Gisons received a summons from his father to join him in Paris.

The messenger who brought the letter to M. du Tillet brought one also for Marie from the marquise, saying that the heads of both families were of opinion that the marriage must be still further postponed, as in the present state of affairs all private plans and interests must be put aside in view of the dangers that surrounded the king. Marie acquiesced in the decision, and bade her lover adieu calmly and bravely.

"They are quite right, Victor; I have felt for some time that when France was on the verge of a precipice it was not the time for her nobles to be marrying. Noblesse oblige. If we were two peasants we might marry and be happy. As it is we must wait, even though we

44

know that waiting may never come to an end. I have a conviction, Victor, that our days of happiness are over, and that terrible things are about to happen."

"But nothing that can happen can separate us, Marie."

"Nothing but death, Victor," she said quietly.

"But surely, Marie, you take too gloomy a view. Death, of course, may separate all lovers; but there seems no reason that we should fear him now more than at other times. A few farmers-general and others who have made themselves obnoxious to the mob have been killed, but what is that! There should at least be no hostility to our order. Many of the nobles have been foremost in demanding reforms. All have cheerfully resigned their privileges. There is no longer the slightest reason for hostility against us."

"My dear Victor," Marie said quietly, "you do not ask a wild beast about to rend his prey, what is the reason for his actions. I hope I may be wrong; but at least, dear, we shall see each other again before long, and, whatever troubles may come, will share them. My mother in her letter yesterday said that she and the marquis had determined that we should join them in Paris; for that although the disorders have abated somewhat they are anxious at the thought of our being alone here, and in the present position of things they have no hope of being able to leave the king. She says my father is very indignant at the great emigration of the nobility that is going on. In the first place, he holds that they are deserting their post in the face of the enemy; and in the second place, by their assemblage across the frontier and their intrigues at foreign courts against France they are causing the people to look with suspicion upon the whole class."

"You have kept your good news till the last, Marie," Victor said. "Here have we been saying good-bye, and it seems that we are going to meet again very shortly."

"I have been bidding farewell," Marie said, "not to you, but to our dream of happiness. We shall meet soon, but I fear that will never return."

"You are a veritable prophet of ill to-day, Marie," Victor said with an attempt at gaiety. "Some day, I hope, dear, that we shall smile together over your gloomy prognostication."

"I hope so, Victor—I pray God it may be so!"

A week later three carriages arrived from Paris to convey the family there; and upon the following day the whole party started; the girls, the gouvernante, the abbe, and some of the female servants occupying the carriages, Monsieur du Tillet, the boys, and several of the men riding beside them as an escort.

They met with no interruption on the road, and arrived in Paris on the last day of April, 1792. Harry was glad at the change. The doings at Paris had been the subject of conversation and thought for nearly two years, and he had caught the excitement which pervaded France. He was tired of the somewhat monotonous life in the country, and had for some time been secretly longing to be at the centre of interest, and to see for himself the stirring events, of which little more than a feeble echo had reached them at the chateau.

The change of life was great indeed; the marquis had thrown himself into the thick of all that was going on, and his salon was crowded every evening with those of the nobility who still remained In Paris. But he was regarded as by no means a man of extreme views, and many of the leaders of the party of the Gironde with whose names Harry was familiar were also frequent visitors— Roland, Vergniaud, Lanjuinais, Brissot, Guader, Lebrun, and Condorcer.

Harry was struck with the variety of conversation that went on at these meetings. Many of the young nobles laughed and chatted with the ladies with as much gaiety as if the former state of things were continuing undisturbed; and an equal indifference to the public state of things was shown by many of the elders, who sat down and devoted themselves to cards. Others gathered apart in little groups and discussed gloomily and in low tones the events of the day; while others who were more liberal in their views gathered round the deputies of the Gironde and joined in their talk upon the meetings of the Assembly and the measures which were necessary to consolidate the work of reform, and to restore peace and happiness to France.

The marquis moved from group to group, equally at home with all, chatting lightly with the courtiers, whispering gravely with the elders, or discussing with the tone of the man of the world the views and opinions of the deputies. Victor de Gisons was constantly at the house, and strove by his cheerfulness and gaiety to dissipate the shade of melancholy which still hung over Marie.

Towards the end of July the Marquis de St. Caux and the little body of royalists who still remained faithful to the king became more and more anxious; the position of the royal family was now most precarious; most of the troops in Paris had been sent to the frontier, and those left behind were disorganized and ready to join the mob. Two out of the three Swiss battalions had been sent away and but one remained at the Tuileries. Of the National Guard only the battalion of Filles St. Thomas and part of the battalion of the Saints Pares could be trusted to defend the king. The rest were opposed to him, and would certainly join the populace.

On the 14th of July a large number of National Guards from the provinces had arrived in Paris; and the battalion from Marseilles, the most violent of all, had, immediately that it arrived in the city, come into collision with one of the loyal battalions.

The royalists were wholly without organization, their sole aim being to defend the king should he be in danger, and if necessary to die by his side.

On the evening before the 10th of August the tocsin was heard to sound and the drums to beat to arms. All day there had been sinister rumours circulating, but the king had sent privately to his friends that the danger was not imminent and that he had no need of them; however, as soon as the alarm sounded the marquis snatched up a sword and prepared to start for the palace. He embraced his wife, who was calm but very pale, and his children. Ernest asked to be allowed to go with him, but the marquis said:

"No, my son, my life is the king's; but yours at present is due to your mother and sisters."

It was twenty-four hours before he returned. His clothes were torn, his head was bound up, and one of his arms disabled. The marquise gave a cry of delight as he entered. No one had slept since he left, for every hour fresh rumours of fighting had arrived, and the sound of cannon and musketry had been heard in the early part of the day.

"It is all over, wife!" he said. "We have done our best, but the king will do nothing. We cannot say we have lost the battle, for we have never tried to win it; but it would be the same thing in the long run."

Before hearing what had passed the marquise insisted upon her husband taking refreshment and having his wounds bound up and attended to. When he had finished his meal the marquis began:

"We had a good deal of difficulty in getting into the Tuileries, for the National Guard tried to prevent our passing. However, we most of us got through; and we found that there were about a hundred assembled, almost all men of family. The Marshal de Mailly led us into the king's apartment.

"'Sire,' he said, 'here are your faithful nobles, eager to replace your majesty on the throne of your ancestors.' The National Guard in the palace withdrew at once, leaving us alone with the Swiss.

"We formed in the courtyard; and the king, with his hat in his hand, walked down our ranks and those of the Swiss. He seemed without fear, but he did not speak a word, and did nothing to encourage us. Several of our party, in trying to make their way to the palace, had been murdered, and the mob cut off their heads and put them on pikes; and these were paraded in the streets within sight of the windows. Roederer, the procureur-general of the department of Paris, came to the king and pressed him to leave the Tuileries.

"'There are not five minutes to lose, sire,' he said. 'There is no safety for your majesty but in the National Assembly.'

"The queen resisted; but upon Roederer saying that an enormous crowd with cannon were coming, and that delay would endanger the lives of the whole of the royal family, he went. But he thought of us, and asked what was to become of us. Roederer said that, as we were not in uniform, by leaving our swords behind us we could pass through the crowd without being recognized. The king moved on, followed by the queen, Madam Elizabeth, and the children. The crowd, close and menacing, lined the passage, and the little procession made their way with difficulty to the Assembly.

"We remained in the palace, and every moment the throng around became more and more numerous. The cannon they brought were turned against us. The first door was burst open, the Swiss did not fire, the populace poured in and mixed with us and the soldiers. Some one fired a gun. Whether it was one of the Swiss or one of the mob I know not, but the fight began. The Swiss in good order marched down the staircase, drove out the mob, seized the cannon the Marseillais had brought, and turning them upon their assailants opened fire. The mob fled in terror, and I believe that one battalion would have conquered all the scum of Paris, had not the king, at the sound of the first shot, sent word to the Swiss to cease firing. They obeyed, and although the mob kept firing upon them from the windows, the great part of them marched calm, and without returning a shot, to the Assembly, where, at the order of the king, they laid down their arms and were shut up in the church of the Feuillants.

"A portion of the Swiss had remained on guard in the Tuileries when the main body marched away. The instant the palace was undefended the mob burst in. Every Swiss was murdered, as well as many of the servants of the queen. The mob sacked the palace and set it on fire. When the Swiss left we had one by one made our way out by a back entrance, but most of us were recognized by the mob and were literally cut to pieces. I rushed into a house when assaulted, and, slamming the door behind me, made my way out by the back and so escaped them, getting off with only these two wounds; then I hurried to a house of a friend, whom I had seen murdered before my eyes, but his servants did not know of it, and they allowed me to remain there till dark, and you see here I am."

"But what has happened at the Assembly and where is the king?" the marquise asked, after the first exclamation of horror at the tale they had heard.

"The king and his family are prisoners in the Temple," the marquis said. "The Commune has triumphed over the Assembly and a National Convention is to be the supreme power. The king's functions are suspended, but as he has not ruled for the last three years that will make little difference. A new ministry has been formed with Danton, Lebrun, and some of the Girondists. He and his family are handed over to the care of the Commune, and their correspondence is to be intercepted. A revolutionary tribunal has been constituted, when, I suppose, the farce of trying men whose only crime is loyalty to the king is to be carried out.

"We must be prepared, my love, to face the worst. Escape is now impossible, and, indeed, so long as the king and queen are alive I would not quit Paris; but we must prepare for sending the children away if possible."

CHAPTER V

THE OUTBURST

"Monsieur le Marquis," M. du Tillet exclaimed, hurrying into the salon, in which the marquis with his family were sitting, on the evening of the 21st of August, "I hear that it is rumoured in the street that all the members of noble families are to be arrested."

The room was lit up as if to receive company, but the crowd which had thronged it a fortnight before were gone. The Girondists had first withdrawn, then the nobles had begun to fall off, for it had become dangerous for them to show themselves in the streets, where they were liable to be insulted and attacked by the mob. Moreover, any meeting of known Royalists was regarded with suspicion by the authorities, and so gradually the gatherings had become smaller and smaller.

The only constant visitor now was the Count de Gisons, but he to-night was absent. The news was not unexpected. The violence of the extremists of the Mountain had been increasing daily. At the Cordeliers and Jacobin Clubs, Danton, Robespierre, and Marat had thundered nightly their denunciations against the aristocrats, and it was certain that at any moment the order for their arrest might be given. Such bad news had been received of the state of feeling in the provinces, that it was felt that it would be more dangerous to send the young ones away than to retain them in Paris, and the marquise had been a prey to the liveliest anxiety respecting her children. It seemed impossible that there could be any animosity against them, but the blind rage of the mob had risen to such a height that it was impossible to say what might happen. Now that she heard the blow was about to fall she drew her younger girls instinctively to her, as if to protect them, but no word passed her lips.

"It might still be possible to fly," M. du Tillet went on. "We have all the disguises in readiness."

"A Marquis de St. Caux does not fly from the canaille of Paris," the marquis said quietly. "No, Du Tillet; the king and queen are in prison, and it is not for their friends to leave their post here in Paris because danger threatens them; come when they may, these wretches will find us here ready for them."

"But the children, Edouard!" the marquise murmured.

"I shall stand by my father's side," Ernest said firmly.

"I do not doubt your courage, my son. I wish now that I had

long ago sent you all across the frontier; but who could have foreseen that the people of France were about to become a horde of wild beasts, animated by hate against all, old and young, in whose veins ran noble blood. However, although it is the duty of your mother and I to stay at our posts, it is our duty also to try and save our house from destruction; therefore, Du Tillet, I commit my two sons to your charge. Save them if you can, disguise them as you will, and make for the frontier. Once there you know all the arrangements we have already made."

"But, father," Ernest remonstrated.

"I can listen to no argument, Ernest," the marquis said firmly. "In this respect my will is law. I know what your feelings are, but you must set them aside, they must give way to the necessity of saving one of the oldest families of France from perishing."

"And the girls?" the marquise asked, as Ernest bent his head in sign of obedience to his father's orders.

"I cannot think," the marquis said, "that they will be included in the order for our arrest. They must go, as arranged, in the morning to the house of our old servant and remain quietly there awaiting the course of events. They will pass very well as three of her nieces who have arrived from the country. You had better send a trusty servant to prepare her for their coming. You, Harry, will, of course, accompany my sons.

"Pardon, marquis," Harry said quietly, "I am firmly resolved to stay in Paris. I may be of assistance to your daughters, and there will be no danger to me in remaining, for I have no noble blood in my veins. Besides, my travelling with M. du Tillet would add to his danger. He will have difficulty enough in traversing the country with two boys; a third would add to that difficulty."

"I cannot help that," the marquis said. "I ought long ago to have sent you home, and feel that I have acted wrongly in allowing you to remain so long. I must insist upon your accompanying my sons."

"I am sorry to disobey you, monsieur le marquis," Harry said quietly but firmly; "but from the moment of your arrest I shall be my own master and can dispose of my actions. I am deeply sensible of all your goodness to me, but I cannot yield, for I feel that I may be of some slight use here. There are so many strangers in Paris that there is little fear of my attracting any notice. A mouse may help a lion, monsieur, and it may be that though but a boy I may be able to be of service to mesdemoiselles."

"Do not urge him further, Edouard," the marquise said, laying a hand on her husband's arm as he was again about to speak. "Harry

51

is brave and thoughtful beyond his years, and it will be somewhat of a comfort to me to think that there is some one watching over our girls. I thank you, Harry, for your offer, and feel sure that you will do all that can possibly be done to protect my girls. You will be freer to do so than any of our friends, for they are likely to become involved in our fate, whatever that may be. Marie, you will view our English friend as joint guardian with yourself over your sisters. Consult him should difficulty or danger arise as if he were your brother, and be guided by his advice. And now, girls, come with me to my room, I have much to say to you.

"I am glad my wife decided as she did, Harry," the marquis said, putting his hand on his shoulder when his wife and daughters left the room, "for I too shall feel comfort in knowing that you are watching over the girls. Now leave us, for I have much to arrange with Monsieur du Tillet."

After a prolonged talk with M. du Tillet the marquis sent for Ernest. As soon as he entered the lad said:

"Of course, sir, I shall obey your commands; but it seems to me an unworthy part for your son to play, to be flying the country and leaving a stranger here to look after your daughters."

"He is hardly a stranger, Ernest," the marquis replied. "He has been with us as one of the family for two years, and he risked his life for your sisters. You could not stay here without extreme risk, for if your name is not already included in the warrant for arrest it speedily will be so, and when they once taste blood these wolves will hunt down every one of us. He, on the other hand, might proceed openly through the streets without danger; nevertheless, I would not have kept him if he would have gone; but I have no power of controlling him, and as he chooses to devote himself to us I thankfully accept his devotion.

"And now, my son, it may be that after our parting to-morrow we shall not meet again, for God alone knows what fate is in store for us. I have, therefore, some serious advice to give you. If anything happens to me, you will, I know, never forget that you are the head of the family, and that the honour of a great name is in your keeping; but do not try to strive against the inevitable. Adapt yourself to the new circumstances under which you will be placed, and lay aside that pride which has had much to do with the misfortunes which are now befalling us.

"As to your sisters, Marie is already provided for, that is if De Gisons is not included in the order for arrest. I have already sent off a message to him to warn him; and as it has already been arranged between us that while his father will stay and face whatever will

52

come, it is his duty, like yours, to escape the danger which threatens our class, I trust that he will at once endeavour to leave the country; but I imagine that he will stop in Paris until some means are devised for getting your sisters away.

"As to the others, if you all reach England and settle down there do not keep up the class distinctions which have prevailed here. Marry your sisters to men who will protect and make them happy. That these must be gentlemen goes without saying; but that is sufficient. For example, if in future time a gentleman of the rank of our English friend here, of whose character you can entirely approve, asks for the hand of either of your younger sisters, do not refuse it. Remember that such a suit would have the cordial approval of your mother and myself."

A look of great surprise passed over Ernest's face. It had seemed to him so much a matter of course that the ladies of his house should marry into noble families that the idea of one of them being given to a gentleman belonging to the professional class was surprising indeed.

"Do you really mean, sir, that if my friend Harry were some day to ask for Jeanne's hand you would approve of the match?"

"That is exactly what I do mean, Ernest. In the stormy times in which we are living I could wish no better protector for her. Were he a Frenchman, in the same position of life, I own that I might view the matter in a different light; but, as I have said, in England the distinction of classes is much less marked than here; and, moreover, in England there is little fear of such an outbreak of democracy as that which is destroying France."

A few minutes later Monsieur du Tillet entered with the clothes which had been prepared for the boys. They were such as would be worn by the sons of workmen; he himself was attired in a blue blouse and trousers. Jules was aroused from the couch on which he had for the last hour been asleep, and he and Ernest retired to dress themselves in their new costume, M. du Tillet accompanying them to assist in their toilet. Both boys had the greatest repugnance to the change, and objected still further when M. du Tillet insisted it was absolutely necessary that they should cut their hair and smear their faces and hands with dirt.

"My dear Monsieur Ernest," he said, "it would be worse than useless for you to assume that attire unless at the same time you assumed the bearing and manners appropriate to it. In your own dress we might for a short time walk the street without observation; but if you sallied out in that blouse with your white hands and your head thrown back, and a look of disdain and disgust on your face, the first gamin who met you would cry out, 'There is an aristocrat in disguise!'

"You must behave as if you were acting in a comedy. You are representing a lad of the lower orders. You must try to imitate his walk and manner. Shove your hands deep in your pockets, shuffle your feet along carelessly; let your head roll about as if it were uneasy on your neck, round your shoulders, and slouch your head forward. As to you Jules, your role should be impertinence. Put your cap on the wrong way; hold your nose in the air; pull your short hair down over your forehead, and let some of it spurt out through that hole in your cap. To be quite correct, you ought to address jeering remarks to every respectable man and woman you meet in the streets; but as you know nothing of Parisian slang, you must hold your tongue. See how thoroughly I have got myself up. You would take me for an idle out-of-elbows workman wherever you met me. I do not like it; but, as I have to disguise myself, I try to do it thoroughly."

It was, however, with a feeling of humiliation that the boys presented themselves before the marquis. He looked at them scrutinizingly.

"You will do, my boys," he said gravely. "I should have passed you in the street without knowing you. Now come in with me and say good-bye to your mother and sisters. The sooner you are out of this house the better, for there is no saying at what hour the agents of the canaille may present themselves."

The parting was a sad one indeed, but it was over at last, and Monsieur du Tillet hurried the two boys away as soon as their father returned with them.

"God bless you, du Tillet!" the marquis said as he embraced his friend. "Should aught happen to us, you will, I know, be a father to them."

"Now, Harry," the marquis said when he had mastered the emotion caused by the parting, which he felt might be a final one, "since you have chosen to throw in your lot with ours, I will give you a few instructions. In the first place, I have hidden under a plank beneath my bed a bag containing a thousand crowns. It is the middle plank. Count an even number from each leg and the centre one covers the bag.

"You will find the plank is loose and that you can raise it easily with a knife; but wax has been run in, and dust swept over it, so that there is no fear of its being noticed by any who may pillage the house, which they will doubtless do after we are arrested. I have already sent an equal sum to Louise Moulin. Here is her address;

but it is possible that you may need money, and may be unable to communicate with my daughters at her house; at any rate do you keep the bag of money in your charge.

"You had best attire yourself at once in the oldest suit of clothes you have got. My daughters will be ready in a few minutes. They are already dressed, so that they can slip out at the back entrance. Should we be disturbed before morning I shall place them under your escort; for although I hope that all the servants are faithful, one can answer for no one in these times. I would send them off now, but that the sight of females moving through the streets at this time of night would be likely to attract attention on the part of drunken men, or of fellows returning from these rascally clubs, which are the centre and focus of all the mischief that is going on.

"I can give you no further advice. You must be guided by circumstances. If, as I trust, the girls can live undisturbed and unsuspected with their mother's old nurse, it were best that they should remain there until the troubles are finally over, and France comes to her senses again. If not, I must leave it to you to act for the best. It is a great trust to place in the hands of a youth of your age; but it is your own choosing, and we have every confidence in you.

"I will do my best to deserve it, sir," Harry said quietly; "but I trust that you and madame la marquise will soon be able to resume your guardianship. I cannot believe that although just at present the populace are excited to fury by agitators, they can in cold blood intend to wreak their vengeance upon all the classes above them."

"I hope you may be right," the marquis said; "but I fear that it is not so. The people are mad so far. All that has been done has in no way mitigated their sufferings, and they gladly follow the preachings of the arch scoundrels of the Jacobin Club. I fear that before all this is over France will be deluged with blood. And now, when you have changed your clothes, lie down, ready to rise at a moment's notice. Should you hear a tumult, run at once to the long gallery. There my daughters will join you prepared for flight. Lead them instantly to the back entrance, avoiding, if possible, any observation from the domestics. As these sleep on the floor above, and know nothing of the dangers which threaten us, they will not awake so quickly, and I trust that you will be able to get out without being seen by any of them. In that case, however closely questioned no one will be able to afford a clue by which you can be traced."

When he had changed his clothes Harry extinguished all the lights in the salon, for the marquis had long before ordered all the servants to retire to rest. Then he opened the window looking into the street and took his place close to it. Sleep under the circumstances was impossible.

As the hours passed he thought over the events of the last few days. He was fully aware that the task he had undertaken might be full of danger; but to a healthy and active English lad a spice of danger is by no means a deterrent. He could, of course, have left his employment before the family left their chateau; but after his arrival in Paris it would have been difficult for him to have traversed the country and crossed the frontier, and he thought that the danger which he now ran was not much greater than would have been entailed by such a step.

In the next place he was greatly attached to the family of the marquis; and the orgies of the mob had filled him with such horror and disgust that he would have risked much to save any unfortunate, even a stranger, from their hands; and lastly, he felt the fascination of the wild excitement of the times, and congratulated himself that he should see and perhaps be an actor in the astonishing drama which was occupying the attention of the whole civilized world.

As he sat there he arranged his own plans. After seeing his charge in safety he would take a room in some quiet locality, alleging that he was the clerk of a notary, and would, in the dress of one of that class, or the attire of one of the lower orders, pass his days in the streets, gathering every rumour and watching the course of events.

Morning was just breaking when he heard the sound of many feet coming along the street, and looking out saw a crowd of men with torches, headed by two whose red scarfs showed them to be officials. As they reached the entrance gate the men at the head of the procession stopped. Harry at once darted away to the long gallery, and as he did so, heard a loud knocking at the door.

Scarcely had he reached the gallery when a door at the further end opened, and three figures, the tallest carrying a lamp, appeared. The girls, too, had been keeping watch with their father and mother. They were dressed in the attire of respectable peasant girls. Virginie was weeping loudly, but the elder girls, although their cheeks bore traces of many tears they had shed during the night, restrained them now. When they reached Harry, the lad, without a word, took the lamp from Marie's hand, and led the way along the corridor and down the stairs towards the back of the house.

Everything was quiet. The knocking, loud as it was, had not yet aroused the servants, and, drawing the bolt quietly, and blowing out the lamp, Harry led the way into the garden behind the house.

Then for a moment he paused. There was a sound of axes hewing down the gate which led from the garden into the street behind.

"Quick, mesdemoiselles!" he said. "There is no time to lose."

He took they key out of the door, and closed and locked it after him. Then throwing the key among the shrubs he took Virginie's hand, and led the way rapidly towards the gate, which was fortunately a strong one.

"In here, mesdemoiselles," he said to Marie, pointing to some shrubs close to the gate. "They will rush straight to the house when the gate gives way, and we will slip out quietly."

For nearly five minutes the gate, which was strongly bound with iron, resisted the attack upon it. Then there was a crash, and a number of men with torches, and armed with muskets and pikes, poured in. Virginie was clinging to Marie, who, whispering to her to be calm and brave, pressed the child closely to her, while Jeanne stood quiet and still by the side of Harry, looking through the bushes.

Some twenty men entered, and a minute later there was the sound of battering at the door through which the fugitives had sallied out.

"Now," Harry said, "let us be going." Emerging from the shelter, a few steps took them to the gate, and stepping over the door, which lay prostrate on the ground, they turned into the lane.

"Let us run," Harry said; "we must get out of this lane as soon as possible. We are sure to have the mob here before long, and should certainly be questioned."

They hurried down the lane, took the first turning away from the house, and then slackened their pace. Presently they heard a number of footsteps clattering on the pavement; but fortunately they reached another turning before the party came up. They turned down and stood up in a doorway till the footsteps had passed, and then resumed their way.

"It is still too early for us to walk through the streets without exciting attention," Harry said. "We had better make down to the river and wait there till the town is quite astir."

In ten minutes they reached the river, and Harry found a seat for them at the foot of a pile of timber, where they were partially screened from observation. Hitherto the girls had not spoken a word since they had issued from the house. Virginie was dazed and frightened by the events of the night, and had hurried along almost mechanically holding Marie's hand. Marie's brain was too full to talk; her thoughts were with her father and mother and with her absent lover. She wondered that he had not come to her in spite of everything. Perhaps he was already a captive; perhaps, in obedience to his father's orders, he was in hiding, waiting events. That he could, even had his father commanded him, have left Paris as a fugitive without coming to see her, did not even occur to her as possible.

With these thoughts there was mingled a vague wonder at her own position. A few weeks since petted and cared for as the eldest daughter of one of the noblest families of France, now a fugitive in the streets under the sole care of this English boy. She had, the evening before, silently sided with Ernest. It had seemed to her wrong that he should be sent away, and the assertion of Harry that he intended to stay and watch over her and her sisters seemed at once absurd and presumptuous; but she already felt that she had been wrong in that opinion.

The decision and coolness with which he had at once taken the command from the moment he met them in the gallery, and the quickness with which he had seized the only mode of escape, had surprised and dominated her. Her own impulse, when on opening the door she heard the attack that was being made on the gate, was to draw back instantly and return to the side of her parents, and it was due to Harry only that she and her sisters had got safely away.

Hitherto, although after the incident of the mad dog she had exchanged her former attitude of absolute indifference to one of cordiality and friendliness, she had regarded him as a boy. Indeed she had treated and considered him as being very much younger than Ernest, and in some respects she had been justified in doing so, for in his light-hearted fun, his love of active exercise, and his entire absence of any assumption of age, he was far more boyish than Ernest. But although her thoughts were too busy now to permit her to analyse her feelings, she knew that she had been mistaken, and felt a strange confidence in this lad who had so promptly and coolly assumed the entire command of the party, and had piloted them with such steady nerve through the danger.

As for Jeanne, she felt no surprise and but little alarm. Her confidence in her protector was unbounded. Prompt and cool as he was himself, she was ready on the instant to obey his orders, and felt a certain sensation of pride at the manner in which her previous confidence in him was being justified.

After placing the girls in their shelter Harry had left them and stood leaning against the parapet of the quay as if carelessly watching the water, but maintaining a vigilant look-out against the approach of danger. The number of passers-by increased rapidly. The washerwomen came down to the boats moored in the stream and began their operation of banging the linen with wooden beaters. Market-women came along with baskets, the hum and stir of life everywhere commenced, and Paris was fairly awake.

Seeing that it was safe now to proceed, Harry returned to his companions. He had scarcely glanced at them before, and now looked approvingly at their disguises, to which the marquise had, during the long hours of the night, devoted the most zealous attention. Marie had been made to look much older than she was. A few dark lines carefully traced on her forehead, at the corners of her eyes and mouth, had added many years to her appearance, and she could have passed, except to the closest observer, as the mother of Virginie, whose dress was calculated to make her look even younger than she was. The hands and faces of all three had been slightly tinged with brown to give them a sun-burnt aspect in accordance with their peasant dresses, and so complete was the transformation that Harry could scarcely suppress a start of surprise as he looked at the group.

"It would be safe now, mademoiselle," he said to Marie, "for us to proceed. There are plenty of people about in the streets; but as the news has, no doubt, already been spread that the daughters of the Marquis de St. Caux had left the house before those charged with their father's arrest arrived, it will be better for you not to keep together. I would suggest that you should walk on with Virginie. I will follow with Jeanne a hundred yards behind, so that I can keep you in sight, and will come up if anyone should accost you."

Marie at once rose, and taking the child's hand set out. They had to traverse the greater part of Paris to reach their destination. It was a trial for Marie, who had never before been in the streets of Paris except with her mother and closely followed by two domestics, and even then only through the quiet streets of a fashionable quarter. However, she went steadily forward, tightly holding Virginie's hand and trying to walk as if accustomed to them in the thick heavy shoes which felt so strangely different to those which she was in the habit of wearing.

From time to time she addressed an encouraging word to Virginie as she felt her shrink as they approached groups of men lounging outside the wine-shops, for there was but little work done in Paris, and the men of the lower class spent their time in idleness, in discussions of the events of the day, or in joining the mobs which, under one pretext or another, kept the streets in an uproar.

Fortunately Marie knew the way perfectly and there was no occasion for her to ask for directions, for she had frequently driven with her mother to visit Louise Moulin. The latter occupied the upper floor of a house in a quiet quarter near the fortifications in the north-western part of the town. A message had been sent to her the night before, and she was on the look-out for her visitors, but she did not recognize them, and she uttered a cry of surprise as Marie and Virginie entered the room.

"Is it you, mademoiselle?" she exclaimed in great surprise. "And you, my little angel? My eyes must be getting old, indeed, that I did not recognize you; but you are finely disguised. But where is Mademoiselle Jeanne?"

"She will be here in a moment, Louise; she is just behind. But you must not call me mademoiselle; you must remember that we are your nieces Marie and Jeanne, and that you are our aunt Louise Moulin, whom we have come to stay with."

"I shall remember in time," the old woman said. "I have been talking about you to my neighbours for the last week, of how your good father and mother have died, and how you were going to journey to Paris under the charge of a neighbour, who was bringing a waggon load of wine from Burgundy, and how you were going to look after me and help me in the house since I am getting old and infirm, and the young ones were to stop with me till they were old enough to go out to service. Ah, here is Mademoiselle Jeanne!"

"Here is Jeanne," Marie corrected; "thank God we have all got here safely. This, Louise, is a young English gentleman who is going to remain in Paris at present, and to whom we are indebted for having got us safely here."

"And your mother," Louise Moulin exclaimed, "the darling lamb I nursed, what of her and your father? I fear, from the message I got last night, that some danger threatens them."

"They have, I fear, been arrested by the sans culottes," Marie said mournfully as she burst into tears, feeling, now that the strain was over, the natural reaction after her efforts to be calm. For her mother's sake she had held up to the last, and had tried to make the parting as easy as possible.

"The wretches!" the old woman said, stamping her foot. "Old as I am I feel that I could tear them to pieces. But there I am chattering away, and you must be faint with hunger. I have a nice soup ready on the fire, a plate of that will do good to you all. And you too, monsieur, you will join us, I hope?"

Harry was nothing loth, for his appetite was always a healthy one. When he had finished he said:

"Madame Moulin, I have been thinking that it would be an advantage if you would take a lodging for me. If you would say that a youth whose friends are known to you has arrived from Dijon, to make his way in Paris, and they have asked you to seek a lodging for him; it will seem less strange than if I went by myself. I should like it to be near, so that you can come to me quickly should anything out of the way occur. I should like to look in sometimes to see that all is well. You could mention to your neighbours that I travelled up with the same waggon with your nieces.

"I will do that willingly," the old woman said; "but first, my dears, you must have some rest; come in here." And she led the way to the next room. "There is a bed for you, Mademoiselle Marie, and one for the two young ones. The room is not like what you are accustomed to, but I dared not buy finer things, though I had plenty of money from your mother to have furnished the rooms like a palace; but you see it would have seemed strange to my neighbours; but, at least, everything is clean and sweet."

Leaving the girls, who were worn out with weariness and anxiety, to sleep, she rejoined Harry.

"Now, monsieur, I will do your business. It is a comfort to me to feel that some one will be near of whom I can ask advice, for it is a terrible responsibility for an old woman in such dreadful times as these, when it seems to me that everyone has gone mad at once. What sort of a chamber do you want?"

"Quite a small one," Harry answered, "just such a chamber as a young clerk on the look-out for employment and with his pocket very slenderly lined, would desire."

"I know just such a one," the old woman said. "It is a house a few doors away and has been tenanted by a friend of mine, a young workwoman, who was married four days ago—it is a quiet place, and the people keep to themselves, and do not trouble about their neighbours' affairs."

"That will just suit me," Harry said. "I suppose there is no porter below, so that I can go in or out without being noticed."

"Oh, we have no porters in this quarter, and you can go in and out as you like."

Half an hour later the matter was settled, and Harry was installed in his apartment, which was a little room scantily furnished, at the top of the house, the window looking into the street in front.

61

CHAPTER VI

AN ANXIOUS TIME

Harry and the girls had brought bundles of clothes with them in their flight, as it would have looked strange had they arrived without any clothes save those they wore. Harry had brought with him only underlinen, as he had nothing else which would be of service to him now. No sooner had Louise Moulin left him than he went out and purchased, at a second-hand shop, a workman's suit. This he carried home, and dressing himself in it descended the stairs again and set out to retrace his steps across Paris.

When he reached the mansion of the marquis he found a crowd of people going in and out. Those leaving the house were laden with articles of furniture, clocks, pictures, bedding, and other things. A complete sack of the mansion was indeed taking place. The servants had all fled after the arrest of the marquis and his wife, and the mob had taken possession of the house. The lofty mirrors were smashed into fragments, the costly hangings torn down, and after they had destroyed much of the elaborate furniture, every man and woman began to lay hands upon whatever they fancied and the mansion was already stripped of the greater part of its belongings.

With his hands in his pockets, whistling carelessly, Harry wandered from room to room watching the proceedings. Several barrels of wine had been brought up into the salon, and round these were gathered a number of already drunken men, singing, shouting, and dancing.

"Drink, drink, my garcon," a woman said, holding a silver goblet full of wine towards him, "drink confusion to the tyrants and liberty and freedom to the people."

Harry drank the toast without hesitation, and then, heartsick at the destruction and ruin, wandered out again into the streets. Knowing the anxiety which Marie would be suffering as to the safety of her lover he next took his way to the mansion of the Duke de Gisons. The house was shut up, but groups of men were standing in the road opposite talking.

Sauntering along Harry stopped near enough to one of these to hear what they were saying. He learned that the duke had been arrested only that morning. It had been effected quietly, the doors had again been locked before those in the neighbourhood knew

62

what was going on, and a guard had been left inside, partly, it was said, in order that the mansion might be preserved from pillage and be used for public purposes, partly that the young count, who was absent, might be arrested when he returned.

As Harry knew that the duke had estates in the neighbourhood of Fontainebleau he thought it probable that Victor might have gone thither, and he at once proceeded towards the gate by which he would enter on his return thence. He sat down a short distance outside the gate and watched patiently for some hours until he perceived a horseman approaching at a gallop and at once recognized Victor de Gisons. Harry went forward on to the road and held out his arms. The young count, not recognizing him, did not check his horse and would have ridden him down had he not jumped aside, at the same time shouting to him by name to stop.

"What do you want, fellow?" Victor exclaimed, reining in his horse.

"You do not recognize me!" Harry said. "I am Harry Sandwith, count, and I am here to warn you of the danger of proceeding."

"Why, what has happened?" Victor exclaimed anxiously; "and why are you in disguise, Monsieur Sandwith?"

"A great number of arrests have taken place in the night, among them that of the Marquis de St. Caux and your father. Men are waiting inside your house to arrest you as you enter."

Victor uttered an exclamation of anger.

"That is why I have been sent away," he said. "My father had no doubt received a warning of what was about to happen, and yesterday at noon he requested me to ride to his estate and have an interview with the steward as to the rents. I wondered at his sending me so suddenly, and, feeling uneasy, rode there post-haste, saw the steward last night, and started again on a fresh horse this morning. This accounts for it. He knew that if I were there nothing would have induced me to separate myself from him, while by sending me away he left it to me to do as I thought fit afterwards, trusting that when I found that he was already imprisoned I might follow the counsel he had urged upon me, to make my escape from the country. And how about the ladies, how about Marie?"

"The marquise was conveyed to prison with the marquis. The three young ladies are all safe with their mother's old servant, Louise Moulin; this is her address. They are in disguise as peasants, and no suspicion will, I hope, arise as to their real position. Not that the marquis thought it probable they would be included in the order of arrest, but he said there was no knowing now to what lengths the mob might go and he thought it better that they should disappear altogether for the present. Ernest and Jules went away in disguise with Monsieur du Tillet. After seeing the young ladies in safety this morning I went down to see what had happened at your father's mansion, in order to assuage Mademoiselle de St. Caux's anxiety respecting your safety, and found, as I expected, that the duke had been arrested, and learned that a party were inside waiting to arrest you on your return.

"I thank you indeed," Victor said, "and most warmly. I do not know what to do. My father is most anxious that I should cross the frontier, but I cannot go so long as he and Marie are in danger."

"If you enter Paris as you are," Harry said, "you are certain to be arrested. Your only chance would be to do as I have done, namely to disguise yourself and take a small lodging, where you might live unsuspected."

"And in that way I can see Marie sometimes," Victor said.

"You could do so," Harry agreed, in a somewhat hesitating way, "but it would greatly add to her danger, and, were you detected, might lead to the discovery of her disguise. Besides, the thought that you were liable to arrest at any time would naturally heighten the anxiety from which she is suffering as to the fate of her father and mother."

"But I cannot and will not run away and leave them all here in danger," Victor said passionately.

"I would not advise you to do so," Harry replied. "I would only suggest, that after seeing Mademoiselle de St. Caux once, you should lead her to believe that you have decided upon making for the frontier, and she will therefore have the happiness of believing that you are safe, while you are still near and watching over her."

"That is all very well," Victor said; "but what opinion would she have of me if she thought me capable of deserting her in that way?"

"You would represent that you were obeying the duke's orders; and besides, if you did suffer in her opinion it would be but temporarily, for when she learned the truth, that you had only pretended to leave in order that her position might be the safer and that her mind might be relieved, she could only think more highly of you. Besides, if necessary, you could at any time again present yourself before her."

"Your counsel is good, Monsieur Sandwith, and I will, at anyrate for a time, follow it. As you say, I can at anytime reappear. Where are you lodging? I will take a room near, and we can meet and compare notes and act together."

Harry gave him his address.

"You have only to walk upstairs to the top story. My room is the one directly opposite the top of the stairs."

"I will call on you to-morrow morning," Victor said. "I will ride my horse a few miles back and turn him loose in some quiet place, and buy at the first village a blouse and workman's pantaloons."

"I think," Harry said, "that would be unwise, count; it would look strange in the extreme for a gentleman dressed as you are to make such a purchase. You might be at once arrested, or a report of the circumstance might be sent into Paris and lead to your discovery. If you will wait here for half an hour I will go back and buy you the things you want at the first shop I come to and bring them out to you. Then you can ride back and loose the horse as you propose; but I should advise you to hide the saddle and bridle, as well as the clothes you are now wearing, most carefully. Whoever finds your horse will probably appropriate it and will say nothing about it, so that all clue to your movements will be lost, and it will be supposed that you have ridden to the frontier."

"Peste, Monsieur Sandwith! You seem to have a head ready for all emergencies. I know what a high opinion the marquis had of you, and I perceive that it is fully justified, and consider myself as fortunate indeed in having you for a friend in such a time as the present."

"We have need of all our wits," Harry said quietly. "The marquis was good enough to accept my offer to do all that I could to look after the safety of mesdemoiselles, and if I fail in my trust it will not, I hope, be from any lack of care or courage."

The meeting had taken place at a point where it could not be observed from the gate, and the count withdrew a few hundred yards farther away while Harry went back into Paris. The latter had no difficulty in purchasing the clothes required by the count and returned with them in little over a quarter of an hour, and then, having seen De Gisons ride off, he sauntered back into Paris and made his way towards the heart of the city.

Crossing the river he found a vast crowd gathered in front of the Hotel de Ville. The news of the wholesale arrests which had been made during the night had filled the populace with joy, and the air was full of shouts of "Down with the Aristocrats!" "Vive Danton! Vive Marat! Vive Robespierre!" Hawkers were selling, in the crowd, newspapers and broadsheets filled with the foulest attacks, couched in the most horrible language, upon the king, the queen, and the aristocracy.

At various points men, mounted upon steps or the pedestals of statues, harangued the mob while from time to time the crowd opened and made way for members of the city council, who were cheered or hooted according to their supposed sentiments for or against the cause of the people. After remaining there for some time Harry made his way to the entrance to the Assembly. A crowd was gathered here, and a tremendous rush was made when the doors were opened. Harry managed to force his way in and sat for some hours listening to the debate, which was constantly interrupted by the people in the galleries, who applauded with frenzy the speeches of their favourite orators, the deputies of the Mountain, as the bank of seats occupied by the Jacobin members was named, and howled and yelled when the Girondists ventured to advocate moderation or conciliation.

It was late in the evening before the sitting was over, and Harry was unable to leave his place earlier. Then he went and had supper at a wineshop, and after sauntering on the Boulevards until the streets began to be deserted he again crossed the river and made his way to the mansion. Not a light was to be seen in the windows and all was still and quiet. The great door stood open. The work of destruction was complete; the house was stripped of everything that could be carried away.

Harry made his way up to the bedroom of the marquis. The massive bedstead still stood in its place, having defied the efforts of destruction which had proved successful with the cabinets and other furniture. Sitting down on the floor Harry counted the boards beneath the bed, and then taking out a strong knife which he had purchased during the day he inserted it by the side of the middle board and tried to raise it. It yielded without difficulty to his effort.

As soon as it was lifted he groped in the cavity below it, and his hand soon came in contact with the heavy bag. Taking this out and putting it beneath his blouse he replaced the board and made his way downstairs. He felt too fatigued to walk across Paris again, and therefore made his way down to the river and curled himself up for the night at the foot of the wood pile where the girls had found shelter in the morning, and, in spite of the novelty of his situation, fell instantly asleep.

It was broad daylight when he woke, and an hour later he regained his lodgings, stopping by the way to breakfast at a quiet estaminet frequented by the better class of workmen. As when he had sallied out the day before, he was fortunate in meeting no one as he made his way up the stairs to his room. His first step was to

66

get up a board and to deposit beneath it the bag of money. Then, having changed his clothes, he went out and made a variety of purchases for housekeeping, as he did not wish to be obliged to take his meals at places where anyone sitting at the table with him might enter into conversation.

His French was quite good enough to pass in the salon of the marquis, but his ignorance of the Parisian slang spoken among the working-classes would have rendered it difficult for him to keep up his assumed character among them, and would have needed the fabrication of all sorts of stories as to his birthplace and past history.

Although in the position in which he was placed Harry felt that it would be impossible always to adhere to the truth, he shrank from any falsehoods that could possibly be avoided.

His first duty in order to carry out the task he had undertaken was to keep up his disguise, and this must be done even at the cost of telling lies as to his antecedents; but he was determined that he would avoid this unpleasant necessity as far as lay in his power.

At nine o'clock he made his way to the apartments of Louise Moulin. His entry was received with a cry of satisfaction from the girls.

"What is the news, Harry?" Jeanne exclaimed. "We expected you here yesterday evening, and sat up till ten o'clock."

"I was over the other side of the river discharging a mission your father had confided to me, and did not get back till this morning."

"I knew he was prevented by something," Jeanne said triumphantly. "I told you so, Marie—didn't I?"

"Yes, dear, I was wrong to be impatient; but you will forgive me, Harry? You can guess how I suffered yesterday."

"It was natural you should expect me, mademoiselle. I was sorry afterwards that I did not tell you when I left you that I should not be able to come in the evening, but indeed I did not think of it at the time."

"And now for your news, Harry," Jeanne asked impatiently; "have you learned anything about our father and mother?"

"I am sorry to say I have not, except that they, with many others, were taken to the prison of Bicetre. But I have good news for you, Mademoiselle Marie. After going first to the house and finding it in the possession of a hideous mob, who were plundering and drinking, I went to see what had taken place at the hotel of the Duc de Gisons. I found that he had, like your father, been arrested in the night. I learned that the count was absent, and that a party were inside in readiness to arrest him on his return. Thinking it probable that he might have gone down to their estate near Fontainebleau, I went out beyond the gate on that road and waited for him. I had the good fortune to meet him, to warn him of his danger, and to prevent his returning to town. He rode away with a suit of workman's clothes I had procured for him, and was to enter Paris in that disguise in the evening. He is to call on me at ten o'clock, and I will then conduct him hither. I thought it best to come in before to let you know that he was coming."

Marie burst into tears of happiness at hearing that her lover had escaped from the danger which threatened. Worn out by the fatigue and anxiety of the previous night, she had slept for some hours after reaching the shelter of the old nurse's roof, but she had lain awake all night thinking over the danger of all those dear to her. She was now completely overcome with the revulsion of feeling.

"You are a dear boy, Harry!" Jeanne said with frank admiration, while Marie sobbed out exclamations of gratitude. "You do seem to think about everything; and now Marie knows that Victor is safe, I do hope she is going to be more like herself. As I tell her, they cannot hurt father or mother. They have done no wrong, and they must let them out of prison after a time. Mamma said we were to be brave; and at anyrate I try to be, and so does Virginie, though she does cry sometimes. And now I hope Marie will be cheerful too, and not go about the rooms looking so downcast and wretched. It seems to me a miserable thing being in love. I should have thought Marie would have been the last person to be downcast, for no one is prouder of being a St. Caux than she is."

"I shall be better now, Jeanne," Marie said smiling, as she wiped away her tears. "You shall not have any reason to complain of me in future.

"But do you not think, Harry," she went on with a return of her anxiety, "that it is very dangerous for Victor to come back into Paris? I know that his father has long been praying him to make for the frontier."

"I do not think it is very dangerous at present, mademoiselle, although it may be later, if this rage against the aristocrats increases; but I hope that when he has once seen you, which is his principal object in returning to Paris, he will carry our his father's wishes and make for the frontier, for his presence here can be of no possible utility."

"Oh, I hope so," Marie said, "for I am sure Victor would soon be found out, he could never make himself look like one of these canaille."

"Why shouldn't he?" Jeanne said indignantly. "Harry does, and he is just as good-looking as Victor."

Marie burst into a fit of laughter.

"What a champion you are, child, to be sure! But you are quite right. Clothes, after all, do go a long way towards making a man. Still, although I think that it is dangerous for Harry, I think it will be more dangerous for Victor; because, you see, he is a man and he has the manner of his race, and would find it more difficult to pass himself off as a workman than Harry, who has got something of English"—and she hesitated.

"Roughness," Harry put in laughing. "You are quite right, mademoiselle. I can assure you that with these thick shoes on I find it quite natural for me to slouch along as the workmen do; and it will be much more difficult for the count, who always walks with his head thrown back, and a sort of air of looking down upon mankind in general."

Marie laughed this time.

"That is a fair retort. Victor certainly has the grand manner. However, I shall order him to go; and if he won't obey his father's wishes, he will have to give way to mine."

"I think, mademoiselle, that it would be wiser for Monsieur de Gisons to meet you elsewhere than here. The arrival of three relations to stop with Madame Moulin is sure to attract some little attention among her neighbours just at first. You will be the subject of talk and gossip. My visit will no doubt be noticed, and it will be as well that there should not be more material for talk. The less we attract attention the better. No doubt many have escaped arrest, and there will be a sharp look-out, for, as they will call us, suspicious persons. I should propose, if you have no objection to such a course, that you should stroll out with your sisters and Louise through the fields to St. Denis. The count will be in my room in a few minutes. We can keep a look-out from my window and follow you at a distance until we get clear from observation beyond the gates."

Marie looked at Madame Moulin, who nodded.

"That would be the best plan, my dear. What Monsieur Sandwith says is very true. The less we give the neighbours to gossip about the better; for though your disguises are good, if sharp eyes are watching you they may note something in your walk or air that may excite suspicion."

"That being arranged then you must excuse me, for it is just the time when the count was to arrive, and I fancy that he will be before rather than behind time."

Indeed, upon reaching the door of his room Harry found the young count standing there.

"Oh, it is you, friend Harry! I have been here ten minutes, and I began to be afraid that something might have happened to you and to imagine all sorts of things."

"It is still three or four minutes before the time we agreed upon, Victor," Harry said in a loud voice, for at this moment one of the other doors opened, and a woman came out with a basket in her arms.

"I have been looking about as usual, but without luck so far. I suppose you have had no better fortune in your search for work?" He had by this time unlocked his door, and the two entered together.

"I must call you by your Christian name, count, and will do so, if you don't mind, when alone as at other times, otherwise the title might slip out accidentally. Will you, on your part, call me Henri? As you know the marquis and his family called me Harry, which is the ordinary way in England of calling anyone whose name is Henry, that is unless he is a soft sort of fellow; but I must ask them to call me Henri now, Harry would never do here."

"Have you seen them?" was the count's first question.

"I have just left them, Victor, and if you look out from that window into the street you will in a few minutes see them also; they are just going for a ramble towards St. Denis, and we will follow them. I thought it safer not to attract attention by going to the house, and I also thought that it would be more pleasant for you to talk to Mademoiselle de St. Caux out there in the fields, than in a little room with us present.

"Much more pleasant; indeed, I was wondering whether I should get an opportunity for a few minutes' talk alone with her."

They both took their places at the open window and leaned out apparently chatting and carelessly watching what was passing in the street.

A quarter of an hour later they saw Louise Moulin and the girls come out of their house.

"We had better come away from the window now," Harry said; "Virginie might look up and nod, we can't be too careful."

They waited three or four minutes to allow the others to get well ahead and then started out after them; they walked fast until they caught sight of the others, and then kept some distance behind until the party had left the town and were out among the fields which lay between Paris and St. Denis. They then quickened their pace and were soon up with them.

The greeting between the lovers was a silent one, few words were spoken, but their faces expressed their joy at meeting again after the perils through which they had passed; there was a little pause, and then Harry, as usual, took the lead.

"I will stroll on to St. Denis and back with Jeanne and Virginie; Madame Moulin can sit down on that log over there, and go on with her knitting; you, Victor, can ramble on with mademoiselle by that path through the field; we will agree to meet here again in an hour."

This arrangement was carried out; Jeanne and Virginie really enjoyed their walk; the latter thought their disguise was great fun, and, being naturally a little mimic, imitated so well the walk and manner of the country children she had seen in her walks near the chateau that her sister and Harry were greatly amused.

"I like this too, Harry," Jeanne said. "It would not be nice to be a peasant girl for many things; but it must be joyful to be able to walk, and run, and do just as you please, without having a gouvernante always with you to say, Hold up your head, Mademoiselle Jeanne; Do not swing your arms, Mademoiselle Jeanne; Please walk more sedately, Mademoiselle Jeanne. Oh, it was hateful! Now we might run, mightn't we, Harry?"

"Oh, by the way, Jeanne, please call me Henri now; Harry is English, and people would notice directly if you happened to say it while anyone is near."

"I like Harry best," Jeanne said; "but, of course, I should not say it before the people; but may we run just for once?"

"Certainly you may," Harry laughed; "you and Virginie can have a race to the corner of that wall."

"Come on, Virginie," Jeanne cried as she started, and the two girls ran at full speed to the wall; Jeanne, however, completely distancing her younger sister. They were both laughing when Harry came up.

"That is the first time I have run a race," Jeanne said. "I have often wanted to try how fast I could run, but I have never ventured to ask mademoiselle; she would have been horrified; but I don't know how it is Virginie does not run faster."

"Virginie has more flesh," Harry said smiling. "She carries weight, as we should say in England, while you have nothing to spare.

"And she is three years older," Virginie put in. "Jeanne is just sixteen, and I am not thirteen yet; it makes a difference."

"A great deal of difference," Harry agreed; "but I don't think you will ever run as fast as she does. That will not matter, you know," he went on, as Virginie looked a little disappointed, "because it is not likely that you will ever race again; but Jeanne looks cut out for a runner—just the build, you see—tall, and slim, and active."

"Yes," Virginie agreed frankly, "Jeanne has walked ever so far and never gets tired, while I get dreadfully tired; mamma says sometimes I am quite a baby for my age."

"Here are some people coming," Harry said; "as we pass them please talk with a little patois. Your good French would be suspicious."

All the children of the marquis, from their visits among the peasants' cottages, had picked up a good deal of the Burgundian patois, and when talking among themselves often used the expressions current among the peasantry, and they now dropped into this talk, which Harry had also acquired, as they passed a group of people coming in from St. Denis.

They walked nearly as far as that town, and then turned and reached the point where the party had separated, a few minutes before the expiration of the appointed hour.

The two girls ran away to Louise Moulin, and chatted to her gaily, while Harry walked up and down until, a quarter of an hour later, the count and Marie made their appearance. The party stood talking together for a few minutes; then adieus were said with a very pale face, but with firmness on Marie's part, and then the girls, with Louise, turned their faces to Paris, while Harry and Victor remained behind until they had got well on their way.

"It was hard to deceive her," Victor said; "but you were right. She insisted that I should go. I seemed to resist, and urged that it was cowardly for me to run away and to leave her here alone, but she would not listen to it. She said it was a duty I owed to my father and family to save myself, and that she should be wretched if she thought I was in Paris in constant danger of arrest. Finally, I had to give way to her, but it went against the grain, for even while she was urging me she must have felt in her heart it would be cowardly of me to go. However, she will know some day that Victor de Gisons is no coward."

"I am sure it is better so," Harry said. "She will have anxiety enough to bear as to her father and mother; it is well that her mind should be at ease concerning you."

"In reality," Victor said, "I shall be safer here than I should be journeying towards the frontier. The papers this morning say that in consequence of the escape of suspected persons, and of the emigration of the nobles to join the enemies of France, orders have been sent that the strictest scrutiny is to be exercised on the roads leading to the frontier, over all strangers who may pass through. All who cannot give a perfectly satisfactory account of themselves and produce their papers en regle, are to be arrested and sent to Paris. Therefore, my chance of getting through would be small indeed, whereas while remaining in Paris there can be little fear of detection."

"Not much risk, I hope," Harry agreed; "but there is no saying what stringent steps they may take as time goes on."

Victor had taken a lodging a few houses from that of Harry. Every day the excitement in Paris increased, every day there were fresh arrests until all the prisons became crowded to overflowing. It was late in August; the Prussians were advancing and had laid siege to Verdun, and terror was added to the emotions which excited to madness the population of Paris. Black flags were hung from the steeples, and Danton and his allies skilfully used the fear inspired by the foreign enemy to add to the general hatred of the Royalists.

"We Republicans," he said in the rostrum of the Assembly, "are exposed to two parties, that of the enemy without, that of the Royalists within. There is a Royalist directory which sits secretly at Paris and corresponds with the Prussian army. To frustrate it we must terrify the Royalists."

The Assembly decreed death against all who directly or indirectly refused to execute or hindered the orders given by the executive power. Rumours of conspiracy agitated Paris and struck alarm into people's minds, while those who had friends within the prison walls became more and more alarmed for their safety.

On the 28th of August orders were issued that all the inhabitants of Paris were to stay in their houses in order that a visit might be made by the delegates of the Commune to search for arms, of which Danton had declared there were eighty thousand hidden in Paris, and to search for suspected persons. As soon as the order was issued, Harry and Victor went to their lodgings, and telling their landlords that they had obtained work at the other end of town, paid their rent and left the city, and for the next two days slept in the woods.

They passed most of their time discussing projects for enabling their friends to escape, for from the stringency of the steps taken, and the violence of the Commune, they could no longer indulge in the hopes that in a short time the prisoners against whom no serious charge could be brought, would be released. At the same time they could hardly persuade themselves that even such men as those who now held the supreme power in their hands, could intend to take extreme measures against so vast a number of prisoners as were now in custody.

Victor and Harry knew that their friends had at first been taken to the prison of Bicetre, but whether they were still confined there they were of course ignorant. Still there was no reason to suppose that they had been transferred to any of the other jails.

The Bicetre was, they had discovered, so strongly guarded that neither force nor stratagem seemed available. The jailers were the creatures of Danton and Robespierre, and any attempt to bribe them would have been dangerous in the extreme. Victor proposed that, as he as well as Harry was well provided with funds, for he had brought to Paris all the money which the steward of the estates had collected, they should recruit a band among the ruffians of the city, and make a sudden attack upon the prison. But Harry pointed out that a numerous band would be required for such an enterprise, and that among so many men one would be sure to turn traitor before the time came.

"I am ready to run all risks, Victor, but I see no chance of success in it. The very first man we spoke to might denounce us, and if we were seized there would be no one to look after the safety of Mademoiselle de St. Caux and her sisters. My first duty is towards them. I gave my promise to their father, and although it is not probable that I can be of any use to them, I will at any rate, if possible, be at hand should occasion arise."

On the evening of the 30th they returned to Paris, and took two fresh apartments at a distance from their former quarters.

They were greatly anxious as to the safety of the girls, and Harry at once hastened there, but found that all was well. The deputies, learning from the landlord that only an old woman and her nieces inhabited the upper story, and having a heavy task before them, had only paid a short visit to the room, and had left after asking Louise one or two questions.

The girls, however, were in a state of terrible anxiety as to their parents, although Louise had avoided repeating to them the sinister rumours which came to her ears when she was abroad doing her marketing, for she now went out alone, thinking it better that the girls should appear as little as possible in the streets.

"It is terrible," Marie said. "I think night and day of our father and mother. Can nothing be done? Surely we might devise some means for their escape."

"I can think of nothing," Harry said. "The prison is too strong to be taken without a considerable force, and it would be impossible to get that together."

"Could we not bribe these wretches?"

"I have thought over that too," Harry replied; "but, you see, it would be necessary to get several men to work together. One might, perhaps, bribe the man who has charge of the cell, but there would be other warders, and the guard at the gate, and the latter are changed every day. I do not see how that could possibly be done."

"Would it be any use, do you think, were I to go to Danton or Robespierre and plead with them for their lives? I would do that willingly if you think there would be the slightest chance of success."

"It would be like a lamb going to plead with a wolf. You would only attract attention to them."

"Could you not get hold of one of these wretches and force him to sign an order for their release?" Jeanne suggested.

"Eh!" Harry exclaimed in surprise. "Jeanne, you have the best head of us all. That idea never occurred to me. Yes, that might be possible. How stupid of me not to think of it!"

"Do not run into any danger, Harry," Marie said earnestly. "Such a scheme could hardly succeed."

"I don't know, mademoiselle. I think it might. I will think it over. Of course there are difficulties, but I do not see why it should not succeed."

"Certainly it will succeed if Harry undertakes it," Jeanne said, with implicit trust in his powers.

Harry laughed, and even Marie, anxious as she was, could not help smiling.

"I will try and deserve your confidence, Jeanne; but I am not a magician. But I will talk it over with"—and he hesitated—"with a young fellow who is, like myself, a Royalist, and in disguise. Luckily, we ran against each other the other day, and after a little conversation discovered each other. He, too, has relatives in prison, and will, I am sure, join me in any scheme I may undertake. Two heads are better than one, and four are much better than two when it comes to acting. And now I must say good-night. I hope when I see you again I shall be able to tell you that I have formed some sort of plan for their release."

CHAPTER VII

THE 2D OF SEPTEMBER

Victor de Gisons was, as usual, waiting near the door when Harry left Louise Moulin's.

"What is the news, Henri? Nothing suspicious, I hope? You are out sooner than usual."

"Yes, for I have something to think of. Here have we been planning in vain for the last fortnight to hit upon some scheme for getting our friends out of prison, and Jeanne has pointed out a way which you and I never thought of."

"What is that, Henri?"

"The simplest thing in the world, namely, that we should seize one of the leaders of these villains and compel him to sign an order for their release."

"That certainly seems possible," Victor said. "I wonder it never occurred to either of us. But how is it to be done?"

"Ah, that is for us to think out! Jeanne has given us the idea, and we should be stupid if we cannot invent the details. In the first place we have got to settle which of them it had better be, and in the next how it is to be managed. It must be some one whose signature the people at the prison would be sure to obey."

"Then," Victor said, "it must be either Danton or Robespierre."

"Or Marat," Harry added; "I think he is as powerful as either of the others."

"He is the worst of them, anyhow," Victor said. "There is something straightforward about Danton. No doubt he is ambitious, but I think his hatred of us all is real. He is a terrible enemy, and will certainly stick at nothing. He is ruthless and pitiless, but I do not think he is double-faced. Robespierre is ambitious too, but I think he is really acting according to his principles, such as they are. He would be pitiless too, but he would murder on principle.

"He would sign unmoved the order for a hundred heads to fall if he thought their falling necessary or even useful for the course of the Revolution, but I do not think he would shed a drop of blood to satisfy private enmity. They call him the 'incorruptible.' He is more dangerous than Danton, for he has no vices. He lives simply, and they say is fond of birds and pets. I do not think we should make much of either Danton or him, even if we got them in our power.

"Danton would be like a wild beast in a snare. He would rage with fury, but I do not think that he would be intimidated into signing what we require, not do I think would Robespierre. Marat is a different creature altogether. He is simply venomous. He hates the world, and would absolutely rejoice in slaughter. So loathsome is he in appearance that even his colleagues shrink from him. He is a venomous reptile whom it would be a pleasure to slay, as it would be to put one's heel upon a rattlesnake. Whether he is a coward or not I do not know, but I should think so. Men of his type are seldom brave. I think if we had him in our hands we might frighten him into doing what we want."

"Then Marat it shall be," Harry said; "that much is settled. Tomorrow we will find out something about his habits. Till we know about that we cannot form any plan whatever. Let us meet at dinner-time at our usual place. Then we will go outside the Assembly and wait till he comes out. Fortunately we both know him well by sight. He will be sure to go, surrounded, as usual, by a mob of his admirers, to the Jacobin Club. From there we can trace him to his home. No doubt anyone could tell us where he lives, but it would be dangerous to ask. When we have found that out we can decide upon our next step."

They were, however, saved the trouble they contemplated, for they learned from the conversation of two men among the mob, who cheered Marat as he entered the Assembly, what they wanted to know.

"Marat is the man for me," one of them said. "He hates the aristocracy; he would bathe in their blood. I never miss reading his articles in the Friend of the People. His cry is always 'Blood! Blood!' He does not ape the manner of the bourgeois. He does not wash his face and put on clean linen. He is a great man, but he is as dirty as the best of us. He still lives in his old lodgings, though he could move if he liked into any of the fine houses whose owners are in the prisons. He wants no servants, but lives just as we do. Vive Marat!"

"Where does the great citizen live?" Victor asked the men in a tone of earnest entreaty. On learning the address they took their way to the dirty and disreputable street where Marat lodged.

"The citizen Marat lives in this street, does he not?" Victor asked a man lounging at the door of a cabaret.

"Yes, in that house opposite. Do you want him?"

"No; only I was curious to see the house where the friend of the people lives, and as I was passing the end of the street turned down. Will you drink a glass?"

"I am always ready for that," the man said, "but in these hard times one cannot do it as often as one would like."

"That is true enough," Victor said as they took their seats at a table. "And so Marat lives over there; it's not much of a place for a great man."

"It is all he wants," the other said carelessly; "and he is safer here than he would be in the richer quarters. There would be a plot against him, and those cursed Royalists would kill him if they had the chance; but he is always escorted home from the club by a band of patriots."

In the evening Harry and Victor returned to the street and watched until Marat returned from the Jacobin Club. His escort of men with torches and bludgeons left him at the door, but two or three went upstairs with him, and until far in the night visitors came and went. Then the light in the upper room was extinguished.

"It is not such an easy affair," Victor said as they moved away; "and you see, as that man in the wine-shop told us, there is an old woman who cooks for him, and it is much more difficult to seize two people without an alarm being given than one."

"That is so," Harry agreed; "but it must be done somehow. Every day matters grow more threatening, and those bands of scoundrels from Marseilles have not been brought all this way for nothing. The worst of it is, we have such a short time to act. Marat does not seem to be ever alone from early morning until late at night. Supposing we did somehow get the order of release from him at night we could not present it till the morning, and before we could present it some one might arrive and discover him fastened up, and might take the news to the prison before we could get them out."

"Yes, that is very serious," Victor agreed. "I begin to despair, Henri."

"We must not do that," Harry rejoined. "You see we thought it impossible before till Jeanne gave us the idea. There must be some way out of it if we could only hit upon it. Perhaps by to-morrow morning an idea will occur to one of us. And there is another thing to be thought of; we must procure disguises for them. It would be of no use whatever getting them out unless we could conceal them after they are freed. It would not do for them to go to Louise Moulin's. She has three visitors already, and the arrival of more to stay with her would be sure to excite talk among the neighbours. The last orders are so strict about the punishment of anyone giving shelter to enemies of the republic, that people who let rooms will all be suspicious. The only plan will be to get them out of the city at once. It will be difficult for them to make their way through France on foot, for in every town and village there is the strictest look-out kept for suspected persons. Still, that must be risked; there is no other way."

"Yes, we must see about that to-morrow, Henri; but I do not think the marquise could support a journey, for they would have to sleep in the fields. Moreover, she will probably elect to stay near her children until all can go together. Therefore I think that it will be best for her to come either to you or me. We can take an additional room, saying that our mother is coming up from the country to keep house for us."

"Yes, that would be much the best plan, Victor. And now here we are close home. I hope by the time we meet in the morning one of us may have hit upon some plan or other for getting hold of this scoundrel."

"I have hit upon an idea, Victor," Harry said when they met the next morning.

"I am glad to hear it, for though I have lain awake all night I could think of nothing. Well, what is your idea?"

"Well, you see, Marat often goes out in the morning alone. He is so well known and he is so much regarded by the lower class that he has no fear of any assault being made upon him during the day.

"My plan is that we should follow him till he gets into some street with few people about. Then I would rush upon him, seize him, and draw a knife to strike, shouting, 'Die, villain!' You should be a few paces behind, and should run up and strike the knife out of my hand, managing at the same moment to tumble over Marat and fall with him to the ground. That would give me time to bolt. I would have a beard on, and would have my other clothes under the blouse. I would rush into the first doorway and run up stairs, pull off my beard, blouse, and blue pantaloons, and then walk quietly down. You would, of course, rush up stairs and meet me on the way. I should say I had just met a fellow running up stairs, and should slip quietly off."

"It would be a frightful risk, Henri, frightful!"

"No, I think it could be managed easily enough. Then, of course, Marat would be very grateful to you, and you could either get him to visit your lodgings or could go up to his, and once you had been there you could manage to outsit his last visitor at night, and then we could do as we agreed."

"But, you know, we thought we should hardly have time in the morning, Henri!"

"No, I have been thinking of that, and I have come to the conclusion that our best plan would be to seize him and hold a dagger to his heart, and threaten to kill him instantly if he did not accompany us. Then we would go down with him into the street and walk arm in arm with him to your lodging. We could thrust a ball of wood into his mouth so that he could not call out even if he had the courage to do so, which I don't think he would have if he were assured that if he made the slightest sound we would kill him. Then we could make him sign the order and leave him fastened up there. It would be better to take him to your lodgings than mine, in case my visits to Louise Moulin should have been noticed, and when he is released there will be a hue and cry after his captors."

"The best plan will be to put a knife into his heart at once the minute you have got the order signed," Victor said savagely; "I should have no more hesitation in killing him than stamping on a snake."

"No, Victor; the man is a monster, but we cannot kill him in cold blood; besides, we should do more harm than good to the cause, for the people would consider he had died a martyr to his championship of their rights, and would be more furious than ever against the aristocracy."

"But his account of what he has gone through will have just the same effect, Henri."

"I should think it probable he would keep the story to himself. What has happened once may happen again; and besides, his cowardice in signing the release of three enemies of the people in order to save his life would tell against him. No, I think he would keep silence. After we have got them safe away we can return and so far loosen his bonds that he would be able, after a time, to free himself. Five minutes' start would be all that we should want."

But the plan was not destined to be carried out. It was the morning of the 2d of September, 1792, and as they went down into the quarter where the magazines of old clothes were situated, in order to purchase the necessary disguises, they soon became sensible that something unusual was in the air. Separating, they joined the groups of men at the corners of the streets and tried to learn what was going on, but none seemed to know for certain. All sorts of sinister rumours were about. Word had been passed that the Jacobin bands were to be in readiness that evening. Money had been distributed. The Marseillais had dropped hints that a blow was to be struck at the tyrants. Everywhere there was a suppressed excitement among the working-classes; an air of gloom and terror among the bourgeois.

After some time Harry and Victor came together again and compared their observations. Neither had learned anything definite, but both were sure that something unusual was about to take place.

"It may be that a large number of fresh arrests are about to be made," Harry said. "There are still many deputies who withstand the violence of the Mountain. It may be that a blow is going to be struck against them."

"We must hope that that is it," Victor said, "but I am terribly uneasy."

Harry had the same feeling, but he did his best to reassure his friend, and proposed that they should at once set about buying the disguises, and that on the following morning they should carry into effect their plan with reference to Marat. The dresses were bought. Two suits, such as a respectable mechanic would wear on Sundays or holidays, were first purchased. There was then a debate as to the disguise for the marquise; it struck them at once that it was strange for two young workmen to be purchasing female attire, but, after some consultation, they decided upon a bonnet and long cloak, and these Victor went in and bought, gaily telling the shopkeeper that he was buying a birthday present for his old mother.

They took the clothes up to Harry's room, agreeing that Louise could easily buy the rest of the garments required for the marquise as soon as she was free, but they decided to say nothing about the attempt that was about to be made until it was over, as it would cause an anxiety which the old woman would probably be unable to conceal from the girls.

Victor did not accompany Harry to his room; they had never, indeed, visited each other in their apartments, meeting always some little distance away in order that their connection should be unobserved, and that, should one be arrested, no suspicion would follow the other. As soon as he had deposited the clothes Harry sallied out again, and on rejoining Victor they made their way down to the Hotel de Ville, being too anxious to remain quiet. They could learn nothing from the crowd which was, as usual, assembled before the Hotel.

There was a general impression that something was about to happen, but none could give any definite reason for their belief. All day they wandered about restless and anxious. They fought their way into the galleries of the Assembly when the doors opened, but for a time nothing new took place.

The Assembly, in which the moderates had still a powerful voice, had protested against the assumption of authority by the council of the Commune sitting at the Hotel de Ville. But the Assembly lacked firmness, the Commune every day gained in power. Already warrants of arrest were prepared against the Girondists, the early leaders of the movement.

Too restless to remain in the Assembly, Victor and Harry again took their steps to the Hotel de Ville. Just as they arrived there twenty-four persons, of whom twenty-two were priests, were brought out from the prison of the Maine by a party of Marseillais, who shouted, "To the Abbaye!" These ruffians pushed the prisoners into coaches standing at the door, shouting: "You will not arrive at the prison; the people are waiting to tear you in pieces." But the people looked on silently in sullen apathy.

"You see them," the Marseillais shouted. "There they are. You are about to march to Verdun. They only wait for your departure to butcher your wives and children."

Still the crowd did not move. The great mass of the people had no share in the bloody deeds of the Revolution; these were the work of a few score of violent men, backed by the refuse of the population. A few shouts were raised here and there of, "Down with the priests!" But more of the crowd joined in the shouts which Victor and Harry lustily raised of, "Shame, down with the Marseillais!" Victor would have pressed forward to attack the Marseillais had not Harry held his arm tightly, exclaiming in his ear:

"Restrain yourself, Victor. Think of the lives that depend upon ours. The mob will not follow you. You can do nothing yourself. Come, get out of the crowd."

So saying he dragged Victor away. It was well that they could not see what was taking place in the coaches, or Victor's fury would have been ungovernable, for several of the ruffians had drawn their swords and were hacking furiously at their prisoners.

"We will follow them," Harry said, when he and Victor had made their way out of the crowd; "but you must remember, Victor, that, come what may, you must keep cool. You would only throw away your life uselessly; for Marie's sake you must keep calm. Your life belongs to her, and you have no right to throw it away."

"You are right, Henri," Victor said gloomily; "but how can one look on and see men inciting others to massacre? What is going to take place? We must follow them."

"I am ready to follow them," Harry said; "but you must not go unless you are firmly resolved to restrain your feelings whatever may happen. You can do no possible good, and will only involve yourself in the destruction of others."

"You may trust me," the young count said; "I will be calm for Marie's sake."

Harry had his doubts as to his friend's power of self-control, but he was anxious to see what was taking place, and they joined the throng that followed the coaches. But they were now in the rear, and could see nothing that was taking place before them. When the carriages reached the Abbaye the prisoners alighted. Some of them were at once cut down by the Marseillais, the rest fled into the hall, where one of the committees was sitting. Its members, however, did nothing to protect them, and looked on while all save two were massacred unresistingly. Then the Marseillais came out brandishing their bloody weapons and shouting, "The good work has begun; down with the priests! Down with the enemies of the people!"

The better class of people in the crowd assembled at the Hotel de Ville had not followed the procession to the Abbaye. They had been horror-struck at the words and actions of the Marseillais, and felt that this was the beginning of the fulfilment of the rumours of the last few days.

The murder of the first prisoner was indeed the signal for every man of thought or feeling and of heart to draw back from the Revolution. Thousands of earnest men who had at first thought that the hour of life and liberty commenced with the meeting of the States-General, and who had gone heart and soul with that body in its early struggles for power, had long since shrunk back appalled at the new tyranny which had sprung into existence.

Each act of usurpation of power by the Jacobins had alienated a section. The nobles and the clergy, many of whom had at first gone heartily with the early reformers, had shrunk back appalled when they saw that religion and monarchy were menaced. The bourgeoisie, who had made the Revolution, were already to a man against it; the Girondists, the leaders of the third estate, had fallen away, and over their heads the axe was already hanging. The Revolution had no longer a friend in France, save among the lowest, the basest, and the most ignorant. And now, by the massacres of the 2d of September, the republic of France was to stand forth in the eyes of Europe as a blood-stained monster, the enemy, not of kings only, but of humanity in general. Thus the crowd following the Marseillais was composed almost entirely of the scum of Paris, wretches who had long been at war with society, who hated the rich, hated the priests, hated all above them—men who had suffered so much that they had become wild beasts, who were the products of that evil system of society which had now been overthrown. The

83

greater proportion of them were in the pay of the Commune, for, two days before, all the unemployed had been enrolled as the army of the Commune. Thus there was no repetition before the Abbaye of the cries of shame which had been heard in front of the Maine. The shouts of the Marseillais were taken up and re-echoed by the mob. Savage cries, curses, and shouts for vengeance filled the air; many were armed, and knives and bludgeons, swords and pikes, were brandished or shaken. Blood had been tasted, and all the savage instincts were on fire.

"This is horrible, Henri!" Victor de Gisons exclaimed. "I feel as if I were in a nightmare, not that any nightmare could compare in terror to this. Look at those hideous faces—faces of men debased by crime, sodden with drink, degraded below the level of brutes, exulting in the thought of blood, lusting for murder; and to think that these creatures are the masters of France. Great Heavens! What can come of it in the future? What is going to take place now?"

"Organized massacre, I fear, Victor. What seemed incredible, impossible, is going to take place; there is to be a massacre of the prisoners."

They had by this time reached the monastery of the Carmelites, now converted into a prison. Here a large number of priests had been collected. The Marseillais entered, and the prisoners were called by name to assemble in the garden.

First the Archbishop of Arles was murdered; then they fell upon the others and hewed them down. The Bishops of Saintes and Beauvais were among the slain, and the assassins did not desist until the last prisoner in the Carmelites had been hacked to pieces. Graves had already been dug near the Barrier Saint Jacques and carts were waiting to convey the corpses there, showing how carefully the preparations for the massacre had been made.

Then the Marseillais returned to the Abbaye, and, with a crowd of followers, entered the great hall. Here the bailiff Maillard organized a sort of tribunal of men taken at random from the crowd. Some of these were paid hirelings of the Commune, some were terrified workmen or small tradesmen who had, merely from curiosity, joined the mob. The Swiss officers and soldiers, who were, with the priests, special objects of hatred to the mob, were first brought out. They were spared the farce of a trial, they were ordered to march out through the doors, outside which the Marseillais were awaiting them. Some hesitated to go out, and cried for mercy.

A young man with head erect was the first to pass through the fatal doors. He fell in a moment, pierced with pikes. The rest followed him, and all save two, who were, by some caprice of the mob, spared, shared his fate. The mob had crowded into the galleries which surrounded the hall and applauded with ferocious yells the murder of the soldiers. In the body of the hall a space was kept clear by the armed followers of the Commune round the judges' table, and a pathway to the door from the interior of the prison to that opening into the street.

When the Swiss had been massacred the trial of the other prisoners commenced. One after another the prisoners were brought out. They were asked their names and occupations, a few questions followed, and then the verdict of "Guilty." One after another they were conducted to the door and there slain. Two or three by the wittiness of their answers amused the mob and were thereupon acquitted, the acquittals being greeted by the spectators as heartily as the sentences of death.

Victor and Harry were in the lowest gallery. They stood back from the front, but between the heads of those before them they could see what was going on below. Victor stood immovable, his face as pale as death. His cap had fallen off, his hair was dank with perspiration, his eyes had a look of concentrated horror, his body shook with a spasmodic shuddering. In vain Harry, when he once saw what was going to take place, urged him in a low whisper to leave. He did not appear to hear, and even when Harry pulled him by the sleeve of his blouse he seemed equally unconscious. Harry was greatly alarmed, and feared that every moment his companion would betray himself by some terrible out-burst.

After the three or four first prisoners had been disposed of, a tall and stately man was brought into the hall. A terrible cry, which sounded loud even above the tumult which reigned, burst from Victor's lips. He threw himself with the fury of a madman upon those in front of him, and in a moment would have bounded into the hall had not Harry brought the heavy stick he carried with all his force down upon his head. Victor fell like a log under the blow.

"What is it? What is it?" shouted those around.

"My comrade has gone out of his mind," Harry said quietly; "he has been drinking for some days, and his hatred for the enemies of France has turned his head. I have been watching him, and had I not knocked him down he would have thrown himself head-foremost off the gallery and broken his neck."

The explanation seemed natural, and all were too interested in what was passing in the hall below to pay further attention to so trivial an incident. It was well that Harry had caught sight of the prisoner before Victor did so and was prepared for the out-break, for it was the Duc de Gisons who had thus been led in to murder. Harry dragged Victor back against the wall behind and then tried to lift him.

"I will lend you a hand," a tall man in the dress of a mechanic, who had been standing next to him, said, and, lifting Victor's body on to his shoulder, made his way to the top of the stairs, Harry preceding him and opening a way through the crowd. In another minute they were in the open air.

"Thank you greatly," Harry said. "I do not know how I should have managed without your aid. If you put him down here I will try and bring him round."

"I live not far from here," the man said. "I will take him to my room. You need not be afraid," he added as Harry hesitated, "I have got my eyes open, you can trust me."

So saying he made his way through the crowd gathered outside. He was frequently asked who he was carrying, for the crowd feared lest any of their prey should escape; but the man's reply, given with a rough laugh—"It is a lad whose stomach is not strong enough to bear the sight of blood, and I tell you it is pretty hot in there,"—satisfied them.

Passing through several streets the man entered a small house and carried Victor to the attic and laid him on a bed, then he carefully closed the door and struck a light.

"You struck hard, my friend," he said as he examined Victor's head. "Ma foi, I should not have liked such a blow myself, but I don't blame you. You were but just in time to prevent his betraying himself, and better a hundred times a knock on the head than those pikes outside the door. I had my eye on him, and felt sure he would do something rash, and I had intended to choke him, but he was too quick for me. How came you to be so foolish as to be there?"

"We had friends in the prison, and we thought we might do something to save them," Harry answered, for he saw that it would be his best policy to be frank. "It was his father whom they brought out."

"It was rash of you, young sir. A kid might as well try to save his mother from the tiger who has laid its paw upon her as for you to try to rescue any one from the clutches of the mob. Mon Dieu! To think that in the early days I was fool enough to go down to the Assembly and cheer the deputies; but I have seen my mistake. What has it brought us? A ruined trade, an empty cupboard, and to be ruled by the ruffians of the slums instead of the king, the clergy, and

86

the upper classes. I was a brass-worker, and a good one, though I say it myself, and earned good wages. Now for the last month I haven't done a stroke of work. Who wants to buy brass-work when there are mansions and shops to pillage? And now, what are you going to do? My wife is out, but she will probably be back soon. We will attend to this young fellow. She is a good nurse, and I tell you I think he will need all we can do for him."

"You don't think I have seriously injured him?" Harry said in a tone of dismay.

"No, no; don't make yourself uneasy. You have stunned him, and that's all; he will soon get over that. I have seen men get worse knocks in a drunken row and be at work again in the morning; but it is different here. I saw his face, and he was pretty nearly mad when you struck him. I doubt whether he will be in his right senses when he comes round; but never fear, we will look after him well. You can stay if you like; but if you want to go you can trust him to us. I see you can keep your head, and will not run into danger as he did."

"I do want to go terribly," Harry said, "terribly; and I feel that I can trust you completely. You have saved his life and mine already. Now you will not be hurt at what I am going to say. He is the son of the Duc de Gisons, the last man we saw brought out to be murdered. We have plenty of money. In a belt round his waist you will find a hundred louis. Please do not spare them. If you think he wants a surgeon call him in, and get everything necessary for your household. While you are nursing him you cannot go out to work. I do not talk of reward; one cannot reward kindness like yours; but while you are looking after him you and your wife must live."

"Agreed!" the man said, shaking Harry by the hand. "You speak like a man of heart. I will look after him. You need be under no uneasiness. Should any of my comrades come in I shall say: 'this is a young workman who got knocked down and hurt in the crowd, and whom, having nothing better to do, I have brought in here.'"

"If he should recover his senses before I come back," Harry said, "please do not let him know it was I who struck him. He will be well-nigh heart-broken that he could not share the fate of his father. Let him think that he was knocked down by some one in the crowd."

"All right! That is easily managed," the man said. "Jacques Medart is no fool. Now you had best be off, for I see you are on thorns, and leave me to bathe his head. If you shouldn't come back you can depend upon it I will look after him till he is able to go about again."

CHAPTER VIII

MARIE ARRESTED

On leaving Victor in the care of the man who had so providentially came to his aid, Harry hurried down the street towards the Abbaye, then he stopped to think—should he return there or make his way to the Bicetre. He could not tell whether his friends had, like the Duc de Gisons, been removed to the Abbaye. If they had been so, it was clearly impossible for him to aid them in any way. They might already have fallen. The crowd was too great for him to regain the gallery, and even there could only witness, without power to avert, their murder. Were they still at the Bicetre he might do something. Perhaps the assassins had not yet arrived there.

It was now nine o'clock in the evening. The streets were almost deserted. The respectable inhabitants all remained within their houses, trembling at the horrors, of which reports had circulated during the afternoon. At first there had been hopes that the Assembly would take steps to put a stop to the massacre, but the Assembly did nothing. Danton and the ministers were absent. The cannon's roar and the tocsin sounded perpetually. There was no secret as to what was going on. The Commune had the insolence to send commissioners to the bar of the Assembly to state that the people wished to break open the doors of the prisons, and this when two hundred priests had already been butchered at the Carmelites.

A deputation indeed went to the Abbaye to try to persuade the murderers to desist; but their voices were drowned in the tumultuous cries. The Commune of Paris openly directed the massacre. Billaud-Varennes went backwards and forwards to superintend the execution of his orders, and promised the executioners twenty-four francs a day. The receipt for the payment of this blood-money still exists.

On arriving in front of the Bicetre Harry found all was silent there, and with a faint feeling of hope that the massacre would not extend beyond the Abbaye, he again turned his steps in that direction.

The bloody work was still going on, and Harry wandered away into the quiet streets to avoid hearing the shrieks of the victims and the yells of the crowd. A sudden thought struck him, and he went along until he saw a woman come out of a house. He ran up to her.

"Madam," he said, "I have the most urgent need of a bonnet and shawl. Will you sell me those you have on? The shops are all shut, or I would not trouble you. You have only to name your price, and I will pay you."

The woman was surprised at this proposition, but seeing that a good bargain was to be made she asked twice the cost of the articles when new, and this Harry paid her without question.

Wrapping the shawl and bonnet into a bundle, he retraced his steps, and sat down on some doorsteps within a distance of the Abbaye which would enable him to observe any general movement of the crowd in front of the prison. At one o'clock in the morning there was a stir, and the body of men with pikes moved down the street.

"They are going to La Force," he said, after following them for some distance. "Oh, if I had but two or three hundred English soldiers here we would make mincemeat of these murderers!"

Harry did not enter La Force, where the scenes that were taking place at the Abbaye—for, in spite of the speed with which the mock trials were hurried through, these massacres were not yet finished there, so great was the number of prisoners—were repeated.

At La Force many ladies were imprisoned, among them the Princess de Lamballe. They shared the fate of the male prisoners, being hewn to pieces by sabres. The head of the princess was cut off and stuck upon a pike, and was carried in triumph under the windows of the Temple, where the king and queen were confined, and was held up to the bars of the room they occupied for them to see. Marie Antoinette, fearless for herself, fainted at the terrible sight of the pale head of her friend.

Harry remained at a little distance from La Force, tramping restlessly up and down, half-mad with rage and horror, and at his powerlessness to interfere in any way with the proceedings of the wretches who were carrying on the work of murder. At last, about eight o'clock in the morning, a boy ran by.

"They have finished with them at the Abbaye," he said with fiendish glee. "They are going from there to the Bicetre."

Harry with difficulty repressed his desire to slay the urchin, and hurried away to reach the prison of Bicetre before the band from the Abbaye arrived there. Unfortunately he came down by a side street upon them when they were within a few hundred yards of the prison. His great hope was that he might succeed in penetrating with the Marseillais and find the marquise, and aid her in making her way through the mob in the disguise he had purchased.

But here, as at the other prisons, there was a method in the work of murder. The agents of the Commune took possession of the hall at the entrance and permitted none to pass farther into the prison, the warders and officials bringing down the prisoners in batches, and so handing them over for slaughter. In vain Harry tried to penetrate into the inner part of the prison. He was roughly repulsed by the men guarding the door; and at last, finding that nothing could be done, he forced his way out again into the open air, and hurrying away for some distance, threw himself on the ground and burst into a passion of tears.

After a time he rose and made his way back to the house where he had left Victor de Gisons. He found him in a state of delirium, acting over and over again the scene in the Abbaye, cursing the judge and executioners, and crying out he would die with his father.

"What does the doctor think of him?" he asked the woman who was sitting by Victor's bed.

"He did not say much," the woman replied. "He shook his head, and said there had been a terrible mental shock, and that he could not answer either for his life or reason. There was nothing to do but to be patient, to keep his head bandaged with wet cloths, and to give him water from time to time. Do not be afraid, sir; we will watch over him carefully."

"I would stay here if I could," Harry said; "but I have others I must see about. I have the terrible news to break to some young ladies of the murder of their father and mother."

"Poor things! Poor things!" the woman said, shaking her head. "It is terrible! My husband was telling me what he saw; and a neighbour came in just now and said it was the same thing at all the other prisons. The priest, too—our priest at the little church at the corner of the street, where I used to go in every morning to pray on my way to market—he was dragged away ten days ago to the Carmelites, and now he is a saint in heaven. How is it, sir, that God allows such things to be?"

"We cannot tell," Harry said sadly. "As for myself, I can hardly believe it, though I saw it. They say there are over four thousand people in the prisons, and they will all be murdered. Such a thing was never heard of. I can hardly believe that I am not in a dream now."

"You look almost like one dead yourself," the woman said

pityingly. "I have made a bouillon for Jacques' breakfast and mine. It is just ready. Do take a mouthful before you go out. That and a piece of bread and a cup of red wine will do you good."

Harry was on the point of refusing; but he felt that he was utterly worn and exhausted, and that he must keep up his strength. Her husband, therefore, took her place by Victor's bedside in readiness to hold him down should he try to get up in his ravings, while the good woman ladled out a basin of the broth and placed it with a piece of bread and some wine on the table. Harry forced himself to drink it, and when he rose from the table he already felt the benefit of the meal.

"Thank you very much," he said. "I feel stronger now; but how I am to tell the story I do not know. But I must make quite certain before I go to these poor girls that their parents were killed. Three or four were spared at the Abbaye. Possibly it may have been the same thing at the Bicetre."

So Harry went back and waited outside the prison until the bloody work was over; but found on questioning those who came out when all was done that the thirst for blood had increased with killing, and that all the prisoners found in the Bicetre had been put to death.

"Ma foi!" the man whom he was speaking to said; "but these accursed aristocrats have courage. Men and women were alike; there was not one of them but faced the judges bravely and went to their death as calmly as if to dinner. There was a marquis and his wife—the Marquis de St. Caux they called him. They brought them out together. They were asked whether they had anything to say why they should not be punished for their crimes against France. The marquis laughed aloud.

"'Crimes!' he said. 'Do you think a Marquis de St. Caux is going to plead for his life to a band of murderers and assassins? Come, my love.'

"He just gave her one kiss, and then took her hand as if they were going to walk a minuet together, and then led her down between the lines of guards with his head erect and a smile of scorn on his face. She did not smile, but her step never faltered. I watched her closely. She was very pale, and she did not look proud, but she walked as calmly and steadily as her husband till they reached the door where the pikemen were awaiting them, and then it was over in a minute, and they died without a cry or a groan. They are wretches, the aristocrats. They have fattened on the life-blood of the people; but they know how to die, these people."

Without a word Harry turned away. He had told himself there was no hope; but he knew by the bitter pang he felt now that he had hoped to the last. Then he walked slowly away to tell the news.

There were comparatively few people about the streets, and these all of the lower order. Every shop was closed. Men with scared faces stood at some of the doors to gather the news from passers-by, and pale women looked timidly from the upper windows. When he reached the house he could not summon courage to enter it, but stood for a long time outside, until at last he saw Louise Moulin put her head from the window. He succeeded in catching her eye, and placing his finger on his lips signed to her to come down. A minute later she appeared at the door.

"Is it all true, Monsieur Sandwith? They say they are murdering the prisoners. Surely it must be false! They could never do such a thing!"

"It is true, Louise. I have seen it myself. I went with a disguise to try and rescue our dear lady, even if I could not save the marquis; but I could not get to her—the wretches have murdered them both."

"Oh, my dear lady!" the old woman cried, bursting into tears. "The pretty babe I nursed. To think of her murdered; and the poor young things upstairs—what shall I do!—what shall I do, Monsieur Sandwith!"

"You must break it to them, Louise. Do they know how great the danger is?"

"No. I have kept it from them. They can see from the window that something unusual is going on; everyone can see that. But I told them it was only that the Prussians were advancing. They are anxious—very anxious—but they are quite unprepared for this."

"Break it gradually, Louise. Tell them first that there are rumours that the prisons have been attacked. Come down again presently as if to get more news, and then tell them that there are reports that the prisoners have been massacred, and then at last tell them all the truth."

"But will you not come up, Monsieur Sandwith—they trust you so much? Your presence will be a support to them."

"I could do nothing now," Harry said sadly. "God only can console them. They had best be by themselves for awhile. I will come in this evening. The first burst of grief will be over then, and my talk may aid them to rouse themselves. Oh, if we had but tried to get them out of prison sooner. And yet who could have foreseen that here in Paris thousands of innocent prisoners, men and women, would be murdered in cold blood!"

Finding that she could not persuade Harry to enter, Louise turned to perform her painful duty; while Harry, thoroughly exhausted with the night of horrors, made his way home, and throwing himself on the bed, fell asleep, and did not wake until evening. His first step was to plunge his head into water, and then, after a good wash, to prepare a meal. His sleep had restored his energy, and with brisk steps he made his way through the streets to Louise Moulin. He knocked with his knuckles at the outer door of her apartments. The old nurse opened it quietly.

"Come in," she said, "and sit down. They are in their room, and I think they have cried themselves to sleep. My heart has been breaking all day to see them. It has been dreadful. Poor little Virginie cried terribly, and sobbed for hours; but it was a long time before the others cried. Marie fainted, and when I got her round lay still and quiet without speaking. Jeanne was worst of all. She sat on that chair with her eyes staring open and her face as white as if she were dead. She did not seem to hear anything I said; but at last, when Virginie's sobs were stopping, I began to talk to her about her mother and her pretty ways when she was a child, and then at last Jeanne broke down, and she cried so wildly that I was frightened, and then Marie cried too; and after a while I persuaded them all to lie down; and as I have not heard a sound for the last hour I hope the good God has sent them all to sleep."

"I trust so indeed, Louise. I will stay here quietly for an hour, and then if we hear nothing I will go home, and be back again in the morning. Sleep will do more for them than anything I can say."

At the end of an hour all was still quiet, and Harry with a somewhat lightened heart took his departure.

At nine o'clock next morning he was again at the house. When he entered Virginie ran to him, and throwing her arms round his neck again burst into a passion of tears. Harry felt that this was the best thing that could have happened, for the others were occupied for some time in trying to soothe her, crying quietly to themselves while they did so. At last her sobs became less violent.

"And now, Harry," Marie said, turning to him, "will you tell us all about it?"

"I will tell you only that your dear father and mother died, as you might be sure they would, calmly and fearlessly, and that they suffered but little. More than that I cannot tell you now. Some day farther on, when you can bear it, I will tell you of the events of the last forty-eight hours. At present I myself dare not think of it, and it would harm you to know it.

"Do not, I pray you, ask me any questions now. We must think of the future. Fortunately you passed unsuspected the last time they searched the house; but it may not be so another time. You may be sure that these human tigers will not be satisfied with the blood they have shed, but that they will long for fresh victims. The prisons are empty now, but they will soon be filled again. We must therefore turn our thoughts to your making your escape from the city. I fear that there is peril everywhere; but it must be faced. I think it will be useless for us to try and reach the frontier by land. At every town and village they will be on the look-out for fugitives, and whatever disguise you might adopt you could not escape observation. I think, then, that we must make for the sea and hire a fishing-boat to take us across to England.

"But we must not hurry. In the first place, we must settle all our plans carefully and prepare our disguises; in the next place, there will be such tremendous excitement when the news of what has happened here is known that it would be unsafe to travel. I think myself it will be best to wait a little until there is a lull. That is what I want you to think over and decide.

"I do not think there is any very great danger here for the next few days. For a little time they will be tired of slaying; and, from what I hear, the Girondists are marked out as the next victims. They say Danton has denounced them at the Jacobin Club. At any rate it will be better to get everything in readiness for flight, so that we can leave at once if we hear of any fresh measures for a search after suspects."

Harry was pleased to find that his suggestion answered the purpose for which he made it. The girls began to discuss the disguises which would be required and the best route to be taken, and their thoughts were for a time turned from the loss they had sustained. After an hour's talk he left them greatly benefited by his visit.

For the next few days Harry spent his time for the most part by the bedside of Victor de Gisons. The fever was still at its height, and the doctor gave but small hopes of his recovery. Harry determined that he would not leave Paris until the issue was decided one way or the other, and when with the girls he discouraged any idea of an immediate flight. This was the more easy, for the news from the provinces showed that the situation was everywhere as bad as it was at the capital.

The Commune had sent to all the committees acting in connection with them in the towns throughout the country the news of the execution of the enemies of France confined in the prisons, and had urged that a similar step should at once be taken with reference to all the prisoners in their hands. The order was promptly obeyed, and throughout France massacres similar to those in Paris were at once carried out. A carnival of murder and horror had commenced, and the madness for blood raged throughout the whole country. Such being the case, Harry found it by no means difficult to dissuade the girls from taking instant steps towards making their escape.

He was, however, in a state of great uneasiness. Many of the moderate deputies had been seized, others had sought safety in flight, and the search for suspected persons was carried on vigorously. Difficult and dangerous as it would be to endeavour to travel through France with three girls, he would have attempted it without hesitation rather than remain in Paris had it not been for Victor de Gisons.

One day a week after the massacres at the prisons he received another terrible shock. He had bought a paper from one of the men shouting them for sale in the street, and sat down in the garden of the Tuileries to read it. A great portion of the space was filled with lists of the enemies of the people who had been, as it was called, executed. As these lists had formed the staple of news for several days Harry scarce glanced at the names, his eye travelling rapidly down the list until he gave a start and a low cry. Under the heading of persons executed at Lille were the names of Ernest de St. Caux, Jules de St. Caux, Pierre du Tillet—"aristocrats arrested, August 15th, in the act of endeavouring to leave France in disguise."

For some time Harry sat as if stunned. He had scarce given a thought to his friends since that night they had left, the affairs of the marquis and his wife, of their daughters, and of Victor de Gisons, almost excluding everything else. When he thought of the boys it had been as already in England, under the charge of du Tillet.

He had thought, that if they had been arrested on the way he should have been sure to hear of it; and he had such confidence in the sagacity of Monsieur du Tillet that he had looked upon it as almost certain he would be able to lead his two charges through any difficulty and danger which might beset them. And now he knew that his hopes had been ill founded—that his friends had been arrested when almost within sight of the frontier, and had been murdered as soon as the news of the massacres in Paris had reached Lille.

He felt crushed with the blow. A warm affection had sprung

up between him and Ernest, while from the first the younger boy had attached himself to him; and now they were dead, and the girls were alone in the world, save for himself and the poor young fellow tossing with fever! It was true that if his friends had reached England in safety they could not have aided him in the task he had before him of getting the girls away; still their deaths somehow seemed to add to his responsibilities.

Upon one thing he determined at once, and that was, that until his charges were safely in England they should not hear a whisper of this new and terrible misfortune which had befallen them.

In order to afford the girls some slight change, and anxious at their pale faces, the result of grief and of their unwonted confinement, Louise Moulin had persuaded them to go out with her in the early mornings when she went to the markets. The fear of detection was small, for the girls had now become accustomed to their thick shoes and rough dress; and indeed she thought that it would be safer to go out, for the suspicions of her neighbours might be excited if the girls remained secluded in the house. Harry generally met them soon after they started, and accompanied them in their walk.

One morning he was walking with the two younger girls, while Marie and the old nurse were together a short distance in front of them. They had just reached the flower-market, which was generally the main object of their walks—for the girls, having passed most of their time in the country, were passionately fond of flowers—when a man on horseback wearing a red sash, which showed him to be an official of the republic, came along at a foot-pace. His eyes fell upon Marie's face and rested there, at first with the look of recognition, followed by a start of surprise and satisfaction. He reined in his horse instantly, with the exclamation:

"Mademoiselle de St. Caux!"

For a moment she shrank back, her cheek paler even than before; then recovering herself she said calmly:

"It is myself, Monsieur Lebat."

"Citizen Lebat," he corrected. "You forget, there are no titles now—we have changed all that. It goes to my heart," he went on with a sneer, "to be obliged to do my duty; but however unpleasant it is, it must be done. Citizens," he said, raising his voice, "I want two men well disposed to the state."

As to be ill disposed meant danger if not death, several men within hearing at once came forward.

"This female citizen is an aristocrat in disguise," he went on, pointing to Marie; "in virtue of my office as deputy of Dijon and member of the Committee of Public Safety, I arrest her and give her into your charge. Where is the person who was with her? Seize her also on a charge of harbouring an enemy of the state!"

But Louise was gone. The moment Lebat had looked round in search of assistance Marie had whispered in Louise's ear: "Fly, Louise, for the sake of the children; if you are arrested they are lost!"

Had she herself been alone concerned, the old woman would have stood by Marie and shared her fate; but the words "for the sake of the children" decided her, and she had instantly slipped away among the crowd, whose attention had been called by Lebat's first words, and dived into a small shop, where she at once began to bargain for some eggs.

"Where is the woman?" Lebat repeated angrily.

"What is she like?" one of the bystanders asked.

But Lebat could give no description whatever of her. He had noticed that Marie was speaking to some one when he first caught sight of her face; but he had noticed nothing more, and did not know whether the woman was young or old.

"I can't tell you," he said in a tone of vexation. "Never mind; we shall find her later on. This capture is the most important."

So saying he set out, with Marie walking beside him, with a guard on either hand. In the next street he came on a party of four of the armed soldiers of the Commune, and ordered them to take the place of those he had first charged with the duty, and directed them to proceed with him to the Maine.

Marie was taken at once before the committee sitting en permanence for the discovery and arrest of suspects.

"I charge this young woman with being an aristocrat in disguise. She is the daughter of the ci-devant Marquis de St. Caux, who was executed on the 2d of September at Bicetre."

"Murdered, you mean, sir," Marie said in a clear haughty voice. "Why not call things by their proper name?"

"I am sorry," Lebat went on, not heeding the interruption, "that it should fall to my lot to denounce her, for I acknowledge that in the days before our glorious Revolution commenced I have visited at her father's chateau. But I feel that my duty to the republic stands before any private considerations."

"You have done perfectly right," the president of the committee said. "As I understand that the accused does not deny that she is the daughter of the ci-devant marquis, I will at once sign the order for her committal to La Force. There is room there still, though the prisons are filling up again fast."

"We must have another jail delivery," one of the committee laughed brutally; and a murmur of assent passed through the chamber.

The order was made out, and Marie was handed over to the armed guard, to be taken with the next batch of prisoners to La Force.

Harry was some twenty yards behind Marie and her companion when Lebat checked his horse before her. He recognized the man instantly, and saw that Marie's disguise was discovered. His first impulse was to rush forward to her assistance, but the hopelessness of any attempt at interference instantly struck him, and to the surprise of the two girls, who were looking into a shop, and had not noticed what was occurring, he turned suddenly with them down a side street.

"What are you doing, Harry? We shall lose the others in the crowd if we do not keep them in sight," Jeanne said.

"I know what I am doing, Jeanne; I will tell you presently." He walked along several streets until he came to an unfrequented thoroughfare.

"There is something wrong, Harry. I see it in your face!" Jeanne exclaimed. "Tell us at once.

"It is bad news," Harry said quietly. "Try and nerve yourselves, my dear girls, for you will need all your courage. Marie is captured."

"Oh, Harry!" Virginie exclaimed, bursting into tears, while Jeanne stood still and motionless.

"Why are you taking us away?" she said in a hard sharp voice which Harry would not have recognized as hers. "Our place is with her, and where she goes we will go. You have no right to lead us away. We will go back to her at once."

"You can do her no good, Jeanne, dear," Harry said gently. "You could not help her, and it would only add to her misery if Virginie and you were also in their hands. Besides, we can be of more use outside. Trust to me, Jeanne; I will do all in my power to save her, whatever the risk."

"You could not save our father and mother," Jeanne said with a quivering lip.

"No, dear; but I would have saved them had there been but a little time to do so. This time I hope to be more successful. Courage,

Jeanne! Do not give way; I depend on your clear head to help me. Besides, till we can get her back, you have to fill Marie's place and look after Virginie."

The appeal was successful, and Jeanne burst into a passion of tears. Harry did not try to check them, and in a short time the sobs ceased and Jeanne raised her head again.

"I feel better now," she said. "Come, Virginie, and dry your eyes, darling; we shall have plenty of time to cry afterwards. Are we to go home, Harry? Have they taken Louise?"

"I do not know, Jeanne; that is the first thing to find out, for if they have, it will not be safe for you to return. Let us push on now, so that if she has not been taken we shall reach home before her. We will place ourselves at the corner of your street and wait for an hour; she may spend some time in looking for us, but if she does not come by the end of that time I shall feel sure that it is because she cannot come, and in that case I must look out for another place for you."

They hurried on until they were nearly home, the brisk walk having, as Harry had calculated it would do, had the effect of preventing their thoughts from dwelling upon Marie's capture. They had not been more than a quarter of an hour at their post when Harry gave an exclamation of satisfaction as he saw Louise Moulin approaching. The two girls hurried to meet her.

"Thank God you are both safe, dears!" she exclaimed with tears streaming down her cheeks. "I thought of you in the middle of it all; but I was sure that Monsieur Sandwith would see what was being done and would get you away."

"And you, Louise," said Harry, who had now come up, "how did you get away? I have been terribly anxious, thinking that they might seize you too, and that would have been dreadful."

"So they would have done," the old woman said; "but when that evil man looked away for a moment, mademoiselle whispered, 'Fly, Louise, for the children's sake!' and I slipped away into the crowd without even stopping to think, and ran into a shop; and it was well I did, for he shouted to them to seize me too, but I was gone, and as I don't think he noticed me before, they could not find me; and as soon as they had all moved away I came out. I looked for you for some time, and then made up my mind that Monsieur Sandwith had come on home with you."

"So I did, you see," Harry said; "but I did not dare to go in until we knew whether you had been taken too. If you had not come after a time we should have looked for another lodging, though I knew well enough that you would not tell them where you lived."

"No, indeed," the old woman said. "They might have cut me in pieces without getting a single word from me as to where I lived. Still they might have found out somehow, for they would have been sure to have published the fact that I had been taken, with a description of me. Then the neighbours would have said, 'This description is like Louise Moulin, and she is missing;' and then they would have talked, and the end of it would have been you would have been discovered. Will you come home with us, Monsieur Sandwith?"

"I will come after it's dark, Louise. The less my visits are noticed the better."

"This is awful!" Harry said to himself as he turned away. "The marquis and his wife massacred, Ernest and Jules murdered, Marie in prison, Victor mad with fever, Jeanne and Virginie with no one to trust to but me, my people at home in a frightful state of mind about me. It is awful to think of. It's enough to drive a fellow out of his senses. Well, I will go and see how Victor is going on. The doctor thought there was a change yesterday. Poor fellow! If he comes to his senses I shall have hard work to keep the truth about Marie from him. It would send him off again worse than ever if he had an idea of it."

"And how is your patient to-day, madame?" he asked, as Victor's nurse opened the door to him.

"He is quieter, much quieter," she replied. "I think he is too weak to rave any longer; but otherwise he's just the same. He lies with his eyes open, talking sometimes to himself, but I cannot make out any sense in what he says. The doctor has been here this morning, and he says that he thinks another two days will decide. If he does not take a turn then he will die. If he does, he may live, but even then he may not get his reason again. Poor young fellow! I feel for him almost as if he were my son, and so does Jacques."

"You are both very good, madame," Harry said, "and my friend is fortunate indeed to have fallen into such good hands. I will sit with him for three or four hours now, and you had better go and get a little fresh air."

"That I will, monsieur. Jacques is asleep. He was up with him all last night, and I had a good night. He would have it so."

"Quite right!" Harry said. "You must not knock yourself up, madame. You are too useful to others for us to let you do that. Tomorrow night I will take my turn."

CHAPTER IX

ROBESPIERRE

After dark Harry presented himself at Louise Moulin's.

"Have you thought of anything, Harry?" was Jeanne's first question. She was alone, for Louise was cooking, and Virginie had lain down and cried herself to sleep.

"I have thought of a number of things," he replied, for while he had been sitting by Victor's bedside he had turned over in his mind every scheme by which he could get Marie out of prison, "but at present I have fixed upon nothing. I cannot carry out our original plan of seizing Marat. It would require more than one to carry out such a scheme, and the friend whom I relied upon before can no longer aid me."

"Who is it?" Jeanne asked quietly. "Is it Victor de Gisons?"

"What! Bless me, Jeanne!" Harry exclaimed in surprise. "How did you guess that?"

"I felt sure it was Victor all along," the girl said. "In the first place, I never believed that he had gone away. Marie told me she had begged and prayed him to go, and that he had only gone to please her. She seemed to think it was right he should go, but I didn't think so. A gentleman would not run away and leave anyone he liked behind, even if she told him. It was not likely. Why, here are you staying here and risking your life for us, though we are not related to you and have no claim upon you. And how could Victor run away? But as Marie seemed pleased to think he was safe, I said nothing; but I know, if he had gone, and some day they had been married, I should never have looked upon him as a brother. But I felt sure he wouldn't do it, and that he was in Paris still. Then, again, you did not tell us the name of the friend who was working with you, and I felt sure you must have some reason for your silence. So, putting the two things together, I was sure that it was Victor. What has happened to him? Is he in prison too?"

"No, he is not in prison, Jeanne," Harry said, "but he is very ill." And he related the whole circumstances of Victor's fever. "I blamed myself awfully at first for having hit him so hard, as you may suppose, Jeanne; but the doctor says he thinks it made no difference, and that Victor's delirium is due to the mental shock and not in any way to the blow on the head. Still I should not like your sister to know it. I am very glad you have guessed the truth, for it is a comfort to talk things over with you."

"Poor Marie!" Jeanne said softly. "It is well she never knew about it. The thought he had got safely away kept her up. And now, tell me about your plans. Could I not take Victor's place and help you to seize Marat? I am not strong, you know; but I could hold a knife, and tell him I would kill him if he cried out. I don't think I could, you know, but he wouldn't know that."

"I am afraid that wouldn't do, Jeanne," Harry said with a slight smile, shaking his head. "It was a desperate enterprise for two of us. Besides, it would never do for you to run the risk of being separated from Virginie. Remember you are father and mother and elder sister to her now. The next plan I thought of was to try and get appointed as a warder in the prison, but that seems full of difficulties, for I know no one who could get me such a berth, and certainly they would not appoint a fellow at my age unless by some extraordinary influence. Then I thought if I let out I was English I might get arrested and lodged in the same prison, and might help her to get out then. From what I hear, the prisoners are not separated, but all live together."

"No, no, Harry," Jeanne exclaimed in a tone of sharp pain, "you must not do that of all things. We have only you, and if you are once in prison you might never get out again; besides, there are lots of other prisons, and there is no reason why they should send you to La Force rather than anywhere else. No, I will never consent to that plan."

"I thought it seemed too doubtful myself," Harry said. "Of course, if I knew that they would send me to La Force, I might risk it. I could hide a file and a steel saw about me, and might cut through the bars; but, as you say, there is no reason why they should send me there rather than anywhere else. I would kill that villain who arrested her—the scoundrel, after being a guest at the chateau!—but I don't see that would do your sister any good, and would probably end in my being shut up. The most hopeful plan seems to me to try and bribe some of the warders. Some of them, no doubt, would be glad enough to take money if they could see their way to letting her out without fear of detection."

"But you know we thought of that before, Harry, and agreed it would be a terrible risk to try it, for the very first man you spoke to might turn round on you."

"Of course there is a certain risk, Jeanne, anyway. There is no getting a prisoner out of La Force without running some sort of risk;

the thing is to fix on as safe a plan as we can. However, we must think it out well before we do try. A failure would be fatal, and I do not think there is any pressing danger just at present. It is hardly likely there will be any repetition of the wholesale work of the 2nd of September; and if they have anything like a trial of the prisoners, there are such numbers of them, so many arrested every day, that it may be a long time before they come to your sister. I do not mean that we should trust to that, only that there is time for us to make our plans properly. Have you thought of anything?"

"I have thought of all sort of things since you left us this morning, Harry, but they are like yours, just vague sort of schemes that do not seem possible when you try to work them out. I do not know whether they let you inside the prisons to sell everything to the prisoners, because if they did I might go in with something and see Marie, and find out how she could be got out."

Harry shook his head.

"I do not think anyone would be allowed in like that, but if they did it would only be a few to whom the privilege would be granted."

"Yes, I thought of that, Harry; but one of them might be bribed perhaps to let me take her place."

"It might be possible," Harry said, "but there would be a terrible risk, and I don't think any advantage to compensate for it. Even if you did get to her and spoke to her, we should still be no nearer to getting her out. Still we mustn't be disheartened. We can hardly expect to hit upon a scheme at once, and I don't think either of our heads is very clear to-day; let us think it over quietly, and perhaps some other idea may occur to one of us, I expect it will be to you. Now, good-night; keep your courage up. I rely very much upon you, Jeanne, and you don't know what a comfort it is to me that you are calm and brave, and that I can talk things over to you. I don't know what I should do if I had it all on my own shoulders."

Jeanne made no answer, but her eyes were full of tears as she put her hands into Harry's, and no sound came from her lips in answer to his good-night.

"That girl's a trump, and no mistake," Harry said to himself as he descended the stairs. "She has got more pluck than most women, and is as cool and calm as if she were twice her age. Most girls would be quite knocked over if they were in her place. Her father and mother murdered, her sister in the hands of these wretches, and danger hanging over herself and Virginie! It isn't that she doesn't feel it. I can see she does, quite as much, if not more, than people who would sit down and howl and wring their hands. She is a trump, Jeanne is, and no mistake. And now about Marie. She must be got out somehow, but how? That is the question. I really don't see any possible way except by bribing her guards, and I haven't the least idea how to set about that. I think to-morrow I will tell Jacques and his wife all about it; they may know some of these men, though it isn't likely that they do; anyhow, three heads are better than one."

Accordingly, next morning he took the kind-hearted couple into his counsel. When they heard that the young lady who had been arrested was the fiance of their sick lodger they were greatly interested, but they shook their heads when he told them that he was determined at all hazards to get her out of prison.

"It isn't the risk so much," Jacques said, "that I look at. Life doesn't seem of much account in these days; but how could it be done? Even if you made up your mind to be killed, I don't see that would put her a bit nearer to getting out of prison; the place is too strong to break into or to break out of."

"No, I don't think it is possible to succeed in that sort of way; but if the men who have the keys of the corridors could be bribed, and the guard at the gate put soundly to sleep by drugging their drink, it might be managed."

Jacques looked sharply at Harry to see if he was in earnest, and seeing that he was so, said drily:

"Yes, if we could do those things we should, no doubt, see our way; but how could it be managed?"

"That is just the point, Jacques. In the first place it will be necessary to find out in which corridor Mademoiselle de St. Caux is confined; in the second, to let her know that we are working for her, and to learn, if possible, from her whether, among those in charge of her, there is one man who shows some sort of feeling of pity and kindness; when that is done we should, of course, try to get hold of him. Of course he doesn't remain in the prison all day. However, we can see about that after we have found out the first points."

"I know a woman who is sister to one of the warders," Elise Medart said. "I don't know whether he is there now or whether he has been turned out. Martha is a good soul, and I know that sometimes she has been inside the prison, I suppose to see her brother, for before the troubles the warders used to get out only once a month. What her brother is like I don't know, but if he is like her he would, I think, be just the man to help you."

"Yes," Jacques assented, "I didn't think of Martha. She is a good soul and would do her best, I am sure."

104

"Thank you both," Harry said; "but I do not wish you to run any risks. You have already incurred the greatest danger by sheltering my friend; I cannot let you hazard your lives farther. This woman may, as you say, be ready to help us, but her brother might betray the whole of us, and screen his sister by saying she had only pretended to enter into the plot in order to betray it."

"We all risk our lives every day," Jacques said quietly. "I am sure we can trust Martha, and she will know whether she can rely completely upon her brother. If she can, we will set her to sound him. Elise will go and see her to-day, and you shall know what she thinks of it when you come this evening for your night's watching."

Greatly pleased with this unexpected stroke of luck, Harry went off at once to tell Jeanne that the outline of a plan to rescue Marie had been fixed upon.

The girl's pale face brightened up at the news.

"Perhaps," she said, "we may be able to send a letter to her. I should like to send her just a line to say that Virginie and I are well. Do you think it can be done?"

"I do not know, Jeanne. At any rate you can rely that, if it is possible and all goes well, she shall have it; but be sure and give no clue by which they might find you out, if the letter falls into wrong hands. Tell her we are working to get her free, and ask if she can suggest any way of escape; knowing the place she may see opportunities of which we know nothing. Write it very small, only on a tiny piece of paper, so that a man can hide it anywhere, slip it into her hand, or put it in her ration of bread."

Jeanne wrote the little note—a few loving words, and the message Harry had given her.

"Do not sign your name to it," Harry said; "she will know well enough who it comes from, and it is better in case it should fall into anyone else's hands."

That evening Harry learned that the woman had consented to sound her brother, who was still employed in the prison. She had said she was sure that he would not betray her even if he refused to aid in the plan.

"I am to see her to-morrow morning," Elise said. "She will go straight from me to the prison. She says discipline is not nearly so strict as it used to be. There is a very close watch kept over the prisoners, but friends of the guards can go in and out without trouble, except that on leaving they have to be accompanied by the guard at the door, so as to be sure that no one is passing out in disguise. She says her brother is good-natured but very fond of money. He is always talking of retiring and settling down in a farm in Brittany, where he comes from, and she thinks that if he thought he could gain enough to do this he would be ready to run some risk, for he hates the terrible things that are being done now."

"He seems just the man for us," Harry said. "Will you tell your friend, when you see her in the morning, that I will give her twenty louis and her brother a hundred if he can succeed in getting Marie out?"

"I will tell them, sir. That offer will set his wits to work, I have no doubt."

Harry then gave her the note Jeanne had written, for the woman to hand to her brother for delivery if he proved willing to enter into their plan. Harry had a quiet night of watching, for Victor lay so still that his friend several times leant over him to see if he breathed. The doctor had looked in late and said that the crisis was at hand.

"To-morrow your friend will either sink or he will turn the corner. He is asleep now and will probably sleep for many hours. He may never wake again; he may wake, recognize you for a few minutes, and then go off in a last stupor; he may wake stronger and with a chance of life. Here is a draught that you will give him as soon as he opens his eyes; pour besides three or four spoonfuls of soup down his throat, and if he keeps awake do the same every half hour."

It was not until ten o'clock in the morning that Victor opened his eyes. He looked vaguely round the room and there was no recognition in his eyes as they fell upon Harry's face, but they had lost the wild expression they had worn while he had lain there, and Harry felt renewed hope as he lifted his head and poured the draught between his lips. Then he gave him a few spoonfuls of soup and had the satisfaction of seeing his eyes close again and his breathing become more and more regular.

The doctor, when he came in and felt Victor's pulse, nodded approval.

"The fever has quite left him," he said; "I think he will do now. It will be slow, very slow, but I think he will regain his strength; as to his mind, of that I can say nothing at present."

About mid-day Elise returned.

"I have good news, monsieur," she said at once. "I waited outside the prison till Martha came out. Her brother has agreed to help if he can, but he said that he did not think that it would be at all possible to get mademoiselle out. There are many of the men of the

106

faubourgs mixed up with the old warders, and there is the greatest vigilance to ensure that none escape. There would be many doors to be opened, and the keys are all held by different persons. He says he will think it over, and if it is any way possible he will risk it. But he wishes first of all to declare that he does not think that any way of getting her out can be discovered. He will give her the note on the first opportunity, and get an answer from her, which he will send to his sister as soon as he gets a chance."

"That is all we can expect," Harry said joyfully. "I did not expect that it would be an easy business, or that the man would be able to hit upon a scheme at once; but now that he has gone so far as to agree to carry notes, the thought that he may, if he succeeds, soon have his little farm in Brittany, will sharpen his wits up wonderfully."

It was three days before an answer came from Marie. Jacques handed it to Harry when he came to take his turn by Victor's bedside. Victor was better; he was no longer unconscious, but followed with his eyes the movements of those in the room. Once he had said, "Where am I?" but the answer "You are with friends; you have been ill; you shall hear all about it when you get stronger," had apparently satisfied him. At Harry he looked with doubtful recognition. He seemed to remember the face, but to have no further idea about it, and even when Harry said cheerfully:

"Don't you remember your friend Harry, Victor?" he had shaken his head in feeble negative.

"I expect it will all come back to him," Jacques said, "as he gets stronger; and after all it is much better that he should remember nothing at present. It will be quite time enough for that when he is better able to stand it."

"I agree with you there," Harry said, "and I am really glad that he did not remember me, for had he done so the past might have come back at once and, feeble as he is, that would have completely knocked him over."

Upon the receipt of Marie's note Harry at once started off at full speed and soon had the satisfaction of handing it to Jeanne.

She tore it open.

"Do you not know what it is, Harry?"

"How could I?" Harry replied. "As you see the letter is addressed to you. Of course I should not think of looking at it."

"Why not? You are as much interested in it as I am. Sit down between me and Virginie and let us read it together. Why, it is quite a long epistle."

It was written in pencil upon what was evidently a fly-leaf of a book, and ran as follows:

"My darling Jeanne and Virginie, you can imagine what joy I felt when I received your little note to-day and heard that you were still safe. I could hardly believe my senses when, on opening the little ball of paper which one of our guards thrust into my hand, I found that it was from you, and that you were both safe and well. I am writing this crouched down on the ground behind Madame de Vigny, and so hidden from the sight of our guards, but I can only write a few lines at a time, lest I should be detected. Tell our good friend that I fear there is little chance of escape. We are watched night and day. We are locked up at night, three or four together, in little cells, but in the day we are in a common hall.

"It is a strange mixture. Here are many of the best blood in France, together with deputies, advocates, and writers. We may talk together as much as we like, and sometimes even a joke and a laugh are heard. Every day some names are called out, and these go and we never see them again. Do not fret about me, my dear sisters, we are all in God's hands. If it is his will, we shall be saved; if not, we must face bravely whatever comes.

"It is a day since I wrote last. A strange thing has happened which will make your blood boil, Jeanne, as it has made mine. I was called out this morning to a little room where questions are sometimes asked us, and who do you think was there? M. Lebat, the son of the Maire of Dijon—the man who denounced and arrested me. What do you think the wretch had the insolence to say? That he loved me, and that if I would consent to marry him he could save me. He said that his influence would suffice, not only to get me free, but to obtain for me some of our estates, and he told me he would give me time to consider his offer, but that I must remember that nothing could save me if I refused. What do you think I did, Jeanne? Something very unladylike, I am afraid. I made a step closer to him, and then I gave him a slap on the face which made my fingers tingle, then I made him a deep curtsy and said, 'That is my answer, Monsieur Lebat,' and walked into the great hall again.

"But do not let me waste a line of this last precious letter that I may be able to write to you by saying more about this wretch. I can see no possible way of escape, dears, so do not buoy yourselves up with hope. I have none. Strange as it may seem to you we are not very unhappy here. There are many of our old friends and some of the deputies of the Gironde, who used to attend our salon. We keep up each other's courage. We talk of other things just as if we were in a drawing-room, and when the list is called out of a morning, those who are named say good-bye bravely; there is seldom a tear shed.

"So do not think of me as wretched or unhappy in these last days. And now, my sisters, I must say adieu. You must trust yourselves entirely to our brave English friend, as you would trust a brother. He will do all that is possible to take you out of this unhappy land and conduct you to England, where you will find Victor, Monsieur du Tillet, and your brothers, who have, I trust, weeks ago arrived there in safety. Thank our friend from me and from our dead parents for his goodness and devotion. That your lives may be happy, my dear sisters, will be the last prayer of your loving Marie."

Inside the letter was another tiny note addressed for Jeanne, "Private." Having read the other Jeanne took the little note and walking to the window opened it. As she did so a burning flush of colour swept across her face to her very brow. She folded it carefully again and stood looking through the window silently for another quarter of an hour before she came back to the table.

"What is it, Jeanne?" Virginie asked; "have you been crying, Jeanne dear? You look so flushed. You must not fret. Harry says we must not give up hope, for that he believes he may hit upon some plan for saving Marie yet. He says it's only natural that she should think there was no means of getting away, but it was only what he expected. It is we who must invent something."

"Yes, dear, we will try," Jeanne said with a quiver in her lip, and then she suddenly burst into tears.

"You mustn't give way, Jeanne," Harry said, when she recovered herself a little. "You know how much I trust to your advice; if you were to break down I should lose heart. Do not think of Marie's letter as a good-bye. I have not lost hope yet, by a long way. Why, we have done wonders already in managing to get a letter in to her and to have her reply. I consider half the difficulty is over now we have a friend in there."

"I will try not to break down again," Jeanne said; "it is not often I give way, but to-day I do not feel quite myself, and this letter finished me. You will see I shall be all right to-morrow."

"I hope so," Harry said as he rose to leave; "but I think you had better ask Louise to give you something—your hands are hot and your cheeks are quite flushed, and you look to me as if you were feverish. Good night, dears!"

"I do hope Jeanne is not going to break down," Harry said as he walked towards his lodging. "If she were to get laid up now that would be the finishing touch to the whole affair; but perhaps, as she says, she will be all right in the morning. No doubt in that note Marie wrote as if she were sure of dying, and such a letter as that would be enough to upset any girl, even such a plucky one as Jeanne.

"However, it is of Marie I must think now. It was a brave letter of hers; it is clear she has given up all hope. This is a bad business about the scoundrel Lebat. I used to wonder why he came so often to the chateau on business that could have been done just as well by a messenger. He saw how things were going, and thought that when the division of the estates came he might get a big slice. However, it's most unfortunate that he should have had this interview with Marie in the prison. If it had not been for that it might have been months before her turn came for trial. As it is, no doubt Lebat will have her name put down at once in the list of those for trial, if such a farce can be called a trial, and will see that no time is lost before it appears on that fatal list for execution.

"He will flatter himself, of course, that when the last moment comes, and she sees that there is no hope whatever, she will change her mind. There is one thing, if she is murdered I will kill him as I would a dog, for he will be her murderer just as much as if he had himself cut her throat. I would do it at once if it were not for the girls. I must not run any unnecessary risks, at any rate I need not think of him now; the one thing at present is to get Marie out."

Turning this over in his mind, he walked about for some hours, scarce noticing where he was going. It seemed to him that there must be some way of getting Marie out if he could only hit upon it. He turned over in his mind every escape he had ever read of, but in most of these the prisoner had been a man, capable of using tools passed in to him to saw through iron bars, pierce walls, or overcome jailers; some had been saved by female relatives, wives or daughters, who went in and exchanged clothes and places with them, but this was not feasible here. This was not a prison where relatives could call upon friends, for to be a relative or friend of a prisoner was quite sufficient in the eyes of the terrorists to mark anyone as being an enemy of the republic.

He was suddenly roused from his reverie by a cry, and beneath the dim light of a lantern, suspended over the narrow street, he saw a man feebly defending himself against two others. He sprang forward just as the man fell, and with his stick struck a sharp blow on the uplifted wrist of one of the assailants, sending the knife he was holding flying through the air. The other turned upon him, but he drew the pistol which he always carried beneath his clothes, and the two men at once took to their heels. Harry replaced his pistol and stooped over the fallen man.

"Are you badly hurt?" he asked.

"No, I think not, but I do not know. I think I slipped down; but they would have killed me had you not arrived."

"Well, let me get you to your feet," Harry said, holding out his hands, but with a feeling of some disgust at the abject fear expressed in the tones of the man's voice. He was indeed trembling so that even when Harry hauled him to his feet he could scarcely stand.

"You had better lean against the wall for a minute or two to recover yourself," Harry said. "I see you have your coat cut on the shoulder, and are bleeding pretty freely, but it is nothing to be frightened about. If you will give me your handkerchief I will bind it up for you."

Harry unbuttoned the man's coat, for his hands shook so much that he was unable to do so, pulled the arm out of the sleeve, and tied the bandage tightly round the shoulder. The man seemed to belong to the bourgeois class, and evidently was careful as to his attire, which was neat and precise. His linen and the ruffles of his shirt were spotlessly white and of fine material. The short-waisted coat was of olive-green cloth, with bright metal buttons; the waistcoat, extending far below the coat, was a light-buff colour, brocaded with a small pattern of flowers. When he had bound the wound Harry helped him on with his coat again. He was by this time recovering himself.

"Oh these aristocrats," he murmured, "how they hate me!"

The words startled Harry. What was this? He had not interfered, as he had supposed, to prevent the robbery of some quiet citizen by the ruffians of the streets. It was a political assassination that had been attempted—a vengeance by Royalists upon one of the men of the Revolution. He looked more closely at the person whose life he had saved. He had a thin and insignificant figure—his face was pale and looked like that of a student. It seemed to Harry that he had seen it before, but where he could not say. His first thought was one of regret that he had interfered to save one of the men of the 2d of September; then the thought flashed through his mind that there might be some benefit to be derived from it.

"Young man," the stranger said, "will you give me your arm and escort me home? You have saved my life; it is a humble one, but perhaps it is of some value to France. I live but two streets away. It is not often I am out alone, for I have many enemies, but I was called suddenly out on business, though I have no doubt now the message was a fraudulent one, designed simply to put me into the hands of my foes."

The man spoke in a thin hard voice, which inspired Harry, he knew not why, with a feeling of repulsion; he had certainly heard it before. He offered him his arm and walked with him to his door.

"Come up, I beg you," the stranger said.

He ascended to the second floor and rang at the bell. A woman with a light opened it.

"Why, my brother," she exclaimed on seeing his face, "you are ill! Has anything happened?"

"I have been attacked in the street," he said, "but I am not hurt, though, had it not been for this citizen it would have gone hardly with me. You have to thank him for saving your brother's life."

They had entered a sitting-room now. It was plainly but very neatly furnished. There were some birds in cages, which, late though the hour was, hopped on their perches and twittered when they heard the master's voice, and he responded with two or three words of greeting to them.

"Set the supper," he said to his sister; "the citizen will take a meal with us. You know who I am, I suppose?" he said to Harry.

"No," Harry replied. "I have a recollection of your face and voice, but I cannot recall where I have met you."

"I am Robespierre," he said.

Harry gave a start of surprise. This man whom he had saved was he whom he had so often execrated—one of the leaders of those who had deluged France with blood—the man who, next only to Marat was hated and feared by the Royalists of France. His first feeling was one of loathing and hatred, but at the same moment there flashed through his mind the thought that chance had favoured him beyond his hopes, and that the comedy which he had planned with Victor to carry out upon the person of Marat had come to pass without premeditation, but with Robespierre as the chief actor.

But so surprised and so delighted was he that for a minute he sat unable to say a word. Robespierre was gratified at the effect which his name had produced. His was a strangely-mixed character—at once timid and bold, shrinking from personal danger, yet ready to urge the extremest measures. Simple in his tastes, and yet very vain and greedy of applause. Domestic and affectionate in

112

his private character, but ready to shed a river of blood in his public capacity. Pure in morals; passionless in his resolves; incorruptible and inflexible; the more dangerous because he had neither passion nor hate; because he had not, like Danton and Marat, a lust for blood, but because human life to him was as nothing, because had he considered it necessary that half France should die for the benefit of the other half he would have signed their death-warrant without emotion or hesitation.

"You are surprised, young man," he said, "but the ways of fate are inscrutable. The interposition of a youth has thwarted the schemes of the enemies of France. Had you been but ten seconds later I should have ceased to be, and one of the humble instruments by which fate is working for the regeneration of the people would have perished."

While Robespierre was speaking Harry had rapidly thought over the role which it would be best for him to adopt. Should he avow his real character and ask for an order for the liberation of Marie as a recompense for the service he had rendered Robespierre, or should he retain his present character and obtain Robespierre's confidence? There was danger in an open appeal, for, above all things, Robespierre prided himself upon his incorruptibility, and he might consider that to free a prisoner for service rendered to himself would be a breach of his duty to France. He resolved, therefore, to keep silence at present, reserving an appeal to Robespierre's gratitude for the last extremity.

"Pardon me, monsieur," he said, after he had rapidly arrived at this conclusion; "my emotion was naturally great at finding that I had unwittingly been the means of saving the life of one on whom the eyes of France are fixed. I rejoice indeed that I should have been the means of preserving such a life."

This statement was strictly true, although not perhaps in the sense in which Robespierre regarded it.

"We will talk more after supper," he said. "My sister is, I see, ready with it. Indeed it is long past our usual hour, and we were just sitting down when I was called out by what purported to be an important message from the Club."

CHAPTER X

FREE

Robespierre chatted continuously as the meal went on, and Harry asked himself in astonishment whether he was in a dream, and if this man before him, talking about his birds, his flowers, and his life before he came to Paris, could really be the dreaded Robespierre. After the meal was over his host said:

"As yet I am ignorant of the name of my preserver."

"My name is Henry Sandwith," Harry replied.

"It is not a French name," Robespierre said in surprise.

"I am of English parentage," Harry said quietly, "but have been resident for some years in France. I was for some time in the service of the ci-devant Marquis de St. Caux; but since the break-up of his household I have been shifting for myself as best I could, living chiefly on the moneys I had earned in his service, and on the look-out for any employment that may offer."

"England is our enemy," Robespierre said, raising his voice angrily; "the enemy of free institutions and liberty."

"I know nothing about English politics," Harry replied with a smile; "nor indeed about any politics. I am but little past eighteen, and so that I can earn my living I do not ask whether my employer is a patriot or an aristocrat. It is quite trouble enough to earn one's living without bothering one's head about politics. If you can put me in the way of doing so I shall consider that I am well repaid for the little service I rendered you."

"Assuredly I will do so," Robespierre said. "I am a poor man, you know. I do not put my hand into the public purse, and I and my sister live as frugally as we did when we first came to Paris from Arras. My only gains have been the hatred of the aristocrats and the love of the people. But though I have not money, I have influence, and I promise to use it on your behalf. Until I hear of something suitable you can, if you will, work here with me, and share what I possess. My correspondence is very heavy. I am overwhelmed with letters from the provinces begging me to inquire into grievances and redress wrongs. Can you read and write well?" For from Harry's words he supposed that he had held some menial post in the household of the Marquis de St. Caux.

"Yes, I can read and write fairly," Harry said.

"And are you acquainted with the English tongue?"

"I know enough of it to read it," Harry said. "I spoke it when I was a child."

"If you can read it that will do," Robespierre said. "There are English papers sent over, and I should like to hear for myself what this perfidious people say of us, and there are few here who can translate the language. Do you accept my proposal?"

"Willingly," Harry said.

"Very well, then, come here at nine o'clock in the morning. But mind you are only filling the post of my secretary until I can find something better for you to do."

"The post will be a better one some day, Monsieur Robespierre. Ere long you will be the greatest man in France, and the post of secretary will be one which may well be envied."

"Ah, I see you know how to flatter," Robespierre said with a smile, much gratified nevertheless with Harry's words. "You must remember that I crave no dignities, that I care only for the welfare of France."

"I know, monsieur, that you are called 'Robespierre the Incorruptible,'" Harry said; "but, nevertheless, you belong to France, and France will assuredly see that some day you have such a reward as you richly merit."

"There was no untruth in that," Harry said to himself as he made his way down stairs. "These human tigers will meet their doom when France comes to her senses. He is a strange contrast, this man; but I suppose that even the tiger is a domestic animal in his own family. His food almost choked me, and had I not known that Marie's fate depends upon my calmness, I should assuredly have broken out and told this dapper little demagogue my opinion of him. But this is glorious! What news I shall have to give the girls in the morning! If I cannot ensure Marie's freedom now I should be a bungler indeed. Had I had the planning of the events of this evening they could not have turned out better for us."

It was the first time that Harry had called at Louise Moulin's as early as eight o'clock in the morning, and Jeanne leaped up as he entered.

"What is it, Harry? You bring us some news, don't you?"

"I do indeed, Jeanne; capital news. Whom do you think I had supper with last night?"

"Had supper with, Harry!" Jeanne repeated. "What do you mean? How can I guess whom you had supper with?"

"I am sure you cannot guess, Jeanne, so I will not puzzle your brain. I had supper with Robespierre."

"With Robespierre!" the two girls repeated in astonishment. "You are not joking, Harry?" Jeanne went on. "But no, you cannot be doing that; tell us how you came to have supper with Robespierre."

"My dear Jeanne, I regard it as a special providence, as an answer from God to your prayers for Marie. I had the good fortune to save his life."

"Oh, Harry," Jeanne exclaimed, "what happiness! Then Marie's life will be saved."

"I think I can almost promise you that, Jeanne, though I do not know yet exactly how it's to be done. But such a piece of good fortune would never have been sent to me had it not been intended that we should save Marie. Now, sit down quietly, both of you, and you too, Louise, and let me tell you all about it, for I have to be with Robespierre again at nine o'clock."

"Oh, that is fortunate indeed!" Jeanne exclaimed when he had finished. "Surely he cannot refuse any request you may make now."

"If he does, I must get it out of him somehow," Harry said cheerfully. "By fair means or foul I will get the order for her release."

"But you don't think he can refuse, Harry?" Jeanne asked anxiously.

"I think he may refuse, Jeanne. He is proud of his integrity and incorruptibility, and I think it quite possible that he may refuse to grant Marie's release in return for a benefit done him personally. However, do not let that discourage you in the least. As I said, I will have the order by fair means or foul."

At nine o'clock Harry presented himself in readiness for work, and found that his post would be no sinecure. The correspondence which he had to go through was enormous. Requests for favours, letters of congratulation on Robespierre's speeches and motions in the Assembly, reports of scores of provincial committees, denunciations of aristocrats, letters of blame because the work of rooting out the suspects did not proceed faster, entreaties from friends of prisoners. All these had to be sorted, read, and answered.

Robespierre was, Harry soon found, methodical in the extreme. He read every letter himself, and not only gave directions how they were to be answered, but read through the answers when written, and was most careful before he affixed his signature to any paper whatever. When it was time for him to leave for the Assembly he made a note in pencil on each letter how it should be answered, and directed Harry when he had finished them to leave them on the table for him on his return.

"I foresee that you will be of great value to me, Monsieur Sandwith," he said, "and I shall be able to recommend you for any office that may be vacant with a feeling of confidence that you will do justice to my recommendation; or if you would rather, as time

116

goes on, attach your fortunes to mine, be assured that if I should rise to power your fortune will be made. When you have done these letters your time will be your own for the rest of the day. You know our meal hours, and I can only say that we are punctual to a second."

When Harry had finished he strolled out. He saw that the task of getting an order for Marie's release would be more difficult than he had anticipated. He had hoped that by placing it with a batch of papers before Robespierre he would get him to sign it among others without reading it, but he now saw that this would be next to impossible. One thing afforded him grounds for satisfaction. Among the papers was a list of the prisoners to be brought up on the following day for trial. To this Robespierre added two names, and then signed it and sent it back to the prison. There was another list with the names of the prisoners to be executed on the following day, and this, Harry learned, was not sent in to the prison authorities until late in the evening, so that even they were ignorant until the last moment which of the prisoners were to be called for by the tumbrils next morning. Thus he would know when Marie was to go through the mockery of a trial, and would also know when her name was put on the fatal list for the guillotine. The first fact he might have been able to learn from his ally in the prison, but the second and most important he could not have obtained in any other way.

The work had been frequently interrupted by callers. Members of the Committee of Public Safety, leaders of the Jacobin and Cordeliers Clubs, and others, dropped in and asked Robespierre's advice, or discussed measures to be taken; and after a day or two Harry found that it was very seldom, except when taking his meals, that Robespierre was alone while in the house; and as his sister was in and out of the room all day, the idea of compelling him by force to sign the order, as they had originally intended to do with Marat, was clearly impracticable.

Each day after his work was over, and this was generally completed by about one o'clock, Harry called to see how Victor was getting on. He was gaining strength, but his brain appeared to make far less progress than his bodily health. He did not recognize Harry in the least, and although he would answer questions that were asked him, his mind appeared a blank as to the past, and he often lay for hours without speaking a word. After leaving him Harry met Louise and the two girls at a spot agreed upon the day before, a fresh meeting-place being arranged each day. He found it difficult to satisfy them, for indeed each day he became more and more doubtful as to his ability to get the order of release from Robespierre. Towards the man himself his feelings were of a mixed kind. He shuddered at the calmness with which, in his letters to the provincial committees, he advocated wholesale executions of prisoners. He wondered at the violence with which, in his shrill, high-pitched voice, he declaimed in favour of the most revolutionary measures. He admired the simplicity of his life, his affection for his sister and his birds, his kindness of heart in all matters in which politics were not concerned.

Among Robespierre's visitors during the next three weeks was Lebat, who was, Harry found, an important personage, being the representative on the Committee of Public Safety of the province of Burgundy, and one of the most extreme of the frequenters of the Jacobin Club. He did not recognize Harry, whom he had never noticed particularly on the occasion of his visits to the chateau, and who, in the somewhat threadbare black suit which he had assumed instead of the workman's blouse, wrote steadily at a table apart, taking apparently no notice of what was going on in the apartment.

But Harry's time was not altogether thrown away. It was his duty the first thing of a morning to open and sort the letters and lay them in piles upon the table used by Robespierre himself, and he managed every day to slip quietly into his pockets several of the letters of denunciation against persons as aristocrats in disguise or as being suspected of hostility to the Commune. When Robespierre left him to go to the Club or the Assembly Harry would write short notes of warning in a disguised hand to the persons named, and would, when he went out, leave these at their doors. Thus he had the satisfaction of saving a considerable number of persons from the clutches of the revolutionists. He would then, two or three days later, slip the letters of denunciation, very few of which were dated, among the rest of the correspondence, satisfied that when search was made the persons named would already have shifted their quarters and assumed some other disguise.

February had come and Harry was still working and waiting, busy for several hours each day writing and examining reports with Robespierre, striving of an evening to keep up the courage and spirits of the girls, calling in for a few minutes each day to see Victor, who, after passing through a long and terrible fever, now lay weak and apparently unconscious alike of the past and present, his mind completely gone; but the doctor told Harry that in this respect he did not think the case was hopeless.

"His strength seems to have absolutely deserted him," he said, "and his mind is a blank like that of a little child, but I by no means despair of his gradually recovering; and if he could hear the voice of the lady you tell me he is engaged to, it might strike a chord now lying dormant and set the brain at work again."

But as to Marie, Harry could do nothing. Do what he would, he could hit upon no plan whatever for getting her out of prison; and he could only wait until some change in the situation or the appearance of her name in the fatal list might afford some opportunity for action. It was evident to him that Lebat was not pushing matters forward, but that he preferred to wait and leave the horror of months in prison to work upon Marie's mind, and so break her down that she would be willing enough to purchase her life by a marriage with him.

There had been some little lull in the work of blood, for in December all eyes had been turned to the spectacle of the trial of the king. From the 10th of August he had remained a close prisoner in the Temple, watched and insulted by his ruffian guards, and passing the time in the midst of his family with a serenity of mind, a calmness, and tranquility which went far to redeem the blunders he had made during the preceding three years. The following is the account written by the princess royal in her journal of the manner in which the family passed their days: "My father rose at seven and said prayers till eight; then dressing himself he was with my brother till nine, when he came to breakfast with my mother. After breakfast my father gave us lessons till eleven o'clock; and then my brother played till midday, when we went to walk together, whatever the weather was, because at that hour they relieved guard and wished to see us to be sure of our presence. Our walk was continued till two o'clock, when we dined. After dinner my father and mother played at backgammon, or rather pretended to play, in order to have an opportunity of talking together for a short time.

"At four o'clock my mother went up stairs with us, because the king then usually took a nap. At six o'clock my brother went down, and my father gave us lessons till supper at nine. After supper my mother soon went to bed. We then went up stairs, and the king went to bed at eleven. My mother worked much at tapestry and made me study, and frequently read alone. My aunt said prayers and read the service; she also read many religious books, usually aloud."

But harmless as was the life of the royal family, Danton and the Jacobins were determined upon having their lives. The mockery of the trial commenced on the 10th of December. Malesherbes, Tronchet, and Deseze defended him fearlessly and eloquently, but it was useless—the king was condemned beforehand. Robespierre and Marat led the assault. The Girondists, themselves menaced and alarmed, stood neutral; but on the 15th of January the question was put to the Assembly, "Is Louis Capet, formerly King of the French, guilty of conspiracy and attempt against the general safety of the state?"

With scarcely a single exception, the Assembly returned an affirmative answer, and on the 17th the final vote was taken. Three hundred and sixty-one voted for death, two for imprisonment, two hundred and eighty-six for detention, banishment, or conditional death, forty-six for death but after a delay, twenty-six for death but with a wish that the Assembly should revise the sentence.

Sentence of death was pronounced. After a sitting which lasted for thirty-seven hours there was another struggle between the advocates of delay and those of instant execution, but the latter won; and after parting with noble resignation from his wife and family, the king, on the 21st, was executed. His bearing excited the admiration even of his bitterest foes.

France looked on amazed and appalled at the act, for Louis had undoubtedly striven his best to lessen abuses and to go with the people in the path of reform. It was his objection to shed blood, his readiness to give way, his affection for the people, which had allowed the Revolution to march on its bloody way without a check. It was the victims—the nobles, the priests, the delicate women and cultured men—who had reason to complain; for it was the king's hatred to resistance which left them at the mercy of their foes. Louis had been the best friend of the Revolution that slew him.

The trial and execution of the king had at least the good effect of diverting the minds of Jeanne and Virginie from their own anxieties. Jeanne was passionate and Virginie tearful in their sorrow and indignation. Over and over again Jeanne implored Harry to try to save the king. There were still many Royalists, and indeed the bulk of the people were shocked and alienated by the violence of the Convention; and Jeanne urged that Harry might, from his connection with Robespierre, obtain some pass or document which would enable the king to escape. But Harry refused to make any attempt whatever on his behalf.

"In the first place, Jeanne, it would be absolutely impossible for the king, watched as he is, to escape; and no pass or permit that Robespierre could give would be of the smallest utility. You must remember, that although all apparently unite against the king, there is a never-ending struggle going on in the Convention between the various parties and the various leaders. Robespierre is but one of them, although, perhaps, the most prominent; but could I wring a pass from him even if only to see the king, that pass would not be respected.

"In the next place, Jeanne, I have nothing to do with these struggles in France. I am staying here to do what little I can to watch over you and Virginie, for the sake of your dear parents and because I love you both; and I have also, if possible, to rescue Marie from the hands of these murderers. The responsibility is heavy enough; and could I, by merely using Robespierre's name, rescue the king and queen and their children and pass them across the frontier, I would not do it if the act in the slightest degree interfered with my freedom of action towards you and Marie."

"But Virginie and I would die for the king!" Jeanne said passionately.

"Happily, Jeanne," Harry replied coolly, "your dying would in no respect benefit him; and as your life is in my eyes of a thousand times more consequence than that of the king, and as your chances of safety to some extent depend upon mine, I do not mean to risk one of those chances for the sake of his majesty. Besides, to tell you the truth, I have a good deal of liking for my own life, and have a marked objection to losing my head. You see I have people at home who are fond of me, and who want to see me back again with that head on my shoulders."

"I know, Harry; I know," Jeanne said with her eyes full of tears. "Do not think that I am ungrateful because I talk so. I am always thinking how wrong it is that you should be staying here risking your life for us instead of going home to those who love you. I think sometimes Virginie and I ought to give ourselves up, and then you could go home." And Jeanne burst into tears.

"My dear Jeanne," Harry said soothingly, "do not worry yourself about me. It would have been just as dangerous at the time your father was taken prisoner for me to have tried to escape from the country as it was to stay here—in fact I should say that it was a good deal more dangerous; and at present, as Robespierre's secretary, I am in no danger at all. It is a little disagreeable certainly serving a man whom one regards in some respects as being a sort of wild beast; but at the same time, in his own house, I am bound to say, he is a very decent kind of man and not at all a bad fellow to get on with.

"As to what I have done for you, so far as I see I have done nothing beyond bringing you here in the first place, and coming to have a pleasant chat with you every evening. Nor, with the best will in the world, have I been able to be of the slightest assistance to Marie. As we say at home, my intentions are good; but so far the intentions have borne no useful fruit whatever. Come, Jeanne, dry your eyes, for it is not often that I have seen you cry. We have thrown in our lot together, and we shall swim or sink in company.

"You keep up my spirits and I keep up yours. Don't let there be any talk about gratitude. There will be time enough for that if I ever get you safely to England. Then, perhaps, I may send in my bill and ask for payment."

Harry spoke lightly, and Jeanne with a great effort recovered her composure; and after that, although the trial and danger of the king were nightly discussed and lamented, she never said a word as to any possibility of the catastrophe being averted.

One day towards the end of February Harry felt a thrill run through him as, on glancing over the list of persons to be tried on the following day, he saw the name of Marie, daughter of the ci-devant Marquis de St. Caux. Although his knowledge of Robespierre's character gave him little ground for hope, he determined upon making a direct appeal.

"I see, citizen," he said—for such was the mode of address universal at that time—"that among the list of persons to be tried is the name of Marie de St. Caux."

"Say Marie Caux," Robespierre said reprovingly. "You know de and St. are both forbidden prefixes. Yes; what would you say about her?"

"I told you, citizen, upon the first night when I came here, that I had been in the service of the father of this female citizen. Although I know now that he was one of those who lived upon the blood of the people, I am bound to say that he always treated his dependants kindly. His daughter also showed me many marks of kindness, and this I would now fain return. Citizen, I did you some service on the night when we first met; and I ask you now, as a full quittance for that aid, that you will grant me the freedom of this young woman. Whatever were the crimes of her father, she cannot have shared in them. She is young, and cannot do harm to any; therefore I implore you to give me her life."

"I am surprised at your request," Robespierre said calmly. "This woman belongs to a race who have for centuries oppressed France, and it is better that they should perish altogether. If she can convince the tribunal that she is innocent of all crime, undoubtedly she will be spared; but I cannot, only on account of the obligation I am under to you, interfere on her behalf; such an act would be treason to the people, and I hope you know me well enough by this time to be aware that nothing whatever would induce me to allow my private inclinations to interfere with the course of justice. Ask of me all I have, it is little enough, but it is yours; but this thing I cannot grant you."

For a moment Harry was on the point of bursting out indignantly, but he checked himself and without a word went on with his writing, although tears of disappointment for a time almost blinded him; but he felt it would be hopeless to urge the point further, and that did he do so he might forfeit the opportunity he now had of learning what was going on.

Another month passed before the name appeared on the fatal list. In the meantime Harry had corresponded regularly with Marie by means of the warder, and had even once seen her and exchanged a few words with her, having been sent by Robespierre with a letter to the governor of the prison.

Marie was greatly changed: her colour had faded away, the former somewhat haughty air and carriage had disappeared, and there was an expression of patient resignation on her face. Harry had only the opportunity to whisper to her "Hope always, all is not lost yet." He had spent hours each day in his lodging imitating the signature of Robespierre, and he had made up his mind that, should all other efforts fail, he would boldly present himself at the prison with an order for Marie's release, with Robespierre's signature forged at the bottom.

He thought he could write it now plainly enough for it to pass; his fear was that the prison authorities would not act upon it, unless presented by a well-known official personage, without sending to Robespierre to have it verified.

Still but little change had taken place in Victor de Gisons' condition. He remained in a state almost of lethargy, with an expression of dull hopelessness on his face; sometimes he passed his hand wearily across his forehead as if he were trying to recollect something he had lost; he was still too weak to stand, but Jacques and his wife would dress him and place him on a couch which Harry purchased for his use. The worthy couple ran no risk now, for the sharpest spy would fail to recognize in the bowed-down invalid with vacant face, the once brilliant Victor de Gisons.

Harry had many talks with Jeanne concerning him. "What should we do, Harry," the girl said over and over again, "if we could get Marie away and all get safe together to England, which I begin to despair now of our ever doing, but if we should do it what should we say to Marie? She thinks Victor is safe there. Only the other day, as you know, she sent us out a letter to him. What would she say when she learned on her arrival in England that Victor has all this time been lying broken down and in suffering in Paris?"

To this question Harry, for a long time, could give no answer. At last he said, "I have been thinking it over, Jeanne, and I feel that we have no right to take Marie away without her knowing the truth about Victor. His misfortunes have come upon him because he would stop in Paris to watch over her. I feel now that she has the right, if she chooses, of stopping in Paris to look after him."

"Oh, Harry, you would never think of our going away and leaving her!"

"I don't know, Jeanne, if it would not be best. She could stay

123

in the disguise of a peasant girl with Jacques and his wife; they would give out that she was Victor's sister who had come to nurse him. I have great hopes that her voice and presence would do what we have to do, namely, awaken him from his sad state of lethargy. They could stay there for months until these evil days are over. Jacques' workmen friends are accustomed now to Victor being with him, and there is no chance of any suspicion arising that he is not what he seems to be, a workman whom Jacques picked up injured and insensible on that terrible night. It would seem natural that his sister or his fiance—Marie could pass for whichever she chose—should come and help take care of him."

"Then if she can stop in Paris with Victor, of course we can stop with Louise?"

"I am afraid not," Harry said. "Every day the search for suspects becomes stricter; every day people are being seized and called upon to produce the papers proving their identity; and I fear, Jeanne, there is no hope of permanent safety for you save in flight."

It was just a month from the mock trial, at which Marie had been found guilty and sentenced to death, that Harry received a double shock. Among the letters of denunciation was the following: "Citizen, I know that you watch over the state. I would have you know that for more than seven months two girls have been dwelling with one Louise Moulin of 15 Rue Michel; there were three of them, but the eldest has disappeared. This, in itself, is mysterious; the old woman herself was a servant in the family of the ci-devant Marquis de St. Caux. She gives out that the girls are relatives of hers, but it is believed in the neighbourhood that they are aristocrats in disguise. They receive many visits from a young man of whom no one knows anything."

Harry felt the colour leave his cheeks, and his hand shook as he hastily abstracted the note, and he could scarcely master the meaning of the next few letters he opened.

This was a sudden blow for which he was unprepared. He could not even think what was best to be done. However, saying to himself that he had at any rate a few days before him, he resolutely put the matter aside, to be thought over when he was alone, and proceeded with his work. After a time he came to the list of those marked out for execution on the following day, and saw with a fresh pang the name of Marie de St. Caux.

So the crisis had arrived. That night or never Marie must be rescued, and his plan of forging Robespierre's signature must be put into effect that day. He opened the next few papers mechanically, but steadied himself upon Robespierre asking him a question. For a time he worked on; but his brain was swimming, and he was on the

124

point of saying that he felt strangely unwell, and must ask to be excused his work for that day, when he heard a ring at the bell, and a moment later Lebat entered the room.

"I have just come from the tribunal, citizen," he said, "and have seen the list for to-morrow. I have come to you, as I know you are just, and abhor the shedding of innocent blood. There is among the number a young girl, who is wholly innocent. I know her well, for she comes from my province, and her father's chateau was within a few miles of Dijon. Although her father was a furious aristocrat, her heart was always with the people. She was good to the poor, and was beloved by all the tenants on the estate. It is not just that she should die for the sins of her parents. Moreover, henceforth, if pardoned, she will be no longer an aristocrat. I respond for her; for she has promised to marry me, the delegate of Burgundy to the Commune. The young woman is the daughter of the man called the Marquis de St. Caux, who met his deserved fate on the 2d of September."

"You are willing to respond for her, citizen?" Robespierre said.

"I am. The fact that she will be my wife is surely a guarantee?"

"It is," Robespierre said. "What you tell me convinces me that I can without damage to the cause of the people grant your request. I am the more glad to do so since my secretary has also prayed for her life. But though he rendered me the greatest service, and I owe to him a debt of gratitude, I was obliged to refuse; for to grant his request would have been to allow private feeling to interfere with the justice of the people; but now it is different. You tell me that, except by birth, she is no aristocrat; that she has long been a friend of the people, and that she is going to be your wife; on these grounds I can with a good conscience grant her release."

Lebat had looked with astonishment at Harry as Robespierre spoke.

"Thank you, citizen," he said to Robespierre. "It is an act of justice which I relied upon from your well-known character. I promise you that your clemency will not be misplaced, and that she will become a worthy citizen. May I ask," he said, "how it is that your secretary, whose face seems familiar to me, is interested in this young woman also?"

"It is simple enough," Robespierre replied. "He was in the service of her father."

"Oh, I remember now," Lebat said. "He is English. I wonder, citizen, that you should give your confidence to one of that treacherous nation."

"He saved my life," Robespierre replied coldly; "a somewhat good ground, you will admit, for placing confidence in him."

"Assuredly," Lebat said hastily, seeing that Robespierre was offended. "And now, citizen, there is another matter of importance on which I wish to confer with you."

Harry rose.

"Citizen, I will ask you to excuse me from further work to-day. My head aches badly, and I can scarce see what I am writing."

"I thought you were making some confusion of my papers," Robespierre said kindly. "By all means put aside your work."

On leaving the room Harry ran up to the attic above, which he had occupied since he had entered Robespierre's service, rapidly put on the blue blouse and pantaloons which he had formerly worn, pulled his cap well down over his eyes, and hurried down stairs. He stationed himself some distance along the street and waited for Lebat to come out. Rapidly thinking the matter over, he concluded that the man would not present himself with the order of release until after dark, in order that if Marie struggled or tried to make her escape it would be unnoticed in the street. Lebat had calculated, of course, that on the presentation of the order the prison officials would at once lead Marie to the gates whether she wished it or not, and would, at his order, force her into a vehicle, when she would be completely in his power, and he could confine her in his own house or elsewhere until she consented to be his wife.

A quarter of an hour later Lebat came out of the house and walked down the street. Harry followed him. After walking for some distance Lebat came to a stand of hackney-coaches and spoke to one of the drivers. When he had gone on again Harry went up to the man.

"Comrade," he said, "do you wish to do a good action and earn a couple of gold pieces at the same time?"

"That will suit me admirably," the coachman replied.

"Let one of your comrades look after your horse, then, and let us have a glass of wine together in that cabaret."

As soon as they were seated at a small table with a measure of wine before them Harry said:

"That deputy with the red sash who spoke to you just now has engaged you for a job this evening?"

"He has," the coachman said. "I am to be at the left corner of the Place de Carrousel at eight this evening."

"He is a bad lot," Harry said; "he is going to carry off a poor girl to whom he has been promising marriage; but of course we know better than that. She is a friend of mine, and so were her parents, and I want to save her. Now what I want to do is to take your place on the box this evening. I will drive him to the place where he is to meet her, and when he gets her to the door of his

126

lodging I shall jump off and give my citizen such a thrashing as will put a stop to his gallivanting for some time. I will give you ten crowns for the use of your coach for an hour."

"Agreed!" the coachman said. "Between ourselves, some of these fellows who pretend to be friends of the people are just as great scoundrels, ay, and worse, than the aristocrats were. We drivers know a good many things that people in general don't; but you must mind, citizen, he carries a sword, you know, and the beating may turn out the other way."

"Oh, I can get a comrade or two to help," Harry said laughing. "There are others besides myself who will not see our pretty Isabel wronged."

"And where shall I get my coach again?"

"At the end of the Rue St. Augustin. I expect I shall be there by nine o'clock with it; but I am sure not to be many minutes later. Here is a louis now. I will give you the other when I change places with you. Be at the Place de Carrousel at half-past seven. I shall be on the look-out for you.

"I won't fail," the coachman said; "you may rely upon that."

Harry now hurried away to his friend Jacques, and rapidly gave an account of what had taken place.

"In the first place, Jacques, I want your wife to see her friend and to get her to take a note instantly to the warder, for him to give to Mademoiselle de St. Caux. It is to tell her to make no resistance when Lebat presents the order for her release, but to go with him quietly; because if she appeals to the warders and declares that she would rather die than go with him, it is just possible that they might refuse to let him take her away, saying that the order was for her release, but not for her delivery to him. I don't suppose they would do so, because as one of the members of the Committee of Public Safety he is all-powerful; still it would be as well to avoid any risk whatever of our scheme failing. I will drive to the Rue Montagnard, which, as you know, is close to La Force. It is a quiet street, and it is not likely there will be anybody about at half-past eight. Will you be there and give me a hand to secure the fellow?"

"Certainly I will," Jacques said heartily. "What do you propose to do with him?"

"I propose to tie his hands and feet and gag him, and then drive to the Rue Bluert, which is close by, and where there are some unfinished houses. We can toss him in there, and he will be safe till morning.

"It will be the safest plan to run him through at once and have done with him," Jacques said. "He will be a dangerous enemy if he

127

is left alive; and as he would kill you without mercy if he had a chance, I don't see why you need be overnice with him."

"The man is a scoundrel, and one of a band of men whom I regard as murderers," Harry said; "but I could not kill him in cold blood."

"You are wrong," Jacques said earnestly, "and you are risking everything by letting him live. Such a fellow should be killed like a rat when you get him in a trap."

"It may be so," Harry agreed; "but I could not bring myself to do it."

Jacques was silent, but not convinced. It seemed to him an act of the extremest folly to leave so dangerous an enemy alive.

"He would hunt us all down," he said to himself, "Elise and I, this poor lad and the girl, to say nothing of the Englishman and the girl's sisters. Well, we shall see. I am risking my head in this business, and I mean to have my say."

Having made all his arrangements, Harry returned to his attic and lay down there until evening, having before he went in purchased a sword. At seven o'clock he placed his pistols in his bosom, girded on his sword, which would attract no attention, for half the rabble of Paris carried weapons, and then set out for the Place de Carrousel. At half-past seven his friend the coachman drew up.

"Ah, here you are!" he said. "You had better take this big cape of mine; you will find it precious cold on the box; besides he would notice at once that you are not the coachman he hired if you are dressed in that blouse."

Harry took off his sword and placed it on the seat, wrapped himself in the great cape, wound a muffler round the lower part of his face, and waited. A few minutes after the clock had struck eight Lebat came along.

"Here we are, citizen," Harry said in a rough voice, "I am glad you have come, for it's no joke waiting about on such nights as this. Where am I to drive you to?"

"The prison of La Force," Lebat said, taking his seat in the coach.

Harry's heart beat fast as he drove towards the prison. He felt sure that success would attend his plans; but the moment was an exciting one. It did not seem that anything could interpose to prevent success, and yet something might happen which he had not foreseen or guarded against. He drove at a little more than a footpace, for the streets a short distance from the centre of town were only lighted here and there by a dim oil lamp, and further away they were in absolute darkness, save for the lights which gleamed through the casements. At last he reached the entrance to the prison. Lebat jumped out and rang at the bell.

"What is it, citizen?" the guard said looking through a grille in the gate.

"I am Citizen Lebat of the Committee of Public Safety, and I have an order here, signed by Citizen Robespierre, for the release of the female prisoner known as Marie Caux."

"All right, citizen!" the man said, opening the gate. "It is late for a discharge; but I don't suppose the prisoner will grumble at that."

Ten minutes later the gate opened again and Lebat came out with a cloaked female figure. She hesitated on the top step, and then refusing to touch the hand Lebat held out to assist her, stepped down and entered the coach.

"Rue Fosseuse No. 18," Lebat said as he followed her.

Harry drove on, and was soon in the Rue Montagnard. It was a dark narrow street; no one seemed stirring, and Harry peered anxiously through the darkness for the figure of Jacques. Presently he heard a low whistle, and a figure appeared from a doorway. Harry at once checked the horse.

"What is it?" Lebat asked, putting his head out of the window.

Harry got off the box, and going to the window said in a drunken voice:

"I want my fare. There is a cabaret only just ahead, and I want a glass before I go further. My feet are pretty well frozen."

"Drive on, you drunken rascal," Lebat said furiously, "or it will be worse for you."

"Don't you speak in that way to me, citizen," Harry said hoarsely. "One man's as good as another in these days, and if you talk like that to me I will break your head in spite of your red sash."

With an exclamation of rage Lebat sprang from the coach, and as his foot touched the ground Harry threw his arms round him; but as he did so he trod upon some of the filth which so thickly littered the thoroughfare, and slipped. Lebat wrenched himself free and drew his sword, and before Harry could have regained his feet he would have cut him down, when he fell himself in a heap from a tremendous blow which Jacques struck him with his sword.

"Jump inside," Jacques said to Harry. "We may have some one out to see what the noise is about. He will be no more trouble."

He seized the prostrate body, threw it up on the box, and taking his seat drove on.

"Marie," Harry said as he jumped in, "thank God you are safe!"

"Oh, Harry, is it you? Can it be true?" And the spirit which

129

had so long sustained the girl gave way, and leaning her head upon his shoulder she burst into tears. Harry soothed and pacified her till the vehicle again came to a stop.

"What is it, Jacques?" Harry asked, putting his head out of the window.

"Just what we agreed upon," the man said. "Here are the empty houses. You stop where you are. I will get rid of this trash."

Harry, however, got out.

"Is he dead?" he asked in a low voice.

"Well, considering his head's cut pretty nigh in two, I should think he was," Jacques said. "It could not be helped, you know; for if I hadn't struck sharp it would have been all over with you. Anyhow it's better as it is a hundred times. If you don't value your neck, I do mine. Now get in again. I sha'n't be two minutes."

He slipped off the red sash and coat and waistcoat of the dead man, emptied his trouser pockets and turned them inside out, then lifting the body on his shoulder he carried it to one of the empty houses and threw it down.

"They will never know who he is," he said to himself "In this neighbourhood the first comer will take his shirt and trousers. They will suppose he has been killed and robbed, no uncommon matter in these days, and his body will be thrown into the public pit, and no one be any the wiser. I will burn the coat and waistcoat as soon as I get back."

CHAPTER XI

MARIE AND VICTOR

"Are you taking me to the girls, Harry?"

"No," Harry said. "It would not be safe to do so. There are already suspicions, and they have been denounced."

Marie gave a cry of alarm.

"I have managed to suppress the document, Marie, and we start with them in a day or two. Still it will be better for you not to go near them. I will arrange for you to meet them to-morrow."

"Where am I going, then?"

"You are going to the house of a worthy couple, who have shown themselves faithful and trustworthy by nursing a friend of mine, who has for nearly six months been lying ill there. You will be perfectly safe there till we can arrange matters."

"But if Robespierre has signed my release, as they said, I am safe enough, surely, and can go where I like."

"I think you will be safe from re-arrest here in Paris, Marie, because you could appeal to him; but outside Paris it might be different. However, we can talk about that to-morrow, when you have had a good night's rest."

Harry did not think it necessary to say, that when Lebat was missed it would probably be ascertained that he was last seen leaving La Force with her, and that if inquiries were set on foot about him she might be sought for. However, Marie said no more on the subject, quite content that Harry should make whatever arrangements he thought best, and she now began to ask all sorts of questions about her sisters, and so passed the time until they were close to the Place de Carrousel; then Harry called Jacques to stop.

"Will you please get out, Marie, and wait with our good friend here till I return. I shall be back in five minutes. I have to hand the coach over to its owner."

Jacques threw Lebat's clothes over his arm and got down from the box. Harry took his seat and drove into the Place, where he found the coachman awaiting him.

"Have you managed the job?"

"That we have," Harry said. "He has a lesson, and Isabel has gone off to her friends again. Poor little girl, I hope it will cure her of her flightiness. Here is your cape and your money, my friend, and thank you."

"You are heartily welcome," the driver said, mounting his box. "I wish I could do as well every day; but these are bad times for us, and money is precious scarce, I can tell you."

Harry soon rejoined Jacques and Marie. There were but few words said as they made their way through the streets, for Marie was weakened by her long imprisonment, and shaken by what she had gone through. She had not asked a single question as to what had become of Lebat; but she had no doubt that he was killed. She had grown, however, almost indifferent to death. Day after day she had seen batches of her friends taken out to execution, and the retribution which had fallen upon this wretch gave her scarcely a thought, except a feeling of thankfulness that she was freed from his persecutions. Completely as she trusted Harry, it was with the greatest difficulty that she had brought herself to obey his instructions and to place herself for a moment in the power of her persecutor, and appear to go with him willingly.

When Lebat told her triumphantly that he had saved her from death, and that she was to have formed one of the party in the tumbril on the following morning had he not obtained her release, she had difficulty in keeping back the indignant words, that she would have preferred death a thousand times. When he said that he had come to take her away, she had looked round with a terrified face, as if to claim the protection of the guards; but he had said roughly:

"It is no use your objecting, you have got to go with me; and if you are a wise woman you had better make the best of it. After all I am not very terrible, and you had better marry me than the guillotine."

So, trembling with loathing and disgust, she had followed him, resolved that if Harry's plan to rescue her failed she would kill herself rather than be the wife of this man.

When they reached the house Elise opened the door.

"So you have come, poor lamb!" she said. "Thanks to the good God that all has turned out well. You will be safe here, my child. We are rough people, but we will take care of you as if you were our own."

So saying she led the girl to the little sitting-room which they had prepared for her, for they had that afternoon taken the other two rooms on the floor they occupied, which were fortunately to let, and had fitted them up as a bed-room and sitting-room for her. There was already a communication existing between the two sets of apartments, and they had only to remove some brickwork between the double doors to throw them into one suite. Telling Marie to sit down, Elise hurried off and returned with a basin of bouillon.

"Drink this, my dear, and then go straight to bed; your friend will be here in good time in the morning, and then you can talk over matters with him." She waited to see Marie drink the broth, and then helped her to undress.

"She will be asleep in five minutes," she said when she rejoined her husband and Harry. "She is worn out with excitement, but a night's rest will do wonders for her. Don't come too early in the morning, Monsieur Sandwith; she is sure to sleep late, and I would not disturb her till she wakes of herself."

"I will be here at nine," Harry said, "and will go round before that and tell her sisters. They will be wondering they have seen nothing of me to-day, but I was afraid to tell them until it was all over. The anxiety would have been too great for them."

It was fortunate that Robespierre went out early on the following morning to attend a meeting at the Jacobins, and Harry was therefore saved the necessity for asking leave to absent himself again. At eight o'clock he was at Louise Moulin's.

"What is it, Harry?" Jeanne exclaimed as he entered. "I can see you have news. What is it?"

"I have news," Harry said, "and good news, but you must not excite yourselves."

"Have you found a way for getting Marie out?"

"Yes, I have found a way."

"A sure, certain way, Harry?" Virginie asked. "Not only a chance?"

"A sure, certain way," Harry replied. "You need have no more fear; Marie will certainly be freed."

The two girls stood speechless with delight. It never occurred to them to doubt Harry's words when he spoke so confidently.

"Have you told us all, Harry?" Jeanne asked a minute later, looking earnestly in his face. "Can it be? Is she really out already?"

"Yes," Harry said, "thank God, dears, your sister is free."

With a cry of delight Virginie sprang to him, and throwing her arms round his neck, kissed him in the exuberance of her happiness. Louise threw her apron over her head and burst into tears of thankfulness, while Jeanne put her hand on his shoulder and said:

"Oh, Harry, how can we ever thank you enough for all you have done for us?"

Six months back Jeanne would probably have acted as

Virginie did, but those six months had changed her greatly; indeed, ever since she received that note from Marie, which she had never shown even to Virginie, there had been a shade of difference in her manner to Harry, which he had more than once noticed and wondered at.

It was some little time before the girls were sufficiently composed to listen to Harry's story.

"But why did you not bring her here, Harry?" Virginie asked. "Why did you take her somewhere else?"

"For several reasons, Virginie. I have not told you before, but there is no reason why you should not know now, that Victor is still in Paris."

Virginie uttered an exclamation of wonder.

"He stopped here to look after you all, but he has had a very bad illness, and is still terribly weak, and does not even know me. Marie will nurse him. I have great hopes that he will know her, and that she may be able in time to effect a complete cure. In the next place I think it would be dangerous to bring her here, for we must leave in a very few days."

"What, go without her?"

"Yes, I am afraid so, Virginie. I have learned, Louise, that some of your neighbours have their suspicions, and that a letter of denunciation has already been sent, so it will be absolutely necessary to make a move. I have suppressed the first letter, but the writer will probably not let the matter drop, and may write to Danton or Marat next time, so we must go without delay. You cannot change your lodging, for they would certainly trace you; besides, at the present time the regulations about lodgers are so strict that no one would dare receive you until the committee of the district have examined you and are perfectly satisfied. Therefore, I think we must go alone. Marie is wanted here, and I think she will be far safer nursing Victor than she would be with us; besides, now she has been freed by Robespierre's orders, I do not think there is any fear of her arrest even if her identity were discovered. Lastly, it would be safer to travel three than four. Three girls travelling with a young fellow like me would be sure to attract attention. It will be difficult enough in any case, but it would certainly be worse with her with us."

"But we are to see her, Harry?" Jeanne said. "Surely we are not to go away without seeing Marie!"

"Certainly not, Jeanne; I am not so cruel as that. This evening, after dark, we will meet in the gardens of the Tuileries. Louise, will you bring them down and be with them near the main entrance? I will bring Marie there at six o'clock. And now I must be off; I have to break the news to Marie that Victor is in the same house with her and ill. I did not tell her last night. She will be better able to bear it after a good night's sleep."

Marie was up and dressed when Harry arrived, and was sitting by the fire in the little kitchen.

"I have just left your sisters, Marie," Harry said, "and you may imagine their delight at the news I gave them. You are to see them this evening in the gardens of the Tuileries."

"Oh, Harry, how good you are! How much you have done for us!"

Harry laughed lightly.

"Not very much yet; besides, it has been a pleasure as well as a duty. The girls have both been so brave, and Jeanne has the head of a woman."

"She is nearly a woman now, Harry," Marie said gently. "She is some months past sixteen, and though you tell me girls of that age in England are quite children, it is not so here. Why, it is nothing uncommon for a girl to marry at sixteen."

"Well, at anyrate," Harry said, "Jeanne has no time for any thought of marrying just at present. But there is another thing I want to tell you about. I have first a confession to make. I have deceived you."

"Deceived me!" Marie said with a smile. "It can be nothing very dreadful, Harry. Well, what is it?"

"It is more serious than you think, Marie. Now you know that when the trouble began I felt it quite out of the question for me to run away, and leave you all here in Paris unprotected. Such a thing would have been preposterous."

"You think so, Harry, because you have a good heart; but most people would have thought of themselves, and would not have run all sorts of risks for the sake of three girls with no claim upon them."

"Well, Marie, you allow then that a person with a good heart would naturally do as I did."

"Well, supposing I do, Harry, what then?"

"You must still further allow that a person with a good heart, and upon whom you had a great claim, would all the more have remained to protect you."

"What are you driving at, Harry, with your supposition?" she said, her cheek growing a little paler as a suspicion of the truth flashed upon her.

135

"Well, Marie, you mustn't be agitated, and I hope you will not be angry; but I ask you how, as he has a good heart, and you have claims upon him, could you expect Victor de Gisons to run away like a coward and leave you here?"

Marie had risen to her feet and gazed at him with frightened eyes.

"What, is it about him that you deceived me! Is it true that he did not go away? Has anything happened to him? Oh, Harry, do not say he is dead!"

"He is not dead, Marie, but he has been very, very ill. He was with me at La Force on that terrible night, and saw his father brought out to be murdered. The shock nearly killed him. He has had brain fever, and has been at death's door. At present he is mending, but very, very slowly. He knows no one, not even me, but I trust that your voice and your presence will do wonders for him."

"Where is he, Harry?" Marie said as she stood with clasped hands, and a face from which every vestige of colour had flown. "Take me to him at once."

"He is in the house, Marie; that is why I have brought you here. These good people have nursed and concealed him for five months."

Marie made a movement towards the door.

"Wait, Marie, you cannot go to him till you compose yourself. It is all-important that you should speak to him, when you see him, in your natural voice, and you must prepare yourself for a shock. He is at present a mere wreck, so changed that you will hardly know him."

"You are telling me the truth, Harry? You are not hiding from me that he is dying?"

"No, dear; I believe, on my honour, that he is out of danger now, and that he is progressing. It is his mind more than his body that needs curing. It may be a long and difficult task, Marie, before he is himself again; but I believe that with your care and companionship he will get round in time, but it may be months before that."

"Time is nothing," Marie said. "But what about the girls?"

"They must still be under my charge, Marie. I shall start with them in a day or two and try to make for the sea-shore, and then across to England. Suspicions have been aroused; they have already been denounced, and may be arrested at any time. Therefore it is absolutely necessary that they should fly at once; but I thought that you would consider it your first duty to stay with Victor, seeing that to him your presence is everything, while you could do nothing to assist your sisters, and indeed the fewer of us there are the better."

"Certainly it is my duty," Marie said firmly.

"You will be perfectly safe here under the care of Jacques and his wife. They have already given out to their neighbours that Victor's fiance is coming to help nurse him, and even if by any possibility a suspicion of your real position arises, you have Robespierre's pardon as a protection. This state of things cannot last for ever; a reaction must come; and then if Victor is cured, you will be able to escape together to England."

"Leave me a few minutes by myself, Harry. All this has come so suddenly upon me that I feel bewildered."

"Certainly," Harry said. "It is best that you should think things over a little. No wonder you feel bewildered and shaken with all the trials you have gone through."

Marie went to her room and returned in a quarter of an hour.

"I am ready now," she said, and by the calm and tranquil expression of her face Harry felt that she could be trusted to see Victor.

"I have a feeling," she went on, "that everything will come right in the end. I have been saved almost by a miracle, and I cannot but feel that my life has been spared in order that I might take my place here. As to the girls, it was a shock at first when you told me that fresh danger threatened them, and that I should not be able to share their perils upon their journey; but I could not have aided them, and God has marked out my place here. No, Harry, God has protected me so far, and will aid me still. Now I am ready for whatever may betide."

"One moment before you enter, Marie. You are prepared, I know, to see a great change in Victor, but nevertheless you cannot but be shocked at first. Do not go up to him or attract his attention till you have overcome this and are able to speak to him in your natural voice. I think a great deal depends upon the first impression you make on his brain. Your voice has a good deal changed in the last six months; it would be strange if it had not; but I want you to try and speak to him in the bright cheerful tone he was accustomed to hear."

Marie nodded. "One moment," she said, as she brushed aside the tears which filled her eyes, drew herself up with a little gesture that reminded Harry of old times, and then with a swift step passed through the door into Victor's room. Whatever she felt at the sight of the wasted figure lying listlessly with half-closed eyes on the couch, it only showed itself by a swift expression of pain which passed for a moment across her face and then was gone.

"Victor," she said in her clear ringing voice, "Victor, my well beloved, I am come to you." The effect upon Victor was instantaneous. He opened his eyes with a start, half rose from his couch and held out his arms towards her.

"Marie," he said in a faint voice, "you have come at last. I have wanted you so much."

Then, as Marie advanced to him, and kneeling by his side, clasped him in her arms, Elise and Harry stole quietly from the room. It was nearly an hour before Marie came out. There was a soft glow of happiness on her face, though her cheeks were pale.

"Not yet!" she said, as she swept past them into her own room.

In a few minutes she reappeared.

"Pardon me," she said, holding out her hands to Harry and Elise, "but I had to thank the good God first. Victor is quite sensible now, but oh, so weak! He remembers nothing of the past, but seems to think he is still in Burgundy, and has somehow had an illness. Then he spoke of the duke and my dear father and mother as being still alive, and that he hoped they would let me come to him now. I told him that all should be as he wished as soon as he got stronger, but that he must not think of anything now, and that I would nurse him, and all would be well. He seemed puzzled about my dress"—for Marie had already put on the simple attire which had been prepared for her—"but I told him that it was fit for a sick-room, and he seemed satisfied. He has just dozed off to sleep, and I will go in and sit with him now till he wakes."

"When he does, mademoiselle, I will have some broth and a glass of good burgundy ready for him," Elise said.

"Thank you; but please call me Marie in future. There are no mesdemoiselles in France now, and I shall call you Elise instead of Madame. And Harry, would you mind telling the girls that I will meet them to-morrow instead of this evening. I long to see them, oh so, so much; but I should not like to leave him for a moment now. I fear so that his memory might go again if he were to wake and miss me."

"I was going to propose it myself, Marie," Harry said. "It is all-important to avoid any agitation now. To-morrow, I hope, it will be safer, and the doctor will give him a sleeping-draught, so that he shall not wake while you are away. But, Marie, remember it will be a farewell visit, for I dare not let them stay more than another day. They may be denounced again at any hour, for the man who wrote to Robespierre, if he finds that nothing comes of it, may go to the local committee, and they will not lose an hour, you may be sure."

"I must see them this evening, then," Marie said hurriedly. "The doctor will be here, you say, soon. Victor must have his sleeping-draught this afternoon instead of to-morrow. They must go at once. I should never forgive myself if, by putting off our parting for twenty-four hours, I caused them to fall into the hands of these wretches; so please hurry on all the arrangements so that they may leave the first thing to-morrow morning."

"It will be best," Harry said, "if you will do it, Marie. I own that I am in a fever of apprehension. I will go there at once to tell them that all must be in readiness by to-night. They will be glad indeed to hear that your presence has done such wonders for Victor. They will be able to leave you with a better heart if they feel that your stay here is likely to bring health to him and happiness to both of you."

"A week since," Marie said, "it did not seem to me that I could ever be happy again; but though everything is still very dark, the clouds seem lifting."

The girls were greatly rejoiced when they heard the good news that Victor had recognized Marie, and that Harry had now hopes that he would do well.

"And now we must talk about ourselves," Harry said. "We must not lose another hour. Now, Louise, you must take part in our council. We have everything to settle, and only a few hours to do it in. I should like, if possible, that we should not come back here this evening after you have once left the house. The man who denounced you will expect that something would be done to-day, and when he sees that nothing has come of his letter he may go this evening to the local committee, and they would send men at once to arrest you. No doubt he only wrote to Robespierre first, thinking he would get credit and perhaps a post of some sort for his vigilance in the cause. But if Louise thinks that it cannot possibly be managed, I will write a letter at once to him in Robespierre's name, saying that his letter has been noted and your movements will be closely watched, and thanking him for his zeal in the public service."

"No, I think we are ready," Jeanne said. "Of course we have been talking it over for weeks, and agreed it was better to be in readiness whenever you told us it was time to go. Louise will tell you all about it."

"The disguises are all ready, Monsieur Sandwith; and yesterday when you said that my dear mademoiselle could not go with them, I settled, if you do not see any objection, to go with the dear children."

"I should be very glad," Harry said eagerly, for although he had seen no other way out of it, the difficulties and inconveniences of a journey alone with Jeanne and Virginie had been continually on his mind. The idea of taking the old woman with them had never occurred to him, but now he hailed it as a most welcome solution of the difficulty.

"That will be a thousand times better in every way, for with you with us it would excite far less remark than three young people travelling alone. But I fear, Louise, that the hardships we may have to undergo will be great."

"It matters little," the old woman said. "I nursed their mother, and have for years lived on her bounty; and gladly now will I give what little remains to me of life in the service of her dear children. I know that everything is turned topsy-turvy in our poor country at present, but as long as I have life in my body I will not let my dear mistress's children be, for weeks perhaps, wandering about with only a young gentleman to protect them, and Mademoiselle Jeanne almost a woman too."

"Yes, it is better in every way," Harry said. "I felt that it would be a strange position, but it seemed that it could not be helped; however, your offer gets us out of the embarrassment. So your disguises are ready?"

"Yes, monsieur," Louise said; "I have a boy's suit for Mademoiselle Virginie. She did not like it at first, but I thought that if mademoiselle went with you it would be strange to have three girls journeying under the charge of one young man."

"I think it a very good plan, Louise, but you must get out of the way of calling me monsieur or else it will slip out before people. Now what I propose is, that when we get fairly away we shall buy a horse and cart, for with you with us we can go forward more boldly than if we were alone.

"You will be grandmother, and we shall be travelling from a farm near Etampes to visit your daughter, who is married to a farmer near Nantes. That will be a likely story now, and we can always make a detour to avoid towns. It will be dark when you go out this evening, so you can take three bundles of clothes with you. The only thing is about to-night. The weather is bitterly cold, and it is out of the question that you should stop out all night, and yet we could not ask for a lodging close to Paris.

"Oh, I see now! The best plan will be for you all to sleep to-night at Jacques'. The good people will manage somehow; then we can start early in the morning. Yes, and in that way it will not be necessary for Marie to go out and leave Victor."

"That will certainly be the best way," Louise said. "I have been wondering ever since you said we must start this evening, what would become of us to-night. When we once get fairly away from Paris it will be easier, for the country people are kind-hearted, and I think we shall always be able to get shelter for the night; but just outside Paris it would be different. Then where shall we meet this evening?"

"I will be at the end of the street," Harry said. "It is quite dark by five, so do you start a quarter of an hour later; hide your bundles under your cloaks, for if that fellow is on the look-out he might follow you if he thought you were leaving. Draw your blinds up when you leave, Louise, so that the room will look as usual, and then it may be some time before anyone suspects that you have left; and if I were you I would mention to some of your neighbours this afternoon that you have had a letter from your friends in Burgundy, and are going away soon with your nieces to stay with them for a while. You had better pay your rent for three months in advance, and tell your landlord the same thing; saying that you may go suddenly anytime, as a compere who is in Paris, and is also going back, is going to take charge of you on the journey, and that he may call for you at any time. Thus when he finds that you have left, your absence will be accounted for; not that it makes much difference, for I hope that when you have seen the girls safely to England you will make your home with them there."

"Yes, I shall never come back here," the old woman said, "never, even if I could. Paris is hateful to me now, and I have no reason for ever wanting to come back."

"In that case," Harry said smiling, "we may as well save the three months' rent."

"Oh, how I long to be in England," Virginie exclaimed, "and to see dear Ernest and Jules again! How anxious they must be about us, not having heard of us all this long time! How shall we know where to find them?"

"You forget, Virginie," Jeanne said, "it was arranged they should go to Harry's father when they got to England, and he will know where they are living; there is sure to be no mistake about that, is there, Harry?"

"None at all," Harry said. "You may rely upon it that directly you get to my father you will hear where your brothers are. And now

141

I will go and tell Marie that there is no occasion for Victor to take a sleeping draught."

Marie was delighted when she heard that she was going to have her sisters with her for the whole evening and night, and Elise busied herself with preparations for the accommodation of her guests. Harry then went back to his attic, made his clothes into a bundle, and took up the bag of money from its hiding-place under a board and placed it in his pocket.

He had, since he had been with Robespierre, gradually changed the silver for gold in order to make it more convenient to carry, and it was now of comparatively little weight, although he had drawn but slightly upon it, except for the payment of the bribe promised to the warder. His pistols were also hidden under his blouse.

He went down stairs and waited the return of Robespierre.

"Citizen," he said when he entered, "circumstances have occurred which render it necessary for me to travel down to Nantes to escort a young girl, a boy, and an old woman to that town; they cannot travel alone in such times as these, and they have a claim upon me which I cannot ignore."

"Surely, friend Sandwith," Robespierre said, "the affairs of France are of more importance than private matters like these."

"Assuredly they are, citizen; but I cannot flatter myself that the affairs of France will be in any way injured by my temporary absence. My duty in this matter is clear to me, and I can only regret that my temporary absence may put you to some inconvenience. But I have a double favour to ask you: the one is to spare me for a time; the second, that you will give me papers recommending me, and those travelling with me, to the authorities of the towns through which we shall pass. In these times, when the enemies of the state are travelling throughout France seeking to corrupt the minds of the people, it is necessary to have papers showing that one is a good citizen."

"But I have no authority," Robespierre said. "I am neither a minister nor a ruler."

"You are not a minister, citizen, but you are assuredly a ruler. It is to you men look more than to any other. Danton is too headstrong and violent. You alone combine fearlessness in the cause of France with that wisdom and moderation which are, above all things, necessary in guiding the state through its dangers."

Robespierre's vanity was so inordinate that he accepted the compliment as his due, though he waved his hand with an air of deprecation.

142

"Therefore, citizen," Harry went on, "a letter from you would be more powerful than an order from another."

"But these persons who travel with you, citizen—how am I to be sure they are not enemies of France?"

"France is not to be shaken," Harry said, smiling, "by the efforts of an old woman of seventy and a young boy and girl; but I can assure you that they are no enemies of France, but simple inoffensive people who have been frightened by the commotion in Paris, and long to return to the country life to which they are accustomed. Come, citizen, you refused the first boon which I asked you, and, methinks, cannot hesitate at granting one who has deserved well of you this slight favour."

"You are right," Robespierre said. "I cannot refuse you, even if the persons who accompany you belong to the class of suspects, of which, mind, I know nothing, though I may have my suspicions. I have not forgotten, you know, that you asked for the life of the daughter of the ci-devant Marquis de St. Caux; and for aught I know these children may be of the same breed. But I will not ask you. Did I know it, not even the obligation I am under to you would you induce me to do what you ask; for although as children they can do no harm, they might do so were they allowed to grow up hating France. All children of suspects are, as you know, ordered to be placed in the state schools, in order that they may there learn to love the people of France and to grow up worthy citizens. Now, how shall I word it?" he said, taking up a pen; and Harry dictated:

"I hereby recommend Citizen Henri Sandwith, age 19, who has been acting as my confidential secretary, to all public authorities, together with Citoyenne Moulin and her two grandchildren, with whom he is travelling."

To this Robespierre signed his name and handed the paper to Harry.

"How long will you be before you return?" he asked.

"I cannot say exactly," Harry replied; "as after I have seen them to their destination I may stop with them for a few weeks."

Robespierre nodded and held out his hand.

"I shall be glad to have you with me again, for I have conceived a strong friendship for you, and think none the worse of you for your showing your gratitude to the family in whom you are interested."

Harry then went into the kitchen, where Robespierre's sister was preparing the next meal, and said good-bye to her.

She had taken a fancy to her brother's young secretary, and expressed a hope that his absence would be but a short one, telling him that Robespierre had said only the day before how much work he had saved him, and that he was determined to push his fortunes to the utmost.

Having thus paved the way for an appeal to Robespierre should he find himself in difficulties on the road, Harry proceeded to Jacques' house and waited there until it was time to go up to meet Louise and the girls.

Victor did not wake until the afternoon. The doctor had called as usual, but had not roused him. He had been told what had taken place, and had held out hope to Marie that Victor's improvement would be permanent, and that he would now make steady progress towards recovery.

At the appointed hour Harry was at his post to meet the party. They came along within a few minutes of the time named, but instead of stopping to greet him they walked straight on, Jeanne saying as she passed him:

"I think we are followed."

Harry at once drew back and allowed them to go fifty yards on before he moved after them. As there were many people about, it was some little time before he could verify Jeanne's suspicions; then he noticed that a man, walking a short distance ahead of him, followed each turning that the others took.

Harry waited until they were in a quiet street, and then quickened his pace until he was close behind the man. Then he drew one of his pistols, and, springing forward, struck him a heavy blow on the head with its butt. He fell forward on his face without a cry; and Harry, satisfied that he had stunned him, ran on and overtook the others, and, turning down the first street they came to, was assured that they were safe from pursuit.

"We had noticed a man lounging against the house opposite all the afternoon," Jeanne said, "and came to the conclusion that he must be watching us; so we looked out for him when we came out, and noticed that as soon as we went on he began to walk that way too. So I told Louise to walk straight on without stopping when we came up to you. I was sure you would manage somehow to get rid of him."

Harry laughed.

"I fancy he will spend to-morrow in bed instead of lounging about. Perhaps it will teach him to mind his own business in future and to leave other people alone. I am very glad that he did follow you; for I felt that I owed him one, and was sorry to leave Paris without paying my debt. Now I think we are pretty well square."

The meeting between the sisters was indeed a happy one.

144

They fell on each other's necks, and for some time scarce a word was spoken; then they stood a little apart and had a long look at each other.

"You are changed, Marie dear," Jeanne said; "you look pale, but you look, too, softer and prettier than you used to."

"All my airs and graces have been rubbed off," Marie said with a slight smile. "I have learned so much, Jeanne, and have been where noble blood has been the reverse of a recommendation. You are changed too—the six months have altered you. Your gouvernante would not call you a wild girl now. You are quite a woman.

"We have suffered too, Marie," Jeanne said as tears came to her eyes at the thought of the changes and losses of the last few months. "We have thought of you night and day; but Louise has been very good to us, and as for Harry, we owe everything to him. He has always been so hopeful and strong, and has cheered us up with promises that he would bring you to us some day."

Marie smiled.

"You are right, Jeanne. I used to laugh a little, you know, at your belief in your hero, and little thought that the time would come when I should trust him as implicitly as you do. You have a right to be proud of him, Jeanne. What thought and devotion and courage he has shown for us! And do you know, he saved Victor too. Jacques has told me all about it—how Victor saw his father brought out to be murdered; and how, half-mad, he was springing out to stand beside him, when Harry as quick as thought knocked him down before he could betray himself; and then Jacques, who was standing by saw it, helped him carry him here. Oh, my dear, how much we owe him!

"And now, Virginie," she said, turning to the youngest, "I must have a good look at you, little one—but no, I mustn't call you little one any longer, for you are already almost as tall as I am. My child, how you have been growing, and you look so well! Louise must have been feeding you up. Ah, Louise, how much we all owe to you too! And I hear you are going to leave your comfortable home and take care of the girls on their journey. It was such a comfort to me when Harry told me!"

"I could not let them go alone, mademoiselle," the old woman said simply; "it was only my duty. Besides, what should I do in Paris with all my children in England?"

"Now, my dears, take your things off," Marie said. "I will just run in and see how Victor is getting on. Harry went straight in to him, and I want to know whether Victor recognized him."

CHAPTER XII

NANTES

Harry was very pleased to see a look of recognition on Victor's face as he came up to the side of his couch.

"Well, Victor," he said cheerfully, "I am glad to see you looking more yourself again."

Victor nodded assent, and his hand feebly returned the pressure of Harry's.

"I can't understand it," he said after a pause. "I seem to be in a dream; but it is true Marie is here, isn't it?"

"Oh yes! She is chatting now with her sisters, Jeanne and Virginie, you know."

"And why am I here?" Victor asked, looking round the room. "Marie tells me not to ask questions."

"No. There will be plenty of time for that afterwards, Victor. It is all simple enough. You were out with me, and there was an accident, and you got hurt. So I and a workman who was passing carried you into his house, and he and his wife have been taking care of you. You have been very ill, but you are getting on better now. Marie has come to nurse you, and she won't leave you until you are quite well. Now, I think that's enough for you, and the doctor would be very angry if he knew I had told you so much; because he said you were not to bother yourself about things at all, but just to sleep as much as you can, and eat as much as you can, and listen to Marie talking and reading to you, and not trouble your brain in any way, because it's your brain that has gone wrong, and any thinking will be very bad for it."

This explanation seemed satisfactory to Victor, who soon after dozed off to sleep, and Harry joined the party in Marie's sitting-room.

"Oh, if I could but keep them here with me, Harry, what a comfort it would be!"

"I know that it would, Marie; but it is too dangerous. You know they were denounced at Louise Moulin's. Already there is risk enough in you and Victor being here. The search for Royalists does not relax, indeed it seems to become more and more keen every day. Victor's extreme illness is your best safeguard. The neighbours have heard that Jacques has had a fellow-workman dangerously ill for

146

some long time, and Victor can no longer be looked upon as a stranger to be suspected, while your coming here to help nurse him will seem so natural a step that it will excite no comment. But any fresh addition of numbers would be sure to give rise to talk, and you would have a commissary of the Commune here in no time to make inquiries, and to ask for your papers of domicile."

"Yes, I know that it would be too dangerous to risk," Marie agreed; "but I tremble at the thought of their journey."

"I have every hope that we shall get through safely," Harry said. "I have some good news I have not yet told you. I have received a paper from Robespierre stating that I have been his secretary, and recommending us all to the authorities, so that we can dispense with the ordinary papers which they would otherwise ask for."

"That is good news, indeed, Harry," Marie said. "That relieves me of half my anxiety. Once on the sea-coast it will be comparatively easy to get a passage to England. My dear Harry, you surprise me more every day, and I am ashamed to think that when our dear father and mother first told me that they had accepted your noble offer to look after us, I was inclined in my heart to think that such protection would be of little use. You see I confess, Harry; and you know that is half-way to forgiveness."

"There is nothing either to confess or forgive," Harry said with a smile. "It was perfectly natural for you to think that a lad of eighteen was a slender reed to lean on in the time of trouble and danger, and that it was only by a lucky accident—for saving Robespierre's life was but an accident—that I have been enabled to be of use to you; and that I have now a pass which will enable me to take your sisters with comparative safety as far as Nantes. Had it not been for that I could have done little indeed to aid you."

"You must not say so, Harry. You are too modest. Besides, was it not your quickness that saved Victor? No, we owe you everything, and disclaimers are only thrown away. As for me, I feel quite jealous of Jeanne's superior perspicacity, for she trusted you absolutely from the first."

"It has nothing to do with perspicacity," Jeanne said. "Harry saved my life from that dreadful dog, and after that I knew if there was danger he would be able to get us out of it. That is, if it were possible for anyone to do so."

"I hope I shall be able to justify your trust, Jeanne, and arrive safely with you at my father's house. I can promise you the warmest of welcomes from my mother and sisters. I fear they must long since have given me up for dead. I shall be like a shipwrecked mariner who has been cast upon an island and given up as lost. But my father always used to say, that if I was a first-rate hand at getting into scrapes, I was equally good at getting out of them again; and I don't think they will have quite despaired of seeing me again, especially as they know, by the last letters I sent them, that you all said I could speak French well enough to pass anywhere as a native."

"How surprised they will be at your arriving with two girls and Louise!" Virginie said.

"They will be pleased more than surprised," Harry replied. "I have written so much about you in my letters that the girls and my mother will be delighted to see you."

"Besides," Jeanne added, "the boys will have told them you are waiting behind with us, so they will not be so surprised as they would otherwise have been. But it will be funny, arriving among people who don't speak a word of our language."

"You will soon be at home with them," said Harry reassuringly. "Jenny and Kate are just about your ages, and I expect they will have grown so I shall hardly know them. It is nearly three years now since I left them, and I have to look at you to assure myself that Jenny will have grown almost into a young woman. Now I shall go out for a bit, and leave you to chat together.

"You need not fidget about Victor, Marie. Elise is with him, and will come and let you know if he wakes; but I hope that he has gone off fairly to sleep for the night. He knew me, and I think I have put his mind at rest a little as to how he came here. I have told him it was an accident in the street, and that we brought him in here, and he has been too ill since to be moved. I don't think he will ask any more questions. If I were you I would, while nursing, resume the dress you came here in. It will be less puzzling to him than the one you are wearing now."

The little party started the next morning at day-light, and at the very first village they came to, found how strict was the watch upon persons leaving Paris, and had reason to congratulate themselves upon the possession of Robespierre's safe-conduct. No sooner had they sat down in the village cabaret to breakfast than an official with a red scarf presented himself, and asked them who they were and where they were going. The production of the document at once satisfied him; and, indeed, he immediately addressed the young man in somewhat shabby garments, who had the honour of being secretary to the great man, in tones of the greatest respect.

Virginie at present was shy and awkward in her attire as a boy, and indeed had there been time the night before to procure a disguise for her as a girl it would have been done, although Harry's opinion that it would attract less attention for her to travel as a boy was unchanged; but he would have given way had it been possible to make the change. As any delay, however, would certainly be dangerous, the original plan was adhered to.

Marie had cut her sister's hair short, and no one would have suspected from her appearance that Virginie was not what she seemed, a good-looking boy of some thirteen years old. With their bundles in their hands they trudged along the road, and stopped for the night at a village about twelve miles out of Paris. After having again satisfied the authorities by the production of the pass, Harry made inquiries, and the next morning went two miles away to a farm-house, where there was, he heard, a cart and horse to be disposed of.

After much haggling over terms—since to give the sum that was first asked would have excited surprise, and perhaps suspicion—Harry became the possessor of the horse and cart, drove triumphantly back to the village, and having stowed Louise and the two girls on some straw in the bottom of the cart, proceeded on the journey.

They met with no adventure whatever on the journey to Nantes, which was performed in ten days. The weather was bitterly cold. Although it was now well on in March the snow lay deep on the ground; but the girls were well wrapped up, and the cart was filled with straw, which helped to keep them warm. Harry walked for the most part by the side of the horse's head, for they could only proceed at foot-pace; but he sometimes climbed up and took the reins, the better to chat with the girls and keep up their spirits. There was no occasion for this in the case of Jeanne, but Virginie often gave way and cried bitterly, and the old nurse suffered greatly from the cold in spite of her warm wraps.

On arriving at Nantes Harry proceeded first to the Maine, and on producing Robespierre's document received a permit to lodge in the town. He then looked for apartments in the neighbourhood of the river, and when he had obtained them disposed of the horse and cart. The statement that he was Robespierre's secretary at once secured for him much attention from the authorities, and he was invited to become a member of the Revolutionary Committee during his stay in the town, in order that he might see for himself with what zeal the instructions received from Paris for the extermination of the Royalists were being carried out.

This offer he accepted, as it would enable him to obtain information of all that was going on. Had it not been for this he would gladly have declined the honour, for his feelings were daily harrowed by arrests and massacres which he was powerless to prevent, for he did not venture to raise his voice on the side of mercy, for had he done so, it would have been certain to excite suspicion. He found that, horrible as were the atrocities committed in Paris, they were even surpassed by those which were enacted in the provinces, and that in Nantes in particular a terrible persecution was raging under the direction of Carrier, who had been sent down from Paris as commissioner from the Commune there.

Harry's next object was to make the acquaintance of some of the fishermen, and to find out what vessels were engaged in smuggling goods across to England; for it was in one of these alone that he could hope to cross the Channel. This, however, he found much more difficult than he had expected.

The terror was universal. The news of the execution of the king had heightened the dismay. Massacres were going on all over France. The lowest ruffians in all the great towns were now their masters, and under pretended accusations were wreaking their hate upon the respectable inhabitants. Private enmities were wiped out in blood. None were too high or too low to be denounced as Royalists, and denunciation was followed as a matter of course by a mock trial and execution. Every man distrusted his neighbour, and fear caused those who most loathed and hated the existing regime to be loudest in their advocacy of it. There were spies everywhere— men who received blood-money for every victim they denounced.

Thus, then, Harry's efforts to make acquaintances among the sailors met with very slight success. He was a stranger, and that was sufficient to cause distrust, and ere long it became whispered that he had come from Paris with special authority to hasten on the work of extirpation of the enemies of the state. Soon, therefore, Harry perceived that as he moved along the quay little groups of sailors and fishermen talking together broke up at his approach, the men sauntering off to the wine-shops, and any he accosted replied civilly indeed, but with embarrassment and restraint; and although any questions of a general character were answered, a profound ignorance was manifested upon the subject upon which he wished to gain information. The sailors all seemed to know that occasionally cargoes of spirits were run from the river to England, but none could name any vessel engaged in the trade. Harry soon perceived that he was regarded with absolute hostility, and one day one of the sailors said to him quietly:

"Citizen, I am a good sans-culotte, and I warn you, you had best not come down the river after dark, for there is a strong feeling against you; and unless you would like your body to be fished out of the river with half a dozen knife-holes in it, you will take my advice."

Harry began to feel almost crushed under his responsibilities. His attendance at the Revolutionary Committee tried him greatly. He made no progress whatever in his efforts to obtain a passage; and to add to his trouble the old nurse, who had been much exhausted by the change from her usual habits, and the inclemency of the weather on her journey, instead of gaining strength appeared to be rapidly losing it, and was forced to take to her bed. The terrible events in Paris, and the long strain of anxiety as to the safety of the girls and the fate of Marie, had completely exhausted her strength, and the last six months had aged her as many years. Harry tried hard to keep up his appearance of hopefulness, and to cheer the girls; but Jeanne's quick eye speedily perceived the change in him.

"You are wearing yourself out, Harry," she said one evening as they were sitting by the fire, while Virginie was tending Louise in the next room. "I can see it in your face. It is of no use your trying to deceive me. You tell us every day that you hope soon to get hold of the captain of a boat sailing for England; but I know that in reality you are making no progress. All those months when we were hoping to get Marie out of prison—though it seemed next to impossible— you told us not to despair, and I knew you did not despair yourself; but now it is different. I am sure that you do in your heart almost give up hope. Why don't you trust me, Harry? I may not be able to do much, but I might try to cheer you. You have been comforting us all this time. Surely it is time I took my turn. I am not a child now."

"I feel like one just at present," Harry said unsteadily with quivering lips. "I feel sometimes as if—as we used to say at school—I could cry for twopence. I know, Jeanne, I can trust you, and it isn't because I doubted your courage that I have not told you exactly how things are going on, but because it is entirely upon you now that Louise and Virginie have to depend, and I do not wish to put any more weight on your shoulders; but it will be a relief to me to tell you exactly how we stand."

Harry then told her how completely he had failed with the sailors, and how an actual feeling of hostility against him had arisen.

"I think I could have stood that, Jeanne; but it is that terrible committee that tries me. It is so awful hearing these fiends marking out their victims and exulting over their murder, that at times I feel tempted to throw myself upon some of them and strangle them."

"It must be dreadful, Harry," Jeanne said soothingly. "Will it not be possible for you to give out that you are ill, and so absent yourself for a time from their meetings? I am sure you look ill—ill enough for anything. As to the sailors, do not let that worry you. Even if you could hear of a ship at present it would be of no use. I couldn't leave Louise; she seems to me to be getting worse and worse, and the doctor you called in three days ago thinks so too. I can see it by his face. I think he is a good man. The woman whose sick child I sat up with last night tells me the poor all love him. I am sure he guesses that we are not what we seem. He said this morning to me:

"' I cannot do much for your grandmother. It is a general break-up. I have many cases like it of old people and women upon whom the anxiety of the times has told. Do not worry yourself with watching, child. She will sleep quietly, and will not need attendance. If you don't mind I shall have you on my hands. Anxiety affects the young as well as the old.'

"At anyrate, you see, we cannot think of leaving here at present. Louise has risked everything for us. It is quite impossible for us to leave her now, so do not let that worry you. We are all in God's hands, Harry, and we must wait patiently what He may send us."

"We will wait patiently," Harry said. "I feel better now, Jeanne, and you shall not see me give way again. What has been worrying me most is the thought that it would have been wiser to have carried out some other plan—to have put you and Virginie, for instance, in some farmhouse not far from Paris, and for you to have waited there till the storm blew over."

"You must never think that, Harry," Jeanne said earnestly. "You know we all talked it over dozens of times, Louise and all of us, and we agreed that this was our best chance, and Marie when she came out quite thought so too. So, whatever comes, you must not blame yourself in the slightest. Wherever we were we were in danger, and might have been denounced."

"I arranged it all, Jeanne. I have the responsibility of your being here."

"And to an equal extent you would have had the responsibility of our being anywhere else. So it is of no use letting that trouble you. Now, as to the sailors, you know I have made the acquaintance of some of the women in our street. Some of them are sailors' wives, and possibly through them I may be able to hear about ships. At anyrate I could try."

"Perhaps you could, Jeanne; but be very, very careful what questions you put, or you might be betrayed."

"I don't think there is much fear of that, Harry. The women are more outspoken than the men. Some of them are with what they call the people; but it is clear that others are quite the other way. You see trade has been almost stopped, and there is great suffering among the sailors and their families. Of course I have been very careful not to seem to have more money than other people; but I have been able to make soups and things—I have learned to be quite a cook from seeing Louise at work—and I take them to those that are very poor, especially if they have children ill, and I think I have won some of their hearts."

"You win everyone's heart who comes near you, Jeanne, I think," Harry said earnestly.

Jeanne flushed a rosy red, but said with a laugh:

"Now, Harry, you are turning flatterer. We are not at the chateau now, sir, so your pretty speeches are quite thrown away; and now I shall go and take Virginie's place and send her in to you."

And so another month went by, and then the old nurse quietly passed away. She was buried, to the girls' great grief, without any religious ceremony, for the priests were all in hiding or had been murdered, and France had solemnly renounced God and placed Reason on His throne.

In the meantime Jeanne had been steadily carrying on her work among her poorer neighbours, sitting up at night with sick children, and supplying food to starving little ones, saying quietly in reply to the words of gratitude of the women:

"My grandmother has laid by savings during her long years of service. She will not want it long, and we are old enough to work for ourselves; besides, our brother Henri will take care of us. So we are glad to be able to help those who need it."

While she worked she kept her ears open, and from the talk of the women learned that the husbands of one or two of them were employed in vessels engaged in carrying on smuggling operations with England. A few days after the death of Louise one of these women, whose child Jeanne had helped to nurse through a fever and had brought round by keeping it well supplied with good food, exclaimed:

"Oh, how much we owe you, mademoiselle, for your goodness!"

"You must not call me mademoiselle," Jeanne said, shaking her head. "It would do you harm and me too if it were heard."

153

"It comes so natural," the woman said with a sigh. "I was in service once in a good family before I married Adolphe. But I know that you are not one of those people who say there is no God, because I saw you kneel down and pray by Julie's bed when you thought I was asleep. I expect Adolphe home in a day or two. The poor fellow will be wild with delight when he sees the little one on its feet again. When he went away a fortnight ago he did not expect ever to see her alive again, and it almost broke his heart. But what was he to do? There are so many men out of work that if he had not sailed in the lugger there would have been scores to take his place, and he might not perhaps have been taken on again."

"He has been to England, has he not?" Jeanne asked.

"Yes; the lugger carries silks and brandy. It is a dangerous trade, for the Channel is swarming with English cruisers. But what is he to do? One must live."

"Is your husband in favour of the new state of things?" Jeanne asked.

"Not in his heart, mademoiselle, any more than I am, but he holds his tongue. Most of the sailors in the port hate these murdering tyrants of ours; but what can we do?"

"Well, Marthe, I am sure I can trust you, and your husband can help me if he will."

"Surely you can trust me," the woman said. "I would lay down my life for you, and I know Adolphe would do so too when he knows what you have done for us."

"Well, then, Marthe, I and my sister and my brother Henri are anxious to be taken to England. We are ready to pay well for a passage, but we have not known how to set about it."

"I thought it might be that," Marthe said quietly; "for anyone who knows the ways of gentlefolk, as I do, could see with half an eye that you are not one of us. But they say, mademoiselle, that your brother is a friend of Robespierre, and that he is one of the committee here."

"He is only pretending, Marthe, in order that no suspicion should fall upon us. But he finds that the sailors distrust him, and he cannot get to speak to them about taking a passage, so I thought I would speak to you, and you can tell me when a boat is sailing and who is her captain."

"Adolphe will manage all that for you, never fear," the woman said. "I know that many a poor soul has been hidden away on board the smuggler's craft and got safely out of the country; but of course it's a risk, for it is death to assist any of the suspects. Still the sailors are ready to run the risk, and indeed they haven't much fear of the consequences if they are caught, for the sailor population here are very strong, and they would not stand quietly by and see some of their own class treated as if they had done some great crime merely because they were earning a few pounds by running passengers across to England. Why they have done it from father to son as far as they can recollect, for there has never been a time yet when there were not people who wanted to pass from France to England and from England to France without asking the leave of the authorities. I think it can be managed, mademoiselle, especially, as you say, you can afford to pay, for if one won't take you, another will. Trade is so bad that there are scores of men would start in their fishing-boats for a voyage across the Channel in the hope of getting food for their wives and families."

"I was sure it was so, Marthe, but it was so difficult to set about it. Everyone is afraid of spies, and it needs some one to warrant that we are not trying to draw them into a snare, before anyone will listen. If your husband will but take the matter up, I have no doubt it can be managed."

"Set your mind at ease; the thing is as good as done. I tell you there are scores of men ready to undertake the job when they know it is a straightforward one."

"That is good news indeed, Jeanne," Harry said, when the girl told him of the conversation. "That does seem a way out of our difficulties. I felt sure you would be able to manage it, sooner or later, among the poor people you have been so good to. Hurry it on as much as you can, Jeanne. I feel that our position is getting more and more dangerous. I am afraid I do not play my part sufficiently well. I am not forward enough in their violent councils. I cannot bring myself to vote for proposals for massacre when there is any division among them. I fear that some have suspicions. I have been asked questions lately as to why I am staying here, and why I have come. I have been thinking for the last few days whether it would not be better for us to make our way down to the mouth of the river and try and bribe some fishermen in the villages there who would not have that feeling against me that the men here have, to take us to sea, or if that could not be managed, to get on board some little fishing-boat at night and sail off by ourselves in the hopes of being picked up by an English cruiser."

Harry indeed had for some days been feeling that danger was thickening round him. He had noticed angry glances cast at him by the more violent of the committee, and had caught sentences expressing doubt whether he had really been Robespierre's secretary. That evening as he came out from the meeting he heard one man say to another:

"I tell you he may have stolen it, and perhaps killed the citizen who bore it. I believe he is a cursed aristocrat. I tell you I shall watch him. He has got some women with him; the maire, who saw the paper, told me so. I shall make it my business to get to the bottom of the affair, and we will make short work with him if we find things are as I believe."

Harry felt, therefore, that the danger was even more urgent than he had expressed it to Jeanne, and he had returned intending to propose immediate flight had not Jeanne been beforehand with her news. Even now he hesitated whether even a day's delay might not ruin them.

"Have you told me all, Harry?" Jeanne asked.

"Not quite all, Jeanne. I was just thinking it over. I fear the danger is even more pressing than I have said;" and he repeated the sentence he had overheard. "Even now," he said, "that fellow may be watching outside or making inquiries about you. He will hear nothing but praise; but that very praise may cause him to doubt still more that you are not what you seem."

"But why can we not run away at once?" Virginie said. "Why should we wait here till they come and take us and carry us away and kill us?"

"That is what I was thinking when I came home, Virginie; but the risk of trying to escape in a fishing-boat by ourselves would be tremendous. You see, although I have gone out sailing sometimes on the river in England, I know very little about it, and although we might be picked up by an English ship, it would be much more likely that we should fall into the hands of one of the French gunboats. So I look upon that as a desperate step, to be taken only at the last moment. And now that Jeanne seems to have arranged a safe plan, I do not like trying such a wild scheme. A week now, and perhaps all might be arranged; but the question is—Have we a week? Have we more than twenty-four hours? What do you think, Jeanne?"

"I do not see what is best to do yet," Jeanne said, looking steadily in the fire. "It is a terrible thing to have to decide; but I see we must decide." She sat for five minutes without speaking, and then taking down her cloak from the peg on which it hung she said; "I will go round to Marthe Pichon again and tell her we are all so anxious for each other, that I don't think we can judge what is really the best. Marthe will see things more clearly and will be able to advise us."

"Yes, that will be the best plan."

It was three-quarters of an hour before she returned.

"I can see you have a plan," Harry said as he saw that there was a look of brightness and hope on Jeanne's face.

"Yes, I have a plan, and a good one; that is to say, Marthe has. I told her all about it, and she said directly that we must be hidden somewhere till her husband can arrange for us to sail. I said, of course, that was what was wanted, but how could it be managed? So she thought it over, and we have quite arranged it. She has a sister who lives in a fishing-village four miles down the river. She will go over there to-morrow and arrange with them to take us, and will get some fisher-girls' dresses for us. She says she is sure her sister will take us, for she was over here yesterday and heard about the child getting better, and Marthe told her all sorts of nonsense about what I had done for it. She thinks we shall be quite safe there, for there are only six or seven houses, and no one but fishermen live there. She proposes that you shall be dressed up in some of her husband's clothes, and shall go out fishing with her sister's husband. What do you think of that, Harry?"

"Splendid, Jeanne! Can the husband be trusted too?"

"Oh, yes, she says so. He is an honest man, she says; and besides, they are very poor, and a little money will be a great help to them. She says she would not propose it unless she was quite, quite sure of them, for if anything happened to us she would be a wretched woman all her life."

"Thank God," Harry said fervently, "that one sees daylight at last! I have felt so helpless lately! Dangers seemed to be thickening round you, and I could do nothing; and now, Jeanne, you have found a way out for us where I never should have found one for myself."

"It is God who has done it, not me," Jeanne said reverently. "I did not begin to go about among the poor people here with any thought of making friends, but because they were so poor and miserable; but He must have put it into my heart to do it, in order that a way of escape might be made for us."

CHAPTER XIII

IN THE HANDS OF THE REDS

The next morning Harry went out, as usual, immediately after breakfast, for a walk for two or three hours. This he did partly to allow the girls to tidy the rooms, an office which had naturally fallen to them since the commencement of their old nurse's illness; partly because in active exercise he found some relief from the burden of his anxieties. To-day he felt more anxious than ever. The conversation with Marthe Pichon had afforded good grounds of hope that in a day or two a fair prospect of escape would be open to them; but this only seemed to make the present anxiety all the sharper. The woman had promised to get disguises, and make the arrangements with her friends at the village below during the course of the day, and by night, if all went well, they might start. He told himself that he had no reason for supposing that the vague suspicions which were, he knew, afloat would suddenly be converted into action. He determined to take his place that afternoon with the committee as usual, and endeavour to allay their doubts by assuming a violent attitude. He felt, however, that the day would be more trying than any he had passed, and that he would give a great deal if the next twenty-four hours were over. Scarcely heeding where he walked he was out longer than usual, and it was nearly three hours after he started before he approached the town again by the road along the river bank. Just when he came to the first houses a woman, who was standing there knitting, came up to him.

"You are the citizen who lives with his two sisters next door to La Mere Pichon, are you not?"

Harry assented hurriedly, with a strange presentiment of evil.

"La Mere Pichon bids me tell you," the woman said, "that half an hour after you started this morning six men, with an official with the red scarf, came to the house and arrested your sisters and carried them off. They are watching there for your return."

Harry staggered as if struck with a blow.

"Poor young man," the woman said compassionately, seeing the ghastly pallor of his face, "but I pity you. The street is furious that these wretches should have carried off that sweet young creature, who was so good to everyone; but what could we do? We hissed the men, and we would have pelted them had we not been afraid of striking your sisters. When they had gone La Mere Pichon said to some of us, 'The best thing we can do for that angel is to save her brother from being caught also. So do one of you post yourself on each road leading to the house, and warn him in time. He generally walks beyond the town. I heard one of his sisters say so.' So some of us came out on all the roads, and two remained, one at each end of the street, in case we should miss you. La Mere said, whoever met you was to tell you to be on this road, by the river, just outside the town, after dark, and she would bring you some clothes, and take you where you would be safe; but till then you were to go away again, and keep far from the town. Do you understand?" she asked, laying her hand on his arm, for he seemed dazed and stupid with the shock he had received.

"I understand," he said in a low voice. "Thank you all for your warning. Yes, I will be here this evening."

So saying he turned and moved away, walking unsteadily as if he were drunk. The woman looked after him pityingly, and then, shaking her head and muttering execrations against the "Reds," she made her way home to tell Mere Pichon that she had fulfilled her mission.

Harry walked on slowly until some distance from the town, and then threw himself down on a bank by the road and lay for a time silent and despairing. At last tears came to his relief, and his broad shoulders shook with a passion of sobbing to think that just at the moment when a chance of escape was opened—just when all the dangers seemed nearly past—the girls should have fallen into the hands of the enemy, and he not there to strike a blow in their defence. To think of Jeanne—his bright, fearless Jeanne—and clinging little Virginie, in the hands of these human tigers. It was maddening! But after a time the passion of weeping calmed down, and Harry sat up suddenly.

"I am a fool," he said as he rose to his feet; "a nice sort of fellow for a protector, lying here crying like a girl when I had begun to fancy I was a man; wasting my time here when I know the only hope for the girls is for me to keep myself free to help them. I need not lose all hope yet. After Marie has been saved, why shouldn't I save my Jeanne? I am better off than I was then, for we have friends who will help. These women whose hearts Jeanne has won will aid if they can, and may get some of their husbands and brothers to aid. The battle is not lost yet, and Jeanne will know I shall move heaven and earth to save her."

Harry's fit of crying, unmanly as he felt it, had afforded him an immense relief, for he hardly knew himself how great the strain had been upon him of late, and with a more elastic step he strode away into the country, and for hours walked on, revolving plan after plan in his mind for rescuing the girls. Although nothing very plausible had occurred to him he felt brighter in mind, though weary in body, when, just after nightfall, he again approached the spot where he had that morning received so heavy a blow. He was not disheartened at the difficulty before him, for he knew that he should have some time yet to hit upon a a plan, and the jails were so crowded with prisoners that he might fairly reckon upon weeks before there was any actual necessity for action. Marthe Pichon was waiting for him.

"Ah, Monsieur," she began, "but this is a terrible day! Oh, if I had but known a day or two earlier they could have moved in time, and now they are in the power of those wolves; but we will try to save them. We have been talking it over. We will all go to the tribunal, and we will take our husbands and our children with us, and we will demand their release. We will not let them be murdered. And now here are the clothes, but you need not put them on now. There will be a boat here in a few minutes. We have told some of the sailors how they misjudged you, and they are sorry, now it is too late, that they would not listen when you spoke to them. However, they will do all they can for you. I have sent a message by a boy to my sister to say that I shall be down this evening, so they will be expecting us. Ah, here is the boat!"

The splash of oars was heard, and a boat rowed along close to the bank.

"Is that you, Pierre?"

"It is us, sure enough, Mere Pichon. Is all right?"

"Yes, we are both here."

In another minute the boat was rowed alongside, and Harry and the woman got on board. There were few words spoken as the two men rowed vigorously down stream. In three quarters of an hour some lights were seen on the opposite bank, and the boat was headed towards them and soon reached a little causeway.

"I shall not be more than twenty minutes," Mere Pichon said as she got out.

"All right, we will wait!" was the reply, and mounting the causeway La Mere Pichon led the way to the farthest cottage in the little fishing-village. A light was burning within, and lifting the latch she entered, followed by Harry. A fisherman and his wife were sitting by the fire.

160

"Here, sister Henriette and brother Pierre," Marthe said; "you have heard from me how a dear angel, who lived next door to me, has nursed and tended my little Julie, and by blessing of the Virgin brought her round from her illness; and those wretches, the Reds, have carried her off to-day with her sister, and you know what it is to fall into their hands. This is her brother, and I am going to ask you to give him shelter and let him stay here with you. I have brought him a suit of clothes with me, and no one will guess that he is not the son of some comrade of yours. He will pay you well for sheltering him till we can put him on board Adolphe's lugger and send him across the water. If it had not been that the Reds had come to-day I should have brought his sisters with him. I was just starting to arrange it with you when those wretches came and took them away, and it may be that they would pay a hundred crowns to you, and that is not a sum to be earned every day."

"No, indeed," her sister said briskly; "that will buy Pierre a new boat, and a good one, such as he can go out to sea in; besides, as you say, after what his sister did for Julie we are bound to help them. What do you say, Pierre?"

Pierre's face had expressed anything but satisfaction until the money was mentioned, but it then changed entirely. The times were bad—his boat was old and unseaworthy—a hundred crowns was a fortune to him.

"I have risked my life often," he said, "to earn five crowns, therefore I do not say no to the offer. Monsieur, I accept; for a hundred crowns I will run the risk of keeping you here, and your sisters too if they should come, until you can cross the water."

"Very well then," Marthe Pichon said. "That's settled, now I shall be off at once. They will be watching the street for monsieur, and to-morrow, when they find he has not come back, they will be asking questions, so the sooner I am back the better."

"We cannot give you much accommodation, monsieur," the fisherman said. "There is only the loft upstairs, and, for to-night, the sails to sleep on; but we will try and make you more comfortable to-morrow."

"I care nothing for comfort," Harry answered, "so make no change for me. Just treat me as if I were what I shall seem to be—a young fisherman who has come to work with you for a bit. I will row with you and help you with your nets. Your sister has promised to send a boy every day with all the news she can gather. Now, if you have a piece of bread I will gladly eat it, for I have touched nothing since breakfast."

"We can do better than that for you," the woman replied, and in a few minutes some fish were frying over the fire. Fortunately the long hours he had been on his feet had thoroughly tired Harry out, and after eating his supper he at once ascended to the loft, threw himself on the heap of sails, and in a few minutes was sound asleep. The next morning he dressed himself in the fisherman's clothes with which he had been provided, and went down stairs.

"You will do," Pierre said, looking at him; "but your hands and face are too white. But I was tanning my sails yesterday, and there is some of the stuff left in the boiler; if you rub your hands and face with that you will do well."

Harry took the advice, and the effect was to give him the appearance of a lad whose face was bronzed by long exposure to the sea and air.

"You will pass anywhere now," Pierre said approvingly. "I shall give out that you belong to St. Nazaire, and are the son of a friend of mine whose fishing-boat was lost in the last gale, and so you have come to work for a time with me; no one would ask you any more. Besides, we are all comrades, and hate the Reds, who have spoilt our trade by killing all our best customers, so if they come asking questions here they won't get a word out of anyone."

For ten days Harry lived with the fisherman. Adolphe had returned in his lugger the day after his arrival there, and came over the next evening to see him. He said that it would be some little time before the lugger sailed again, but that if he was ready to start before she sailed he would manage to procure him a passage in some other craft. He said that he had already been talking to some of the sailors on the wharves, and that they had promised to go to the Tribunal when the girls were brought up before it, and that he would manage to get news from a friend employed in the prison when that would be.

Harry frequently went up in a boat to Nantes with Pierre with the fish they had caught. He had no fear of being recognized, and did not hesitate to land, though he seldom went far from the boat. Adolphe was generally there, and he and two or three of his comrades, who were in the secret, always hailed him as an old acquaintance, so that had any of the spies of the Revolutionists been standing there, no suspicion that Harry was other than he seemed would have entered their minds.

One evening, three weeks after Harry's arrival at the hut, Adolphe came in with his head bound up by a bandage.

"What is the matter, Adolphe?" Harry exclaimed.

"I have bad news for you, monsieur. I learned this morning

that mesdemoiselles were to-day to be brought before the Tribunal, and we filled the hall with women and two or three score of sailors. Mesdemoiselles were brought out. The young one seemed frightened, but the elder was as calm and brave as if she feared nothing. They were asked their names, and she said:

"'I am Jeanne de St. Caux, and this is my sister Virginie. We have committed no crime.'

"Carrier himself was there, and he said:

"'You are charged with being enemies of France, with being here in disguise, and with trying to leave France contrary to the laws against emigration, and with being in company with one who, under false pretenses, obtained admission to the Committee of Safety here, but who is an enemy and traitor to France. What do you say?'

"'I do not deny that we were in disguise,' she said in her clear voice. 'Nor do I deny that we should have escaped if we could. And as you treat us as enemies, and our lives are in danger, I cannot see that we were to blame in doing so. I deny that we are enemies of France, or that the gentleman who was with us was so either. He did not obtain a place on the committee by fraud, for he was really the secretary of Monsieur Robespierre, and he could not refuse the post when it was offered to him.'

"Then we thought it was time to speak, and the women cried out for mercy, and said how good she had been to the poor; and we men cried out too. And then Carrier got into a passion, and said they were traitors and worthy of death, and that they should die. And we shouted we would not have it, and broke into the Tribunal and surrounded mesdemoiselles, and then the guards rushed in and there was a fight. We beat them off and got outside, and then a regiment came up, and they were too strong for us, though we fought stoutly, I can tell you, for our blood was up; but it was no use. The dear ladies were captured again, and many of us got severe wounds. But the feeling was strong, I can tell you, among the sailors when the news spread through the town, for some of the women got hurt, too, in the melee, and I think we could get five hundred men together to storm the jail."

Harry was bitterly disappointed, for he had hoped that the intercession of the women might have availed with the judges, and doubtless would have done so had not Carrier himself been present. However, he thanked the sailor warmly for the efforts he had made and gave him some money to distribute among the wounded, for he always carried half his money concealed in a belt under his clothes. The other half was hidden away under a board in his lodgings, so that in case of his being captured the girls would still have funds available for their escape. As to the prospects of storming the jail he did not feel sanguine. It was strongly guarded, and there were three regiments of troops in the town, and these could be brought up before the fishermen could force the strong defences of the jail. However, as a last resource, this might be attempted.

Two days later Adolphe again returned, and was obliged to confess in answer to Harry's inquiries that he feared the sailors as a body would not join in the attempt.

"I can hardly blame them, monsieur. For though I myself would risk everything, and some of the others would do so too, it is a terrible thing for men with wives and families to brave the anger of these monsters. They would think nothing of putting us all to death. It isn't the fighting we are afraid of, though the odds are heavy against us, but it's the vengeance they would take afterwards, whether we happened to win or whether we didn't."

"I cannot blame them," Harry said. "As you say, even if they succeeded there would be a terrible vengeance for it afterwards. No; if the girls are to be rescued it must be by some other way. I have been quiet so long because I hoped that the intercession of the women would have saved them. As that has failed I must set to work. I have thought of every method, but bribery seems the only chance. Will you speak to the man you know in the prison, and sound him whether it will be possible to carry out any plan in that way?"

"I will speak again to him," Adolphe said. "But I have already sounded him, and he said that there were so many guards and jailers that he feared that it would be impossible. But I will try again."

The next day, soon after dinner, Adolphe came again, and there was a white scared look upon his face which filled Harry with alarm.

"What is it, Adolphe? What is your news?"

"Monsieur, I can hardly tell it," Adolphe said in a low awe-stricken voice. "It is too awful even for these fiends."

"What is it, Adolphe? Tell me. If they have been murdered I will go straight to Nantes and kill Carrier the first time he leaves his house, though they may tear me to pieces afterwards."

"They are not murdered yet," Adolphe said; "but they are to be, and everyone else." And this time the sailor sat down and cried like a child.

At last, in answer to Harry's entreaties, he raised his head and

164

told the story. The Revolutionary Committee had that day been down at the wharf, and had taken for the public service four old luggers past service which were lying on the mud, and they had openly boasted that an end was going to put to the aristocrats; that the guillotine was too slow, that the prison must be cleared, and that they were going to pack the aristocrats on board the luggers and sink them.

Harry gave a cry of horror, in which the fisherman and his wife joined, the latter pouring out voluble curses against Carrier and the Reds.

After his first cry Harry was silent; he sank down on to a low chair, and sat there with his face hidden in his hands for some minutes, while the fisherman and his wife poured question after question upon Adolphe. Presently Harry rose to his feet, and saying to Adolphe, "Do not go away, I shall be back presently, I must think by myself," went out bareheaded into the night.

It was half an hour before he returned.

"Now, Adolphe," he said, "I can think again. Now, how are they to be saved?"

"I cannot say, monsieur," Adolphe said hesitatingly. "It does not seem to me—"

"They have to be saved," Harry interrupted him in a grave, steady voice. "The question is how?"

"Yes, monsieur," Adolphe agreed hesitatingly, "that is the question. You can rely upon me, monsieur," he went on, "to do my best whatever you may decide; but I have no head to invent things. You tell me and I will do it."

"I know I can rely upon you, Adolphe. As far as I can see there are but two ways. One is for me to go to Carrier's house, find the monster, place a pistol at his head, compel him to order them to be released, stand with him at the prison door till they come out, embark with him and them in a boat, row down the river, and put to sea."

"And then, monsieur?" Adolphe asked after a pause, seeing that Harry was speaking to himself rather than to him.

"Yes, that is the question that I cannot answer," Harry replied. "I can see all the rest as if it were passing. I can feel Carrier trembling in my grasp, and shrinking as the pistol touches his forehead. I can hear him giving his orders, I can see the crowd falling back as I walk with him through the street, I can hear him crying to the people to stand aside and let us pass, I can see us going down the river together; but what am I to do in a boat with two ladies at sea?"

165

"Could you not embark in a lugger?" Adolphe exclaimed, carried away by the picture which Harry seemed to be describing as if he saw it. "Why not start in a lugger at once? I might have the Trois Freres ready, and the men will all stand by you; and when we are once outside the river we will throw Carrier over to the fishes and make for England."

"Thank you, Adolphe. If the other plans seem impossible we will try that, but only as a last resource; for I know the chances are a hundred to one against its success. I should have no fear as to Carrier himself, but as I went through the streets some one else might place a musket at the back of my head and shoot me. If I could get him alone it would be different. You could go with me; I would force him to sign the order of release; you could take it; and I would stand over him till you had time to embark with them; then I would blow out his brains and make my way down to the river. But there would be no chance of finding him alone. Monsters like this are always fearful of assassination."

"And what is monsieur's other plan?"

"The other plan is to get on board the boat in which they are to be placed—you might find out which it is from your friend in prison—hide down in the hold until the guards leave her; then join them; and when she sinks fasten them to a spar and drift down the river with them till out of sight of the town, when Pierre could row off and pick them up."

"They say there are to be soldiers on each side of the river," Adolphe said despondently, "to shoot down any who may try to swim to shore. But there would not be many who would try. Most of them, they say, will be women and children; but the heads would be seen as you drifted down."

"Yes; but we must think of something, Adolphe—think, man, think—and you, Pierre, think; if you were in a sinking ship, and you wanted something which would hide you from the eyes of people a hundred yards away, what would you take?"

"But you would be seen on anything you climbed on to or clung to, monsieur.

"But we need not climb on to it," Harry said. "I can take pieces of cork with me and wrap round them so as to keep their faces just afloat. I should only want something that would hide their faces."

"A hatch might do," Pierre said.

"The very thing!" Harry exclaimed with a fresh ring of animation and hopefulness in his voice. "The very thing! Of course there would be a hatchway to the forecastle of the lugger. We might get that loosened beforehand, so that it would float off. What is the size of such a hatch?"

"Some four feet square, monsieur."

"That will be enough," Harry said; "but how high would a hatch float out of water, because there must be room between the top of the water for us to breathe as we lie on our backs. Four inches would be enough. Are the sides buoyant enough to keep the top that much out of water?"

"I do not think so, monsieur," Pierre said with a shake of the head. "It would float nearly level with the water."

"But see here, monsieur," Adolphe said eagerly; "I have an idea! The hatches are covered with tarpaulin. If you could hide in the forecastle during the night you might cut away all the top underneath the tarpaulin and prop it up, so that if anyone trod on it in the morning they would not notice what had been done. Then when they have pushed off you could knock away the props, the board would tumble down, and there would be only the tarpaulin cover on the sides. It would float then quite four inches out of the water, and that in the middle of the stream would look almost level with it."

"I will try it," Harry said; "there is a chance of success."

"It is a terrible risk, monsieur," Pierre said.

"I know it," Harry replied; "but it is just possible. The chances are a hundred to one against it, but it may succeed. Well, Pierre, do you be with your boat on the river just below the point where the town can be seen. If you see a hatch floating down row to it. If we are beneath it, well and good; if not—"

"If not, monsieur," the fisherman's wife said solemnly, "we will pray for your souls."

"Adolphe will send down to you in the morning the two fisher-girls' dresses his wife had prepared for the ladies. Have some brandy in the boat and your little charcoal stove, and keep water boiling. They will want it. And now good-bye, my good friends! Pray for us to-night. Now, Adolphe, let us hasten back to the town, for there is much to be done. And first of all you must see your friend in the prison; find out if mesdemoiselles are on the list of those to be murdered. I have no doubt they will be, for after the emeute there has been about them they are almost sure to be among the first victims. But above all, find out, if you can, which vessel they are to be placed in.

"But if I cannot find that out, monsieur; if there is no arrangement made at all—though I should think there would be, for the butchers will like to have everything done in order—"

"Then I will get you to find a dozen men you can trust to volunteer to row the boats to put them on board. And you must be sure to take the boat in which they are to the lugger we have prepared."

"I will try," Adolphe said, "though I would rather cut off my hand than pull an oar to take these poor creatures out to be murdered. But I will do it, monsieur. But except for that I warrant me they will not get a sailor in Nantes to put his hand to an oar to aid their accursed work."

It was four o'clock when they arrived at Nantes. Adolphe went straight to the prison, while Harry walked along the quay. When he came abreast the centre of the town a number of sailors and fishermen were standing talking in low tones, and looking with horror at four luggers moored in a line in the centre of the river. A number of men drawn from the scum of the town were painting them white, while a strong body of troops were drawn up on the quay in readiness to put a summary stop to any demonstration of hostility on the part of the sailors. These did not indeed venture to express openly their detestation of the proceedings, but the muttered execrations and curses that rose from the little group showed how deep were their feelings.

Harry joined a little knot of three or four men who had been, with Adolphe, in the habit of greeting him when he landed.

"All is lost, you see!" one of them said in a tone of deep commiseration. "There is nothing left but vengeance—we will take that one of these days—but that is a poor consolation for you now."

"All is not quite lost," Harry said. "I have yet one hope."

"We dare not try force," one of the other men said. "They have marched three more regiments of Reds in to-day. What can we do against them without arms? I could cry to think that we are so helpless in the face of these things."

"No; I know force is useless," Harry said. "Still I have just one hope left. It is a desperate one, and I cannot tell you what it is now; but to-night, maybe, Adolphe may ask you to help us. I expect him here soon."

In half an hour Adolphe returned, and Harry at once joined him.

"I have got the news I wanted," he said. "Mesdemoiselles are to be in the first batch brought out. Boats have already been bought by the Reds to row them out, and men hired. They were forced to buy the boats, for not a man would let his craft for such a purpose. It would be accursed ever afterwards, no sailor would ever put a foot on board. The first boats will go to the ship lying lowest in the stream; then they will come back and take the next batch out to the vessel next above; and so until all are on board. There will be fifty placed on board each lugger; and I hear, monsieur, that is only the first of it, and that the drownings will go on until the prisons are cleared."

"Thank God we know that much, Adolphe! Now, in the first place, I want you to get me some tools—a sharp saw, a chisel, a large screw-driver, and half a dozen large screws; also, two beams of wood to fasten across the hatchway and keep the boards up after I have sawn through them; also, I want three bundles of cork—flat pieces will be the best if you can get them, but that doesn't matter much. I may as well have an auger too. When you go back to your house will you go in next door and ask our landlady, Mere Leflo—"

"She died three days ago," the man said.

"Then go into the house without asking, and in the farthest corner to the right-hand side of the kitchen scratch away the earth, and you will find a little bag of money. If I fail to-morrow, keep it for yourself; if I succeed, bring it to me at Pierre's. When does your lugger sail for England?"

"In three days, monsieur. I have already sounded the captain, and I think he will take you. And what shall I do next?"

"At nine o'clock this evening have a boat with the things on board half a mile below the town. Give a low whistle, and I will answer it. Wrap some flannel round the rowlocks to muffle the sound. It will be a dark night, and there's a mist rising already from the river. I do not think there's much chance of our meeting any boats near those vessels."

"No, indeed," Adolphe agreed. "It makes me shiver to look at them. There will be no boat out on the river to-night except ours. Will you not come home with me, monsieur, until it is time to start? You will need supper, for you must keep up your strength."

Harry accepted the sailor's invitation; and after partaking of a meal with Adolphe and his wife, who was informed of the attempt which was about to be made, he sat looking quietly into the fire, arranging in his mind all the details of the enterprise, uttering many a silent but fervent prayer that he might be permitted to save the lives of the two girls.

Adolphe went in and out making his preparations. At half-past eight he said, touching Harry on the shoulder: "It is time to start, monsieur. I have got the bag of money. Everything is in the boat, and I saw the men start with it. It is time for us to go and meet them."

169

Marthe burst into tears as she said good-bye to Harry.

"I shall spend all night on my knees," she said, "praying God and the Holy Virgin to aid you and save those dear angels. Here is a packet, monsieur, with some food for you to eat in the morning, and a bottle of good wine. You will want strength for your adventure."

Three or four minutes after Harry and Adolphe had gained the appointed spot they heard a low whistle on the water. Adolphe whistled in return, and in another minute a dark object appeared through the mist. They took their places in the stern, and the boat rowed quietly off again. So well were the oars muffled that Harry could hear no sound save an almost imperceptible splash each time they dipped into the water.

The town was very still and scarce a sound was heard. The awe of the horrible event which was about to take place hung over the town, and although there was drinking and exultations among the ruffians in the back lanes, even these instinctively avoided the neighbourhood of the river.

So thick was the fog that they were some little time before they found the white luggers. When they did so they rowed to that moored lowest down the stream and made fast alongside. Noiselessly the tools and beams were handed on board. Then Harry said:

"That is all, Adolphe."

"Not at all, monsieur. We are not going to leave you till the work is done. We have settled that four sets of hands can work better than one, and besides, we may hit on some idea. No one can say."

Finding it useless to remonstrate, Harry let the good fellows have their way. The men had already removed their boots, and noiselessly made their way to the hatch of the forecastle.

"Ah, it is just as well I brought a file with me," Adolphe said in a low voice, as he knelt down and felt the hatch. "It is fastened down with a staple and padlock. They are old, but you might have some trouble in breaking them. But let us see first. No, it moves. Now, a wrench all together."

As he spoke the staple came up through the rotten wood of the deck. The hatch was then lifted.

"Lower it down corner-ways into the fo'castle," Adolphe said. "We can work all the better at it there. Jacques, do you get that sail up out of the boat and throw it over the hatch. It isn't likely anyone will come out here through the fog; but it's just as well not to run any risk."

170

As soon as all were below, and the sail spread over the opening above, Adolphe produced a dark lantern from the great pocket of his fisherman's cloak, together with two or three candles. These were lit at the lantern, and the party then set to work.

Two saws had been brought on board, and a piece three feet square was cut out of the top of the hatch, leaving six inches of wood all round. Great pains were taken not to saw through the tarpaulin cover.

"Now, the next thing to do," Harry said, "is to fix the beams so as to hold the wood in its place again." Four pieces of wood, each three inches long, were screwed against the combing of the hatchway in such a position that when the beams were placed upon them they were exactly level with the top, and supported the piece cut out from the hatchway in its original position.

"That will do rarely," Adolphe said, when it was finished and the hatchway experimentally placed in its position. "Now, all you have to do is just to knock the ends of the beams off their ledges. The bit we have cut out will fall down, and you will be able easily enough to lift the hatchway from its place. It is no great weight now."

"It will do capitally," Harry agreed, "and when it floats the tarpaulin will certainly be three inches above the water. Yes, I have no fear of that part of the adventure going wrong. You don't think that it will be noticed from the shore, Adolphe?"

"Not it," Adolphe answered confidently. "Why, from the shore it will look awash with the water. No one will ever dream that there could be a soul alive underneath it. I begin to think you will do it, monsieur. At first it seemed hopeless. Now I really do think there is a chance. I should feel pretty confident if it was you and two of us who had to do it; but the difficulty will be to get the young ladies under it, and then to get them to lie quiet there."

"That is the difficulty," Harry admitted. "I am sure of the eldest. Her nerves are as good as mine; what I fear is about the younger."

"I'll tell you what, monsieur," one of the other men said; "if you take my advice you will have a piece of rope in readiness and tie it round her arms so as to prevent her struggling."

"That would be the best way," Harry agreed. "Yes, if I see she won't be calm and do as I tell her, that is what I will do."

"Now, monsieur, I will bore a couple of auger-holes through the bulkhead here so that you can see what is going on in the hold. They have got the hatch off there. I suppose it wasn't padlocked, and they will no doubt go down to bore the holes the last thing. Like enough they have bored them already, and will only have to knock out the plugs. I will just go and see anyhow. If that is so you may set your mind at rest that none of them will come down here in the morning."

So saying, taking the dark lantern he climbed up on deck, and descended the hold.

"That's it," he said when he returned; "there are six holes bored with plugs in them, so they won't be coming down here. When we go up we will put the staple into its hole again, so that it will look all right. Now, monsieur, we will just have one nip of brandy apiece out of this bottle, and then we will be off. It's just gone midnight, and it were best we should leave you to sleep for a few hours. You will want your strength in the morning, unless, of course, you would rather we stopped with you for a bit."

"No, thank you, Adolphe, I don't think I shall sleep; I shall sit and think out every detail."

"Then good night, monsieur. May the good God bless you and aid you to-morrow, and I think he will! I do think you are the bravest man I ever met."

"I am not brave for myself, Adolphe, but for them."

The three men shook hands with Harry, and one after another in husky voices gave him their good wishes. Then they ascended to the deck, put on the hatch, pressed the staple down through its holes in the deck, got into the boat, cast off the head-rope, and got out the oars.

"Mon Dieu, what courage!" one of them exclaimed. "His hand is as steady, and his voice as firm as if he were going fishing to-morrow."

"I think he will succeed;" Adolphe said, "anyhow, we will have our boat out below the bend of the river, and lend a hand to Pierre to get them out."

CHAPTER XIV

THE NOYADES

When left alone Harry blew out the other candles, but left that in the lantern burning, and threw himself down on the locker and thought over every detail of the work for the next day. As he had said, the great danger was of Virginie struggling and being too frightened to follow his instructions. Certainly he could fasten a rope round her, but even then it might be difficult to manage her. The next danger was, that other persons might cling to the hatchway. Harry felt the long knife which was concealed in his breast.

"God grant I may not have to use it!" he said. "But, if it must be, I shall not hesitate. They would simply destroy us without saving themselves, that is certain; therefore, I am justified in defending the girls, as I would against any other enemy."

He knelt down and prayed for some time. Then he replaced the piece they had cut out from the hatch, and fixed the beams beneath it, and then lay down again. He was worn out by the excitement of the day, and in spite of his anxiety about the morrow he presently fell off to sleep.

It was long before he woke. When he did so, he looked through one of the auger-holes into the hold and saw the light streaming down the open hatchway, and could tell that the sun was already up.

He ate the food which Marthe had put into his pocket just as he was starting; saw that the bundles of corks were ready at hand, and the ropes attached to them so placed that they could be fastened on in an instant. Then there was nothing to do but to wait. The time passed slowly. Presently he heard the sound of drums and bugles, and knew that the troops were taking up their positions on the quays. At last—it seemed many hours to him—he heard the splash of oars, and presently a slight shock as a boat ran alongside the lugger. Then there were voices, and the sound of feet above as persons mounted on to the deck. There was a scraping noise by the lugger's side, and immediately afterwards another bump as the second boat took the place of the first.

This, as far as Harry could hear, did not leave the lugger. There was a great hum of talking on deck, principally in women's voices, and frequently persons stepped on the hatch, and Harry congratulated himself that the beams gave a solid support to it.

Half an hour passed, as well as Harry could judge, then the boom of a cannon was heard, and immediately two men leapt down into the hold, knocked the six plugs out of their place, and climbed up on deck again. There was again the scraping noise, and Harry knew the boat had pushed off this time for good. He watched as if fascinated the six jets of water for a minute or two. Then, saying to himself, "It is time," he knocked the beams from their ledges, allowed the square of wood to fall, lifted the hatch, and pushed it off its combing, and then clambered on to the deck with the corks and ropes. There were some fifty persons on board, for the most part women and children, but with two or three men among them. They were gathered near the stern, and were apparently watching the scene ashore with astonishment. He hurried aft, having no fear that at this distance from the shore his figure would be recognized from the rest, and, if it were, it mattered not. Two or three turned round as the supposed sailor came aft, exclaiming:

"What does this mean? Why are we put here on board these white ships? What are they going to do with us?"

"Alas, ladies," he said, "they have put you here to die; they have bored holes in the ships' bottoms, and in a few minutes they will sink. It is a wholesale execution."

As he began to speak one of the ladies in the stern pushed her way through the rest.

"Oh, Harry, is it you!" she exclaimed as he finished. "Is it true, are we to die together?"

"We are in God's hands, Jeanne, but there is hope yet. Bring Virginie forward with me."

At Harry's first words a panic had seized all around; one or two ran to the hatchway and looked down into the hold, and screamed out that the water was rushing in; then some cried to the distant crowd to send to save them; others ran up and down as if demented; while some threw themselves on their knees. But the panic soon passed away; all had for weeks looked death in the face, and though the unexpected form in which it appeared had for the moment shaken them, they soon recovered. Mothers clasped their daughters to their breasts for a last farewell, and then all with bowed heads kneeled and listened in silence to an old man who began to pray aloud.

Jeanne, without another word, had taken Virginie's hands and accompanied Harry forward to the fore part of the deck.

"Jeanne, I am going to try to save you and Virginie, but everything depends upon your being cool and brave. I need not urge you, because I am sure of you. Virginie, will you try to be so for Jeanne's sake and your own? If you do not we must all die together."

"What are we to do, Harry?" Jeanne said steadily, while Virginie clung to her sister sobbing bitterly.

"Fasten this bundle of corks between Virginie's shoulders high up-yes, there."

While Jeanne was doing this, Harry fastened a rope to a ring in the side of the hatch, then he tied the corks on to Jeanne's shoulders, and adjusted the third bundle to his own. "Now, Jeanne," he said, "I will tell you what we are going to do. You see this hatch; when the vessel sinks it will float, and we must float on our backs with our faces underneath it so that it will hide us from the sight of the wretches on shore; and even if they put out in boats to kill any who may be swimming or clinging to spars, they will not suspect that there is anyone under this. We may not succeed; an accident may betray us, but there is a possibility. At anyrate, dear, we shall live or die together."

"I am content," Jeanne said quietly.

"You know, Jeanne," Harry said, putting his hands on the girl's shoulders, "that I love you; I should never have told you so until I got you home if it hadn't been for this; but though I have never said it, you know I love you."

"I know, Harry, and I love you too with all my heart; so much that I can feel almost happy that we are going to die together. We are affianced now, dear, come what will." And she lifted her face to his.

He gave her one long kiss, then there was a crash. Impatient at the length of time the vessels were in sinking, those ashore had opened fire with cannons upon them, and the shot had struck the lugger just above the water.

With a little cry Virginie fell senseless on the deck.

"That's the best thing that could have happened," Harry said as Jeanne stooped over her sister. "Lie down on the deck, dear, or you may be struck; they are firing with muskets now. I am going to lie down too," he said in answer to her look, "but I shall first twist this cord round Virginie so as to keep her arms by her side, otherwise when the water touches her she may come to her senses and struggle. That's all right."

Then he lay down on the deck between the girls with his head against the hatch, and holding the rope.

175

"Put your head on my shoulder, Jeanne, and I will put my arm round you; I will hold Virginie the same way the other side. Hold tight by me for a moment as we sink, I may have to use my arms to get the hatch over our faces. Do not breathe while you are under the water, for we shall, no doubt, go down with the lugger, although I shall try to keep you afloat; when you are under the hatch you will find you will float with your mouth well out of the water, and will be able to breathe, the corks will keep you up."

"I understand, Harry; now let us pray until the time comes."

Shot after shot struck the lugger, then Harry felt her give a sudden lurch. There was a wild cry and the next moment she went down stern first. She was so nearly even with the water when she sank, that there was less downward suck than Harry had expected, and striking out with his feet his head was soon above the surface. The cord had kept the hatch within a couple of feet of him, and with some difficulty, owing to the buoyancy of the corks, he thrust himself and the girls under it. The tarpaulin was old and rotten, and the light penetrated in several places, and Harry could see that, in the position in which they were lying, the faces of both girls were above the water.

It was useless to speak for their ears were submerged; but a slight motion from Jeanne responded to a pressure of his arm, and he knew that she was sensible although she had not made the slightest motion from the moment the vessel sank. Virginie had not, as he feared would be the case, recovered her senses with the shock of the immersion, but lay insensible on his shoulder. He could see by the movement of Jeanne's lips that she was praying, and he too thanked God that He had given success to the plan so far, and prayed for protection to the end.

With every minute that passed, his hopes rose; everything had answered beyond his expectation. The other victims had apparently not even noticed what he was doing, and therefore had not, as he feared might be the case, interfered with his preparations, nor had any of them striven to gain a hold on the hatchway. The sinking of the vessels, and the tearing up of the water by the shot, would render the surface disturbed and broken, and decrease the chances of the floating hatch attracting attention. After ten minutes had passed he felt certain that they must be below the point where the troops were assembled.

The tide was running out strong, for the time for the massacre had been fixed at an hour which would ensure the bodies being swept down to sea. Half an hour would, he thought, take them past the bend, where their friends would be waiting for them. The time seemed endless, for although Harry felt the coldness of the water but little for himself, he knew that it must be trying indeed for Jeanne. As far as he could see her face it was as white as her sister's; but he had hold of one of her hands now, and knew that she was still conscious.

At last he heard the sound of oars. It might not be one of the friendly boats; but the probability was that it was one or other of them. Had they seen any other fisherman's boat near the point they would have rowed high up so as to intercept the hatch before it reached the stranger. Harry could not hear voices; for although the water had conveyed the sound of the oars a considerable distance, he could hear no sound in the air.

The oars came nearer and nearer, and by the quickness with which the strokes followed each other he knew that two boats were at hand. Then the hatch was suddenly lifted, and as Harry raised his head above water there was a loud cheer, and he saw Adolphe and Pierre, one on each side, stretch out their arms to him. The girls were first lifted into Pierre's boat, for Jeanne was as incapable of movement as her sister, then Harry was dragged in, the rough sailors shaking his hand and patting him on the shoulder, while the tears ran down their cheeks.

"Give them some hot brandy and water," were his first words. Pierre had a kettle boiling. A glass of hot liquor was placed to Jeanne's lips.

At first she could not swallow, but after a few drops had passed her lips she was able to take a sip, and would then have stopped, but Harry insisted upon her drinking the whole contents of the glass.

"You must do as you are told, Jeanne," he said in her ear. "You belong to me now, you know. It can do you no harm chilled as you are, and may save you from illness."

In the meantime Pierre had poured several spoonfuls of nearly neat brandy between Virginie's lips. Adolphe, and one of the men with him, had changed over into Pierre's boat, and were rowing lustily down the river.

As soon as Jeanne was able to sit up she began to chafe one of Virginie's hands, while Harry took the other.

"Take off her shoes, Pierre, and soak a swab with the hot water and put it to her feet."

But with all these efforts it was not until they were close to Pierre's village that Virginie opened her eyes. When they arrived at the little causeway the two girls were wrapped up in the peasants cloaks which Pierre had brought with him. Jeanne took Harry's arm, while Adolphe lifted Virginie and carried her up. Henriette was standing at the door as Jeanne staggered in with Harry.

"That is right, mademoiselle. Thank God who has brought you straight through the danger. Now, do not stop a moment, but come in here and get into bed, it is all ready for you. The blankets have been before the fire until the moment you landed; they will soon give you warmth. Hurry in, mademoiselle; I will undress your sister. And do you, Monsieur Sandwith, hurry up to the loft and get on dry clothes."

Harry soon rejoined the party in the kitchen. The strong glass of hot spirits he had drunk had sent the blood quickly through his veins, and he felt in a glow of warmth.

"Now," he said, "my friends, I can thank you all for the aid you have given us. It is to you we owe our lives, for without your aid I never should have succeeded."

"Say nothing about it, monsieur. We are happy to have saved such a brave young man, and to have rescued two victims from those monsters."

"Do you think there is any danger of anyone here taking the news of our landing to the town?" Harry asked. "They must have seen us come up to the cottage."

"There is no fear," Pierre said confidently. "There is not a man or woman here who would not tear the scelerats to pieces if they had the chance. Have they not spoiled our market by killing all our best customers? And now how are we to earn our living, I should like to know? Why, not even the poorest beggar in Nantes would buy fish out of the river for months after this. No, you need have no fear of them. They may guess who you are, but it is no business of theirs, and they will hold their tongues."

"At anyrate, Pierre, you had better distribute a few crowns among them, to help them live till the fishing is good again."

"That I will do, monsieur. It is quite safe; but it is as well to make it even safer."

In half an hour Pierre's wife came in from the inner room, and said that both girls were sound asleep.

"Now, Adolphe, it only remains for you to arrange with your captain for our passage."

"That I will do this afternoon," Adolphe said confidently. "Consider it as good as done."

After Adolphe had started for the town, Harry was persuaded

by Pierre to lie down for a bit; but he soon gave up the idea of going to sleep. His brain was in a whirl from the events of the last twenty-four hours, and above all he felt so brimming over with happiness that the girls had been saved that he soon found it impossible to lie still. He therefore went down again and joined Pierre, who was doing some repairs to his boat.

"It is no use my trying to sleep, Pierre. I am too delighted that everything has turned out right. I want to break out into shouting and singing."

"I can understand, monsieur. Yes, yes. After great trouble great joy. I know it myself. I was once adrift in a boat for three weeks. I was on a voyage to Guadaloupe when we were blown in a hurricane on a 'key,' as they call the low sandy islands out there. It was in fact no more than a sand-bank. More than half of those on board were drowned; but eight of us got ashore, and we managed to haul up a woman with her child of two years old in her arms.

"We thought at first the mother was dead, but she came round. The ship went to pieces and we saved nothing. The currents swept everything away but a boat, which had been thrown up beyond the reach of the waves. For two days we had no food or water, and suffered terribly, for the sun had shone down straight on our heads, and we envied those who had died at once. The woman set us a good example. She spent her time tending her child and praying to God; and we sailors, who are rough, you know—but who know that God protects us, and never go for a long voyage without going to the chapel and paying for a mass for our safety—we prayed too, and the third morning there were three turtles asleep on the shore. We turned them over on their backs, and there was meat for us for a long time.

"We killed one and drank the blood, and ate our first meal raw. Then we cut up the rest of the flesh and hung it up in the sun to dry. That very night we saw the clouds banking up, and knew it was going to rain.

"'Now,' our mate said, 'if we had but a barrel we could catch water and start in our boat, but without that the water will last only a day or two; for if we kill all the turtles and fill their shells, it will evaporate in a day under this hot sun, and it may be weeks before there is rain again, and we might as well have died at once.

"'For shame,' the woman said. 'You are doubting the good God again, after he has saved your life and has sent you food and is now going to send you water. Do you think he has done all this for nothing? There must be some way out of the difficulty if we could but think of it.'

"She sat looking at the turtle for two or three minutes, and then said:

"'It is easy. Why have you not thought of it? See there. Cut off one of their heads, and then you can get your arm in, if you take the biggest. Then cut out all the meat and bones piece by piece, and there is a great bottle which will hold gallons.'

"We shouted for joy, for it was as she had said, though I am sure none of us would ever have thought of it if God had not given her the idea. We soon set to work and got the shell ready. The rain storm came quickly. We had turned the boat over, the oars had been washed away, but the mast and sail were lashed to the thwarts. We made a little hollow in the sand and stretched out the sail, and by the time this was done and the men were ready with the turtle-shell the rain came. When it rains in those parts it comes down in bucketfuls, and we soon had enough in the sail to drink our fill and to fill up the turtle-shell to the top.

"The next morning we got the boat afloat, put the other turtle in, with our stock of dried flesh and our shell of water, and set sail. But our luck seemed gone. We lay for days scarce moving through the water, with the sail hanging idle and the sun blazing down upon us. We had not been careful enough of the water at first, making sure that in three or four days we should sight land, and when after three days we put ourselves on short rations, there was scarce a gallon of water left.

"It was a week after that before we saw a sail. Two of the men had jumped overboard raving mad, the rest were lying well-nigh senseless in the bottom of the boat. Only the woman was sitting up, holding her child in her arms. She was very weak, too; but she had never complained, never doubted for a moment. Her eyes went from the child's face over the sea to look for the help she felt would come, and back again, and at last she said quite quiet and natural:

"'There is the ship. I knew it must come to-day, for my child could not live through another night.'

"We thought she was dreaming or off her head. But one of us made a shift to stand up and look, and when he screamed out 'A sail! A sail!' two of us who were strong enough looked out also. There she was and sailing, as we could soon see, on a line as directly for us as if they had our bearings, and had been sent to fetch us.

"It was not until evening that she came up, though she was bringing a light breeze along with her. And when we were lifted on to her deck, and had water held to our lips, and knew that we were safe, we felt, I expect, much the same as you do now, monsieur, that it was the good God himself who had assuredly saved us from death. That was my last voyage, for Henriette was waiting for me at home, and I had promised her that after we had gone to church together I would go no more to distant countries, but would settle down here as a fisherman."

"That was a narrow escape indeed, Pierre," Harry said as he worked away with the tar brush. "That idea of the turtle was a splendid one, and you may well say that God put it into the woman's head, for without it you could never have lived till the ship found you."

In the meantime Henriette had made her rounds to the cottage to see what remarks had been made as to the coming of her visitors. She saw that everyone had guessed that the girls who had been picked up by Pierre were victims of the massacre, but no one supposed that it was the result of intention.

"Ah, Mere Gounard, but your good man was fortunate to-day," one of the women said. "My man did not go out. We heard what was doing at Nantes, and he had not the heart to go; besides, who would buy fish caught to-day? If he had thought of it he would have gone too, and perhaps he would have picked up somebody, as you have done. Poor things, what an escape for them!"

"It is wonderful that they have come round," Henriette said. "It was lucky my husband had some brandy in the boat. He thought for a time he would never bring the youngest round. They are only young girls. What harm could they have done that those monsters at Nantes should try to murder them? There is no fear, I hope, that any in the village will say a word about it."

"What!" the woman said indignantly. "Do you think that anyone here would betray a comrade to the Reds? Why, we would tear him to pieces."

"No, no," Henriette said; "I never thought for a moment that anyone would do it intentionally; but the boys might let slip a word carelessly which might bring them down upon us."

"We will take care of that," the woman said. "Make your mind easy. Not a soul outside the village will ever know of it."

"And," Henriette added, "one of them has some money hidden upon her, and she told me just before I came out, when I was saying that the village would have a bad time now the fishing was spoiled— that as she hoped to cross to England in a few days, and would have no need of the money, for it seems that she can get plenty over there, she will give five crowns to each house in the village as a thank-offering."

"Well, that is not to be despised," the woman said. "We shall have a hard time of it for a bit, and that will carry us on through it. You are sure she can spare it; because we would rather starve than take it if she cannot."

Henriette assured her that her visitor said she could afford it well.

"Well, then, it's a lucky day for the village, Mere Gounard, that your husband picked them up."

"Well, I will go back now," Henriette said. "Will you go round the village and tell the others about silencing the children? I must get some broth ready by the time these poor creatures wake."

The next morning Jeanne appeared at breakfast in her dress as a fish-girl, but few words were spoken between her and Harry, for the fisherman and his wife were present.

"How is Virginie?" he asked.

"She's better, but she is weak and languid, so I told her she must stop in bed for to-day. Do not look anxious. I have no doubt that she will be well enough to be up to-morrow. She has been sleeping ever since she went to bed yesterday, and when she woke she had a basin of broth. I think by to-morrow she will be well enough to get up. But it will be some time before she is herself again. It is a terrible strain for her to have gone through, but she was very brave all the time we were in prison. She had such confidence in you, she felt sure that you would manage somehow to rescue us."

After breakfast Jeanne strolled down with Harry to the river-side.

"I feel strange with you, Harry," she said. "Before you seemed almost like a brother, and now it is so different."

"Yes; but happier?" Harry asked gently.

"Oh, so much happier, Harry! But there is one thing I want to tell you. It might seem strange to you that I should tell you I loved you on my own account without your speaking to the head of the family."

"But there was no time for that, Jeanne," Harry said smiling.

"No," Jeanne said simply. "I suppose it would have been the same anyhow; but I want to tell you, Harry, that in the first letter which she sent me when she was in prison, Marie told me, that as she might not see me again, she thought it right I should know that our father and mother had told her that night we left home that they thought I cared for you. You didn't think so, did you, Harry?" she broke off with a vivid blush. "You did not think I cared for you before you cared for me?"

"No, indeed, Jeanne," he said earnestly. "It never entered my mind. You see, dear, up to the beginning of that time I only felt as a boy, and in England lads of eighteen or nineteen seldom think about such things at all. It was only afterwards, when somehow the danger and the anxiety seemed to make a man of me, when I saw how brave and thoughtful and unselfish you were, that I knew I loved you, and felt that if you could some day love me, I should be the happiest fellow alive. Before that I thought of you as a dear little girl who inclined to make rather too much of me because of that dog business. And did you really care for me then?"

"I never thought of it in that way, Harry, any more than you did, but I know now that my mother was right, and that I loved you all along without knowing it. My dear father and mother told Marie that they thought I was fond of you, and that, if at any time you should get fond of me too and ask for my hand, they gave their approval beforehand, for they were sure that you would make me happy.

"So they told Marie and Ernest, who, if ill came to them, would be the heads of the family, that I had their consent to marry you. It makes me happy to know this, Harry."

"I am very glad, too, dear," Harry said earnestly.

"It is very satisfactory for you, and it is very pleasant to me to know that they were ready to trust you to me. Ah!" he said suddenly, "that was what was in the letter. I wondered a little at the time, for somehow after that, Jeanne, you were a little different with me. I thought at first I might somehow have offended you. But I did not think that long," he went on, as Jeanne uttered an indignant exclamation, "because if anything offended you, you always spoke out frankly. Still I wondered over it for some time, and certainly I was never near guessing the truth."

"I could not help being a little different," Jeanne said shyly. "I had never thought of it before, and though I am sure it made me happy, I could not feel quite the same with you, especially as I knew that you never thought of me like that."

"But you thought of me so afterwards, Jeanne?"

"Sometimes just for a moment, but I tried not to think of it, Harry. We were so strangely placed, and it made it easier for you to be a brother, and I felt sure you would not speak till we were safely in England, and I was in Ernest's care. But," she said with a little laugh, "you were nearly speaking that evening in the cottage when you felt so despairing."

"Very nearly, Jeanne; I did so want comfort."

And so they talked happily together for an hour.

"I wonder Pierre does not come down to his boat," Harry said at last. "There were several more things wanting doing to it. Why, there he is calling. Surely it can never be dinner-time; but that's what he says. It doesn't seem an hour since breakfast."

Jeanne hurried on into the hut.

"Why, Pierre," Harry said to the fisherman, who was waiting outside for him, "I thought you were going on with your boat."

"So I was, monsieur, but Henriette told me I should be in the way."

"In the way, Pierre!" Harry repeated in surprise.

"Ah, monsieur," Pierre said with a twinkle in his eye, "you have been deceiving us. My wife saw it in a moment when the young lady came to breakfast.

"'Brother!' she said to me when you went out; 'don't tell me! Monsieur is the young lady's lover. Brother and sister don't look at each other like that. Why, one could see it with half an eye.'

"Your wife is right, Pierre; mademoiselle is my fiance. I am really an Englishman. She and her sister had their old nurse with them, till the latter died some three weeks since; but I have always been called their brother, because it made it easier for her."

"Quite right, monsieur; but my wife and I are glad to see that it is otherwise, and that, after all you have risked for that pretty creature, you are going to be happy together. My wife was not surprised. Women are sharper than men in these matters, and she said to me, when she heard what you were going to do to save them, 'I would wager, Pierre, that one of these mesdemoiselles is not monsieur's sister. Men will do a great deal for their sister, but I never heard of a man throwing away his life as he is going to do on the mere chance of saving one.'"

"I should have done just the same had it been one of my sisters," Harry said a little indignantly.

"Perhaps you would, monsieur, I do not say no," the fisherman said, shaking his head; "but brothers do not often do so."

A stop was put to the conversation by Henriette putting her head outside the door and demanding angrily what they were stopping talking there for when the fish was getting cold.

In the evening Adolphe and his wife came in.

"Ah, mademoiselle," the woman said as she embraced Jeanne with tears in her eyes, "how thankful I am to see you again! I never thought I should do so. My heart almost stopped beating yesterday when I heard the guns. I and my little one were on our knees praying to the good God for the dear lady who had saved her life. Adolphe had spoken hopefully, but it hardly seemed to me that it could be, and when he brought back the news that he had left you all safely here, I could hardly believe it was true."

"And I must thank you also, mademoiselle," Adolphe said, "for saving the life of my little one. I never expected to see her alive again, and when the lugger made fast to the wharf I was afraid to go home, and I hung about till Marthe had heard we were in and came down to me with Julie in her arms, looking almost herself again. Ah, mademoiselle, you cannot tell how glad I was when she told me that there was a way of paying some part of my debt to you."

"You have been able to pay more than your debt," Jeanne said gently; "if I saved one life you have helped to save three."

"No, we shall be only quits, mademoiselle, for what would Marthe's life and mine be worth if the child had died?

"There are fresh notices stuck up," he went on, "warning all masters of ships, fishermen, and others, against taking passengers on board, and saying that the penalty of assisting the enemies of France to escape from justice is death."

"That is rather serious," Harry said.

"It is nothing," Adolphe replied confidently. "After yesterday's work there is not a sailor or fisherman in the port but would do all he could to help people to escape from the hands of the butchers, and once on board, it will help you. You may be sure the sailors will do their best to run away if they can, or to hide any on board, should they be overhauled, now they know that they will be guillotined if anyone is found. However, our captain has made the agreement, and he is a man of his word; besides, he hates the Reds. I have been helping ship the casks to-day, and we have stowed them so as to leave space into which your sisters can crawl and the entrance be stopped up with casks, if we should be overhauled. As for you, monsieur, you will pass anywhere as one of the crew, and we have arranged that one of the men shall at the last moment stay behind, so that the number will be right, and you will answer to his name. We have thought matters over, you see, and I can tell you that the captain does it more because he hates the Reds than for the money. The day before, he would give me no answer. He said he thought the risk was too great; but when I saw him last night he was a different man altogether. His face was as white as a sheet, and his eyes seemed on fire, and he said, 'I will take your friends, Adolphe. I would take them without a penny. I should never sleep again if, owing to me, they fell into the hands of these monsters.' So you see he is in it heart and soul."

After half an hour's talk Adolphe and Marthe took their leave. Both refused the reward which Harry had promised, but Harry insisted, and at last Jeanne said:

"You can refuse for yourselves, but you will make me unhappy if you do not take it. Put it by for Julie; it will help swell her dot when she marries, and will set her husband up in a good fishing-boat if she takes to a sailor."

So it was arranged, and Adolphe and his wife went off invoking blessings on the heads of the fugitives. At daybreak the party took their places in the boat with the fishermen. Virginie was still weak, but was able to walk with Harry's help. Half an hour later a lugger was seen coming down with the wind and tide. She carried a small white flag flying on the mizzen.

"That is her," the fisherman said; "that is the signal."

He rowed out into the middle of the river. In a few minutes the lugger came dashing along, her course took her within a few feet of the boat, a rope was thrown, and in an instant the boat was tearing through the water alongside her. Half a dozen hands were stretched out, the girls and Harry sprang on board, the rope was cast off, and the fisherman, with a cheery "God speed you," put out his oars again and rowed to shore.

CHAPTER XV

ENGLAND

"Go below, mesdemoiselles," the captain of the lugger said as soon as they had put foot on the deck. "If anyone on the shore were to see us as we ran down, and notice women on deck, he would think it strange. At anyrate it's best to be on the safe side."

So saying he led the way to his cabin below.

"It is a rough place, mesdemoiselles," he said, removing his cap, "but it is better than the prisons at Nantes. I am sorry to say that when we get down near the forts I shall have to ask you to hide down below the casks. I heard last night that in future every boat going out of the river, even if it is only a fishing-boat, is to be searched. But you needn't be afraid; we have constructed a hiding-place, where they will never find you unless they unloaded the whole lugger, and that there is no chance of their doing."

"We do not mind where we hide, captain," Jeanne said. "We have been hiding for the last six months, and we are indeed grateful to you for having consented to take us with you."

"I hope that you will not be the last that the Trois Freres will carry across," the captain said. "Whatever be the risk, in future I will take any fugitives who wish to escape to England. At first I was against the government, for I thought the people were taxed too heavily, and that if we did away with the nobles things would be better for those who work for their living, but I never bargained for bloodshed and murder, and that affair I saw yesterday has sickened me altogether; and fond as I am of the Trois Freres, I would myself bore holes in her and sink her if I had Carrier and the whole of his murderous gang securely fastened below hatches. This cabin is at your disposal, mesdemoiselles, during the voyage, and I trust you will make yourselves as comfortable as you can. Ah, here is the boy with coffee. Now, if you will permit me, I will go on deck and look after her course."

In the meantime Harry was chatting with Adolphe, who introduced him to the crew, whom he had already told of the services Jeanne had rendered, and as several of them lived in the same street they too had heard from their wives of the young woman who lodged with Mere Leflo, and had done so much for those who were suffering. He was therefore cordially received by the sailors, to each of whom the captain had already promised double pay for the voyage if they got through safely.

"You will remember," Adolphe said, "that you are Andre Leboeuf. Andre had to make a cold swim of it this morning, for there was the commissary on the wharf when we started, and he had the captain's list of the crew, and saw that each man was on board and searched high and low to see that there was no one else. So Andre, instead of slipping off home again, had to go with us. When we were out of sight of the town the captain steered as near the bank as he could and Andre jumped over and swam ashore. It is all the better as it has turned out, because the commissary signed the list of the crew and put a seal to it."

In four hours the Trois Freres was approaching the forts at the mouth of the river, and the captain came down to the cabin, in which Harry was chatting with the two girls.

"Now, mesdemoiselles," he said, "it is time for you to go to your hiding-place, for it will take us nearly half an hour to close it up again. As soon as the Reds have left us we will let you out."

The hatch was lifted and they descended into the hold of the vessel, which was full of kegs to within three feet of the deck. The captain carried a lantern.

"Please follow me, mesdemoiselles, you must crawl along here."

The girls followed him until they were close to the bulkhead dividing the hold from the forecastle. Two feet from this there was a vacant space.

"Now, mesdemoiselles, if you will give me your hands I will lower you down here. Do not be afraid—your feet will touch the bottom; and I have had some hay put there for you to sit upon. Adolphe, you had better go down first with that lantern of yours to receive them."

The girls were lowered down and found themselves in a space of five feet long and two feet wide. One side was formed by the bulkhead, on the other there were kegs. Four feet from the bottom a beam of wood had been nailed against the bulkhead. The captain now handed down to Adolphe some short beams; these he fixed with one end resting on the beam, the other in a space between the kegs.

"This is to form the roof, mesdemoiselles," he said. "I am going up now, and then we shall place three tiers of kegs on these beams, which will fill it up level with the rest above. I think you will have plenty of air, for it can get down between the casks, and the captain will leave the hatchway open. Are you comfortable?"

"Quite," Jeanne said firmly, but Virginie did not answer; the thought of being shut up down there in the dark was terrible to her.

However, the warm, steady pressure of Jeanne's hand reassured her, and she kept her fears to herself. The kegs were lowered into their places, and all was made smooth just as one of the men called down the hatchway to the captain:

"There is a gunboat coming out from the port, captain."

After a last look round the captain sprang on to the deck and ordered the sails to be lowered, and in a few minutes the gunboat ran alongside.

"Show me your papers," an officer said as he leaped on board followed by half a dozen sailors. The captain went down into his cabin and brought up the papers.

"That is all right," the officer said glancing at them; "now, where is the list of your crew?"

"This is it," the captain said taking it from his pocket; "a commissary at Nantes went through them on starting and placed his seal to it, as you see."

"Form the men up, and let them answer to their names," the officer said. The men formed in line and the officer read out the names; Harry answering for Andre Leboeuf. "That is all right, so far," the officer said. "Now, sir, I must, according to my orders, search your vessel to see that no one is concealed there."

"By all means," the captain said, "you will find the Trois Freres carries nothing contraband except her cargo. I have already taken off the hatch, as you see, in order to save time."

The forecastles and cabin were first searched closely. Several of the sailors then descended into the hold. Two lanterns were handed down to them.

"It looks all clear, sir," one of the sailors said to their officer. The latter leaped down on to the kegs and looked round.

"Yes, it looks all right, but you had better shift some of the kegs and see that all is solid."

Some of the kegs were moved from their position, and in a few places some of the second tier were also lifted. The officer himself superintended the search.

"I think I can let you go on now, Captain Grignaud," he said. "Your men can stow the cargo again. A good voyage to you, and may you meet with no English cruisers by the way."

The captain at once gave orders for the sails to be run up again, and by the time the officer and his men had climbed over the bulwarks into the gunboat the Trois Freres had already way upon her. The captain then gave the order for the men to go below and stow the casks again. Adolphe and Harry were the first to leap down, and before the vessels were two hundred yards apart they had removed the two uppermost tiers of kegs next to the bulkhead, and were able to speak to the girls.

"Are you all right down there, Jeanne?" Harry asked.

"Yes, quite right, Harry, though the air is rather close. Virginie has fainted; she was frightened when she heard them moving the kegs just over our heads; but she will come round as soon as you get her on deck."

The last tier was removed, and Harry lowered himself into the hold; he and Jeanne raised Virginie until Adolphe and one of the other sailors could reach her. Jeanne was lifted on to the cross beams, and was soon beside her sister, and Harry quickly clambered up.

"They must not come on deck yet," the captain said, speaking down the hatchway. "We are too close to the gunboat, and from the forts with their glasses they can see what is passing on our deck. Don't replace the kegs over the hole again, Adolphe; we may be overhauled again, and had better leave it open in case of emergencies."

Virginie was carried under the open hatchway; some water was handed down to Jeanne, who sprinkled it on her face, and this with the fresh air speedily brought her round. When the lugger was a mile below the forts, the captain said that they could now safely come up, and they were soon in possession of the cabin again. Before evening the lugger was out of sight of land. The wind was blowing freshly, and she raced along leaving a broad track of foam behind her. The captain and crew were in high spirits at having succeeded in carrying off the fugitives from under the noses of their enemies, and at the progress the lugger was making.

"We shall not be far from the coast of England by to-morrow night," the captain said to Harry, "that is if we have the luck to avoid meeting any of the English cruisers. We don't care much for the revenue cutters, for there is not one of them that can overhaul the Trois Freres in a wind like this. They have all had more than one try, but we can laugh at them; but it would be a different thing if we fell in with one of the Channel cruisers; in a light wind we could keep away from them too, but with a brisk wind like this we should have no chance with them; they carry too much sail for us. There is the boy carrying in the supper to your sisters; with their permission, you and I will sup with them."

The captain sent in a polite message to the girls, and on the receipt of the answer that they would be very pleased to have the captain's company, he and Harry went down. The meal was an excellent one, but the girls ate but little, for they were both beginning to feel the effects of the motion of the vessel, for they had, when once fairly at sea, kept on deck. The captain perceiving that they ate but little proposed to Harry that coffee should be served on deck, so that the ladies might at once lie down for the night.

"Now, captain," Harry said as the skipper lit his pipe, "I daresay you would like to hear how we came to be fugitives on board your ship."

"If you have no obligation to tell me, I should indeed," the captain replied; "I have been wondering all day how you young people escaped the search for suspects so long, and how you came to be at Nantes, where, as Adolphe tells me, your sister was an angel among the poor, and that you yourself were a member of the Revolutionary Committee; that seemed to me the most extraordinary of all, but I wouldn't ask any questions until you yourself volunteered to enlighten me."

Harry thereupon related the whole story of their adventures, concealing only the fact that the girls were not his sisters; as it was less awkward for Jeanne that this relationship should be supposed to exist.

"Sapriste, your adventures have been marvellous, monsieur, and I congratulate you heartily. You have a rare head and courage, and yet you cannot be above twenty."

"I am just nineteen," Harry replied.

"Just nineteen, and you succeeded in getting your friend safely out of that mob of scoundrels in the Abbaye, got your elder sister out of La Force, you fooled Robespierre and the Revolutionists in Nantes, and you carried those two girls safely through France, rescued them from the white lugger, and got them on board the Trois Freres! It sounds like a miracle."

"The getting them on board the Trois Freres was, you must remember, my sister's work. I had failed and was in despair. Suspicions were already aroused, and we should assuredly have been arrested if it had not been that she had won the heart of Adolphe's wife by nursing her child in its illness."

"That is so," the captain agreed; "and they must have good courage too that they didn't betray themselves all that time. And now I tell you what I will do, monsieur. If you will write a letter to your sister in Paris, saying that you and the other two have reached England in safety, I will when I return send it by sure hand to Paris. To make all safe you had better send it to the people she is staying with, and word it so that no one will understand it if they were to read it. Say, for example:

"'My dear Sister, You will be glad to hear that the consignment

191

of lace has been safely landed in England,' Then you can go on saying that 'your mother is better, and that you expect to be married soon, as you have made a good profit out of the lace,' and so on; and just sign your name—'Your brother Henri.'

"I can trust the man who will deliver it in Paris, but it is just as well always to be on the safe side. If your letter is opened and read, anyone will suppose that it is written by a sailor belonging to one of the Nantes luggers."

Harry thanked the captain warmly for the offer, and said that the letter would indeed be an immense comfort to his sister and friend.

"I will tell the man that he is to ask if there is any answer," the captain said. "And if your sister is as sharp as you are she will write the same sort of letter, and I will bring it across with me to England the first voyage I make after I get it."

Harry slept down in the forecastle with the crew, the captain keeping on deck all night. He was awoke by an order shouted down the forecastle for all hands to come on deck; and hurrying up with the rest found that the sun had just risen. The day was beautifully fine, and to Harry's surprise he found that those on deck had already lowered the great lugsails.

"What is it, captain?" he asked.

"There is a sail there I don't like," the captain said. "If I am not mistaken that is an English frigate."

There were several sails in sight, but the one to which the captain pointed was crossing ahead of the lugger. Her hull could not be seen, and indeed from the deck only her topsails and royals were visible above the water.

"I hope she will not see us," the captain said. "We are low in the water, and these stump masts could not be seen at that distance even by a look-out at the mast-head.

"We are already somewhat astern of her, and every minute will take her further away. If she does not see us in a quarter of an hour, we shall be safe. If she does, there is nothing for it but to run back towards the French coast. We should have such a long start that with this wind she would never catch us. But she may fire her guns and bring another cruiser down upon us and cut us off. There are a dozen of them watching on different parts of the coast."

Harry kept his eye anxiously upon the ship, but she sailed steadily on; and in half an hour the sails were again hoisted and the Trois Freres proceeded on her way. She passed comparatively near several merchantmen, but these paid no attention to her. She was too small for a privateer, and her object and destination were easily guessed at. The girls soon came on deck, and the captain had some cushions placed for them under shelter of the bulwark; for although the sun was shining brightly the wind was keen and piercing.

"Are we beyond danger?" was Virginie's first question as Harry took his seat by her.

"Beyond all danger of being overtaken—that is to say, beyond all danger of meeting a French vessel-of-war. They very seldom venture to show themselves many miles from port, except, of course, as a fleet; for single vessels would soon get picked up by our cruisers. Yes, I think we are quite out of danger. There is only one chance against us."

"And what is that, Harry?" Jeanne asked.

"It is not a serious one," Harry replied; "it is only that we may be chased by English revenue cutters and forced to run off from the English coast again. But even then we should soon return. Besides, I have no doubt the captain would let us have a boat, so that we could be picked up by the cutter in pursuit of us."

"I don't think that would be a good plan," Jeanne said; "because they might not stop to pick us up, and then we might have a long way to reach the shore. No, I think it will be better to stay on board, Harry; for, as you say, if she does have to run away for a time, she is sure to come back again to unload her cargo. But of course do whatever you think best."

"I think your view is the best, Jeanne. However, I hope the opportunity will not occur, and that the Trois Freres will run her cargo without interference. The captain tells me he is making for a point on the Dorsetshire coast, and that he is expected. Of course he could not say the exact day he would be here. But he told them the day on which, if he could get his cargo on board, he should sail, and they will be looking out for him."

Before sunset the English coast was visible.

"We could not have timed it better," the captain said. "It will be getting dark before they can make us out even from the cliffs."

Every sail was now scrutinized by the captain through his glass, but he saw nothing that looked suspicious. At nine o'clock in the evening the lugger was within three miles of the coast.

"Get ready the signal lanterns," the captain ordered. And a few minutes later three lanterns were hoisted, one above the other. Almost immediately two lights were shown in a line on top of the cliff.

"There is our answer," the captain said. "There is nothing to be done to-night. That means 'The revenue men are on the look-out; come back to-morrow night.'"

"But they are always on the look-out, are they not?" Harry asked.

"Yes," the captain said; "but when our friends on shore know we are coming they try to throw them off the scent. It will be whispered about to-morrow that a run is likely to be made ten miles along the coast, and they will take care that this comes to the ears of the revenue officer. Then to-morrow evening after dusk a fishing-boat will go out and show some lights two miles off shore at the point named, and a rocket will be sent up from the cliff. That will convince them that the news is true, and the revenue officers will hurry away in that direction with every man they can get together. Then we shall run here and land our cargo. There will be plenty of carts waiting for us, and before the revenue men are back the kegs will be stowed safely away miles inland. Of course things go wrong sometimes and the revenue officers are not to be fooled, but in nine cases out of ten we manage to run our cargoes without a shot being fired. Now I must get off shore again."

The orders were given, and the Trois Freres was soon running out to sea. They stood far out and then lowered the sails and drifted until late in the afternoon, when they again made sail for the land. At ten o'clock the signal lights were again exhibited, and this time the answer was made by one light low down by the water's edge.

"The coast is clear," the captain said, rubbing his hands. "We'll take her in as close as she will go, the less distance there is to row the better."

The Trois Freres was run on until within a hundred yards of the shore, then a light anchor was dropped. The two boats had already been lowered and were towed alongside, and the work of transferring the cargo at once began.

"Do you go in the first boat, monsieur, with the ladies," the captain said. "The sooner you are ashore the better. There is no saying whether we may not be disturbed and obliged to run out to sea again at a moment's notice."

"Thank God!" he exclaimed, as after wading through the shallow water he stood on the shore, while two of the sailors carried the girls and put them beside him. "Thank God, I have got you safe on English soil at last. I began to despair at one time."

"Thank God indeed," Jeanne said reverently; "but I never quite despaired, Harry. It seemed to me He had protected us through so many dangers, that He must mean that we should go safely through them all, and yet it did seem hopeless at one time."

"We had better stand on one side, girls, or rather we had better push on up the cliff. These people are all too busy to notice

194

us, and you might get knocked down; besides, the coastguard might arrive at any moment, and then there would be a fight. So let us get well away from them."

But they had difficulty in making their way up the cliff, for the path was filled with men carrying up tubs or coming down for more after placing them in the carts, which were waiting to convey them inland. At last they got to the top. One of the carts was already laden, and was on the point of driving off when Harry asked the man if he could tell him of any farmhouse near, where the two ladies who had landed with him could pass the night.

"Master's place is two miles away," the man said; "but if you like to walk as far, he will take you in, I doubt not."

The girls at once agreed to the proposal, and in three quarters of an hour the cart drew up at a farmhouse.

"Is it all right, Bill?" a man asked, opening the door as the cart stopped.

"Yes, it be all right. Not one of them revenue chaps nigh the place. Here be the load of tubs; they was the first that came ashore."

"Who have you got here?" the farmer asked as Harry came forward with the girls.

"These are two young ladies who have crossed in the lugger," Harry replied. "They have narrowly escaped being murdered in France by the Revolutionists, and have gone through a terrible time. As they have nowhere to go to-night, I thought perhaps you would kindly let them sit by your fire till morning."

"Surely I will," the farmer said. "Get ye in, get ye in. Mistress, here are two young French ladies who have escaped from those bloody-minded scoundrels in Paris. I needn't tell you to do what you can for them."

The farmer's wife at once came forward and received the girls most kindly. They had both picked up a little English during Harry's residence at the chateau, and feeling they were in good hands, Harry again went out and lent his assistance to the farmer in carrying the tubs down to a place of concealment made under the flooring of one of the barns.

The next day the farmer drove them in his gig to a town some miles inland. Here they procured dresses in which they could travel without exciting attention, and took their places in the coach which passed through the town for London next day.

That evening Harry gently broke to the girls the news of their brothers' death, for he thought that it would otherwise come as a terrible shock to them on their arrival at his home. Virginie was terribly upset, and Jeanne cried for some time, then she said:

"Your news does not surprise me, Harry. I have had a feeling all along that you knew something, but were keeping it from me. You spoke so very seldom of them, and when you did it seemed to me that what you said was not spoken in your natural voice. I felt sure that had you known nothing you would have often talked to us of meeting them in London, and of the happiness it would be. I would not ask, because I was sure you had a good reason for not telling us; but I was quite sure that there was something."

"I thought it better to keep it from you, Jeanne, until the danger was all over. In the first place you had need of all your courage and strength; in the next place it was possible that you might never reach England, and in that case you would never have suffered the pain of knowing anything about it."

"How thoughtful you are, Harry!" Jeanne murmured. "Oh how much we owe you! But oh how strange and lonely we seem—everyone gone except Marie, and we may never see her again!"

"You will see her again, never fear," Harry said confidently. "And you will not feel lonely long, for I can promise you that before you have been long at my mother's place you will feel like one of the family."

"Yes; but I shall not be one of the family," Jeanne said.

"Not yet, Jeanne. But mother will look upon you as her daughter directly I tell her that you have promised to become so in reality some day."

Harry's reception, when with the two girls he drove up in a hackney coach to the house at Cheyne Walk, was overwhelming, and the two French girls were at first almost bewildered by the rush of boys and girls who tore down the steps and threw themselves upon Harry's neck.

"You will stifle me between you all," Harry said, after he had responded to the embraces. "Where are father and mother?"

"Father is out, and mother is in the garden. No, there she is"—as Mrs. Sandwith, pale and agitated, appeared at the door, having hurried in when one of the young ones had shouted out from a back window: "Harry has come!"

"Oh, my boy, we had given you up," she sobbed as Harry rushed into her arms.

"I am worth a great many dead men yet, mother. But now let me introduce to you Mesdemoiselles Jeanne and Virginie de St. Caux, of whom I have written to you so often. They are orphans, mother, and I have promised them that you and father will fill the place of their parents."

"That will we willingly," Mrs. Sandwith said, turning to the

196

girls and kissing them with motherly kindness. "Come in, my dears, and welcome home for the sake of my dear boy, and for that of your parents who were so kind to him. Never mind all these wild young people," she added, as the boys and girls pressed round to shake hands with the new-comers. "You will get accustomed to their way presently. Do you speak in English?"

"Enough to understand," Jeanne said; "but not enough to speak much. Thank you, madame, for receiving us so kindly, for we are all alone in the world."

Mrs. Sandwith saw the girl's lip quiver, and putting aside her longing to talk to her son, said:

"Harry, do take them all out in the garden for a short time. They are all talking at once, and this is a perfect babel."

And thus having cleared the room she sat down to talk to the two girls, and soon made them feel at home with her by her unaffected kindness. Dr. Sandwith soon afterwards ran out to the excited chattering group in the garden, and after a few minutes' happy talk with him, Harry spoke to him of the visitors who were closeted with his mother.

"I want you to make them feel it is their home, father. They will be no burden pecuniarily, for there are money and jewels worth a large sum over here."

"Of course I know that," Dr. Sandwith said, "seeing that, as you know, they were consigned to me, and the marquis wrote to ask me to act as his agent. The money is invested in stock, and the jewels are in the hands of my bankers. I had begun to wonder what would become of it all, for I was by no means sure that the whole family had not perished, as well as yourself."

"There are only the three girls left," Harry said.

"In that case they will be well off, for the marquis inclosed me a will, saying that if anything should happen to him, and the estates should be altogether lost, the money and proceeds of the jewels were to be divided equally among his children. You must have gone through a great deal, old boy. You are scarcely nineteen, and you look two or three and twenty."

"I shall soon look young again, father, now I have got my mind clear of anxiety. But I have had a trying time of it, I can tell you; but it's too long a story to go into now, I will tell you all the whole yarn this evening. I want you to go in with me now to the girls and make them at home. All this must be just as trying for them at present as the dangers they have gone through."

The young ones were all forbidden to follow, and after an hour spent with his parents and the girls in the dining-room, Harry was pleased to see that the latter were beginning to feel at their ease, and that the strangeness was wearing off.

That evening, before the whole circle of his family, Harry related the adventures that they had gone through, subject, however, to a great many interruptions from Jeanne.

"But I am telling the story, not you, Jeanne," he said at last. "Some day when you begin to talk English quite well you shall give your version of it."

"But he is not telling it right, madame," Jeanne protested, "he keeps all the best part back. He says about the dangers, but he says noting about what he do himself." Then she broke into French, "No, madame, it is not just, it is not right; I will not suffer the tale to be told so. How can it be the true story when he says no word of his courage, of his devotion, of the way he watched over us and cheered us, no word of his grand heart, of the noble way he risked his life for us, for our sister, for our parents, for all? Oh, madame, I cannot tell you what we all owe to him;" and Jeanne, who had risen to her feet in her earnestness, burst into passionate tears. This put an end to the story for the evening, for Mrs. Sandwith saw that Jeanne required rest and quiet, and took the two girls up at once to the bed-room prepared for them. From this Jeanne did not descend for some days. As long as the strain was upon her she had borne herself bravely, but now that it was over she collapsed completely.

After the young ones had all gone off to bed, Harry said to his father and mother:

"I have another piece of news to tell you now. I am afraid you will think it rather absurd at my age, without a profession or anything else, but I am engaged to Jeanne. You see," he went on, as his parents both uttered an exclamation of surprise, "we have gone through a tremendous lot together, and when people have to look death in the face every day it makes them older than they are; and when, as in this case, they have to depend entirely on themselves, it brings them very closely together. I think it might have been so had these troubles never come on, for somehow we had taken very much to each other, though it might have been years before anything came of it. Her poor father and mother saw it before I knew it myself, and upon the night before they were separated told her elder sister and brother that, should I ever ask for Jeanne's hand, they approved of her marrying me. But although afterwards I came to love her with all my heart, I should never have spoken had it not been that I did so when it seemed that in five minutes we should neither of us be alive. If it hadn't been for that I should have brought her home and waited till I was making my own way in life."

"I do not blame you, Harry, my boy," his father said heartily. "Of course you are very young, and under ordinary circumstances would not have been thinking about a wife for years to come yet; but I can see that your Jeanne is a girl of no ordinary character, and it is certainly for her happiness that, being here with her sister alone among strangers, she should feel that she is at home. Personally she is charming, and even in point of fortune you would be considered a lucky fellow. What do you say, mother?"

"I say God bless them both!" Mrs. Sandwith said earnestly. "After the way in which Providence has brought them together, there can be no doubt that they were meant for each other."

"Do you know I half guessed there was something more than mere gratitude in Jeanne's heart when she flamed out just now; did not you, mother?"

Mrs. Sandwith nodded and smiled. "I was sure there was," she said.

"I did not say anything about it when we came in," Harry said, "because I thought it better for Jeanne to have one quiet day, and you know the young ones will laugh awfully at the idea of my being engaged."

"Never you mind, Harry," his father said; "let those laugh that win. But you are not thinking of getting married yet, I hope."

"No, no, father; you cannot think I would live on Jeanne's money."

"And you still intend to go into the army, Harry?"

"No, father; I have had enough of bloodshed for the rest of my life. I have been thinking it over a good deal, and I have determined to follow your example and become a doctor."

"That's right, my boy," Dr. Sandwith said heartily. "I have always regretted you had a fancy for the army, for I used to look forward to your becoming my right hand. Your brothers, too, do not take to the profession, so I began to think I was going to be alone in my old age. You have made me very happy, Harry, and your mother too, I am sure. It will be delightful for us having you and your pretty French wife settled by us; will it not, mother?"

"It will indeed," Mrs. Sandwith said in a tone of deep happiness. "You are certainly overworked and need a partner terribly, and who could be like Harry?"

"Yes, I have been thinking of taking a partner for some time, but now I will hold on alone for another three years. By that time Harry will have passed."

The next morning the young ones were told the news. The elder girls were delighted at the thought of Jeanne becoming their sister, but the boys went into fits of laughter and chaffed Harry so unmercifully for the next day or two that it was just as well that Jeanne was up in her room. By the time she came down they had recovered their gravity. Mrs. Sandwith and the girls had already given her the warmest welcome as Harry's future wife, and the boys received her so warmly when she appeared that Jeanne soon felt that she was indeed one of the family.

Three years later, on the day after Harry passed his final examination, Jeanne and he were married, and set up a pretty establishment close to Cheyne Walk, with Virginie to live with them; and Harry, at first as his father's assistant, and very soon as his partner, had the satisfaction of feeling that he was not wholly dependent on Jeanne's fortune.

They had received occasional news from Marie. Victor had steadily recovered his strength and memory, and as soon as the reign of terror had come to an end, and the priests were able to show themselves from their hiding-places in many an out-of-the-way village in the country, Marie and Victor were quietly married. But France was at war with all Europe now, and Victor, though he hated the revolution, was a thorough Frenchman, and through some of his old friends who had escaped the wave of destruction, he had obtained a commission, and joined Bonaparte when he went to take the command of the army of Italy. He had attracted his general's attention early in the campaign by a deed of desperate valour, and was already in command of a regiment, when, soon after Jeanne's marriage, Marie came over to England by way of Holland to stay for a time with her sisters. She was delighted at finding Jeanne so happy, and saw enough before she returned to France to feel assured that before very long Virginie would follow Jeanne's example, and would also become an Englishwoman, for she and Harry's next brother Tom had evidently some sort of understanding between them. It was not until many years later that the three sisters met again, when, after the fall of Napoleon, Jeanne and Virginie went over with their husbands and stayed for some weeks with General De Gisons and his wife at the old chateau near Dijon. This the general had purchased back from the persons into whose hands it had fallen at the Revolution with the money which he had received as his wife's dowry.